DAIRY, DAIRY, QUITE CONTRARY

AMY LILLARD

Kensington Publishing Corp.
www.kensingtonbooks.com

KENSINGTON BOOKS are published by

Kensington Publishing Corp.
119 West 40th Street
New York, NY 10018

All Kensington titles, imprints, and distributed lines are available at special quantity discounts for bulk purchases for sales promotion, premiums, fund-raising, educational, or institutional use.

Special book excerpts or customized printings can also be created to fit specific needs. For details, write or phone the office of the Kensington Sales Manager: Attn.: Sales Department. Kensington Publishing Corp., 119 West 40th Street, New York, NY 10018. Phone: 1-800-221-2647.

The K and Teapot logo is a trademark of Kensington Publishing Corp.

First Printing: July 2022
ISBN: 978-1-4967-3345-0

ISBN: 978-1-4967-3346-7 (ebook)

10 9 8 7 6 5 4 3 2 1

Printed in the United States of America

My family became blended when most of the children on both sides were grown. Basically, this means I gained stepsiblings that I never shared a house with. But we had all lived in the same little town, had all attended the same little school, and had all gone to the same little church for all our lives. Friends now kin by marriage.

When I was writing this book, my stepsister lost her husband, tragically and unexpectedly.

This book is dedicated to them and their family who suffered through such a terrible loss.

To Patti and Phillip Duke, the Dukes of York. This one is for you! Thanks for lending me your name for my favorite character. I hope he lives up to the honor.

ACKNOWLEDGMENTS

This is the part of writing that I dread the most. There are so many people who contribute to the making of a book—multiple editors, my agent, my family, my friends, my bestie, and of course the readers. All the usual suspects. I'm always worried that I'll leave someone out or violate someone's privacy. Anyway, you know who you are and I thank you all!

As for the new players in this production . . . I want to thank the wonderful town of Yoder, Kansas, for welcoming me so graciously into your midst. Most of you didn't blink an eye at the two strange blondes driving up and down and back and around in the little white convertible Beetle. You are truly my favorite Amish destination!

I also need to give a shout out to Becky Yates Spencer and her husband, Tracy. When I traveled to Kansas for the first time, I stayed with Becky at her beautiful B&B in Buhler, Kansas. The Grand Staff is a grand destination and one of the best places to stay when you're in the area. (Side note: Becky and her husband do wonderful mission work in Africa. Gavin's Buhler interview is a nod to Becky and all that she does.) Becky, you are truly a wonderful soul. The world needs more like you.

My second trip to Yoder was shorter but just as much fun as the first. And this time I stayed in the infamous Chicken House. (Yes, Sissy's new Yoder residence is patterned after this Airbnb.) Kendra is a fabulous host, a caring part of such a unique community, and a VW Beetle lover. What more could you ask for? Kendra, thanks for allowing me time in the Chicken House and for allowing me to loosely include it in my stories. Good luck with the coffee shop, and I hope to stop in again on my next Yoder jaunt.

For more information on what is real in Yoder, what I've changed, and what's completely fiction see my website:

AmyWritesMysteries.com

Or if you're more interested in the many pictures I've taken on my research trips to Yoder (and even to other Amish communities) go to:

AmysAmishAdventures.com

And as always, I apologize if I missed someone in my acknowledgments. It's not that I truly forgot, my writer's brain just gets too far ahead of me most of the time.

Thank you for reading! I appreciate you more than you will ever know.

Blessings and hugs!

Amy

CHAPTER ONE

Life is like a game of chess. To win, you first have to make a move.
—Aunt Bess

"I need an Adam and Eve on a raft, and cry over it."

As Sissy Yoder watched, a woman with a heavy frown stuck her face in the small window that joined the front of the café with the kitchen. Sissy could barely see her, but she thought—hoped, even—that it was her aunt.

"How many times do I have to tell you, Lottie? English. I need you to tell me the order in English."

Lottie, a middle-aged woman with a chubby face and short, gray-streaked blond hair, planted her hands on her wide hips and squared off with the woman in the kitchen. "That *is* English, Bethel. And I thought Josie told you to go home."

"Josie can't—never mind." Bethel waved a hand, as if none of it were of any importance; then she disappeared from view.

So that was her aunt. Well, it had to be her aunt, now, didn't it? Because her aunt was named Bethel, and she owned the Sunflower Café. And since Sissy was in the Sunflower Café and the woman's name was Bethel, it stood to reason. After all, what were the chances that there were two women named Bethel who worked in the Sunflower Café in itty-bitty Yoder, Kansas? Not likely.

It's just that Sissy hadn't seen her aunt in many, many years. She had fond memories of her cousin Lizzie, Bethel's daughter, who had worked at the café part-time until recently. Lizzie had contacted Sissy's mother to see if anyone in the family would be willing to help Bethel in her time of need. A call that reached all the way from Kansas to Oklahoma, to the wayward Yoders, who had gone so far as to leave the Amish church for greener pastures.

At first, Sissy had been a little confused by the call. After all, there were plenty of relations around the tiny town of Yoder, Kansas—more than plenty, in truth. Even Amish ones. But it seemed as if everyone was either under the weather—Lizzie herself had just been put on bed rest for the remainder of her pregnancy—or busier than usual.

After the brief glimpse Sissy had just received of her aunt, she thought it was more likely that everyone had been run off.

Well, not her.

She lifted her chin and pulled on the tails of her pink-checked, button-down shirt. She had a job to do. For the family.

The woman named Bethel burst through the swinging aluminum doors that hung between the dining area and the kitchen, one hand braced on a single crutch as she hobbled into view.

Solid. That was the best word she could find to describe her aunt. Bethel Yoder was stout, her homemade black dress a little tight across the middle. The matching black apron concealed little of her girth. Her aunt looked as if she could hold her own in a wrestling tournament. A *men's* wrestling tournament.

She wore the traditional black walking shoes and black tights, but instead of a white prayer covering, she boasted a faded yellow bandana tied over her hair. If it hadn't been for the dress and the apron, Sissy might not have known she was Amish at all.

"The doctor said—" Lottie started again.

"Bah," Bethel grumbled. "The doctor can't say much unless he wants to come over here and help me." She pulled the order ticket from Lottie's hand, studied it a second, then started for the kitchen once again. "Hard to find good help these days. Hard to find any help at all . . ."

Sissy cleared her throat.

Both women turned to look at her, as if until that moment, neither had been aware of her presence.

"Can I help you?" Lottie asked. Her sweet blue eyes made it seem as if she wanted to help, and they definitely held a different light than Bethel's narrowed ones.

"I'm here to help you." Sissy smiled, completely satisfied with herself. Perfect.

"Are you here about the ad?" Lottie asked.

"No," Sissy replied.

"Ad?" Bethel turned toward Lottie, her cast scraping against the floor. It wasn't one of those walking casts, but a great hulking thing made of off-white fiberglass. Strips of silver duct tape had been added to the bottom, as if to help protect it from the damage of being walked on. "You put out an ad?"

"Well, I mean . . . not me. But . . . yeah . . ." Lottie stumbled over every word.

"I'm Sissy," she said. As if that explained all they needed to know.

"Who?" Bethel asked.

"Virgil," Lottie admitted.

"Sissy Yoder," Sissy continued.

"Virgil, my son Virgil?"

"Do you know any others?" Lottie asked.

"I'm your niece," Sissy explained. "Mary and James's daughter."

"Does it matter how many I know?" Bethel asked.

"We need help," Lottie protested.

"We wouldn't if everyone showed up for work when they're supposed to," Bethel continued.

"Excuse me." A somewhat timid voice sounded behind Sissy.

She turned to find a young girl standing there. She was no more than six, with long blond hair parted down the middle and pulled up into silky pigtails.

Until that moment, not one of the guests had batted an eye at the exchange between aunt, niece, and waitress. Sissy supposed they were accustomed to such displays, and once again, the idea that the help her aunt needed might have been run off flitted through her thoughts.

"Yes?" Sissy asked.

"I'd like some water, please." She turned back toward the table where her family sat. The parents nodded and smiled encouragingly to whom appeared to be their oldest child. A boy of about four sat next to the father, who held a baby swathed in blue. In her arms, the mother cradled a pink bundle that had to be his twin. The little girl turned back to Sissy and held up two baby bottles with powdery formula in the bottom of each. "For our babies."

Sissy looked at the bottles, to the smiling family, then back to the bickering couple that was her aunt and a woman named Lottie.

"Of course," Sissy said. "Warm, but not too warm. Am I right?"

The girl smiled. "That's right."

Sissy edged past Lottie and Bethel without either one noticing that she was going to the back. She filled the bottles with the filtered water from the waitress stand, then added a little bit of hot water from the coffeepot. On her way to the table where the family sat, she could feel her aunt's gaze upon her.

Well, more like boring a hole through her back.

"Thank you," the young mother said with a smile.

"Not a problem." Sissy smiled in return and headed back over to where her aunt waited.

"Who are you again?" Bethel asked, eyes narrowed even more than before.

"Sissy Yoder. Mary and James's daughter. From Tulsa. Well, not originally. They were from here, but you know that." She laughed and wondered why she always had the tendency to talk too much. Maybe because Bethel didn't look pleased that she was there or that she had fetched water for the family at the large corner table. Or maybe she was still a little upset that Virgil had put an ad in the paper.

"Look at you," Lottie gushed. "Little Sissy, all grown up."

Sissy frowned. "I'm sorry. Do I know you?" It had been years and years since she had been to Yoder. Fifteen, if she was counting right. Not since she was fourteen and her *mammi*—her grandmother—had died. After that, her mother, Mary, had come to visit by herself. But in the last couple of years, she didn't think her mother had made the trip, either.

"I'm Lottie Foster." She paused, as if to let that knowledge sink in. "Your grandmother's next-door neighbor." For a moment, Sissy thought Lottie might burst into tears. Instead, Lottie grasped Sissy by the shoulders and pulled her into a suffocating hug.

"Ahmememer," Sissy mumbled into Lottie's ample shirtfront.

Lottie pulled away, allowing Sissy the much-needed air. "What was that?"

"I remember," she repeated. "You had the trampoline." Sissy gulped up another big breath in case Lottie went for a second hug.

"That's right. Heavens above, I would know that freckled face of yours anywhere."

And such was the problem with having bright red hair and more freckles than waves on the ocean—everyone remembered.

"It's good to see you again, Miss Lottie."

Bethel shifted her weight and crossed her arms. "All the way up from Tulsa, huh?"

Sissy smiled. "That's right."

"Bah." Bethel waved her away as if she were nothing more than a pesky fly, then turned and hobbled back into the kitchen.

"I can't say we don't need the help." Lottie tossed a cross look over one shoulder, directing it at the kitchen and Bethel. "But all the way from Tulsa?"

"I don't mind." Even as she said the words, she thought

to take a small step to one side, lest the heavens open up and lightning shoot down and fry her liver. She stayed firmly in place. After all, it wasn't a *complete* lie. She didn't mind, but if her own life hadn't fallen apart in the last couple of weeks, she might not be free to travel four hours from her home to help a family member she hadn't seen since she was fourteen. But she wasn't thinking about that sort of thing right now. Maybe tomorrow.

It's just that her life hadn't fallen completely *completely* apart. Just sort of completely apart. She still had her job as Aunt Bess, one of the most widely read newspaper columns in the South Central region. But no one knew she was Aunt Bess. No one except her editor, who had been sworn to secrecy. The last thing Sissy wanted everyone to know about her was that her alter ego was a seventy-year-old grandmother of eight with a know-it-all, tell-it-like-it-is sass mouth. She had enough trouble getting dates as it was.

Still . . . it paid the bills.

"My mama always told me not to look a gift horse in the mouth, but I'm not the horse in question here." Lottie nodded to the man who had come up to the register. "Just a minute, hun."

Sissy waited as Lottie rang up the meal for his family. She still wasn't sure how to sort through the gift-horse comment. She allowed her gaze to drift around the café, taking in details and imperfections alike. The one wall not broken by long windows was covered in cheap pine paneling and faded sunflower decorations—wreaths, pictures, plates, even prints and oil reproductions.

The Sunflower Café.

Her family merely called it the café. As did everyone on Yelp. And it had some good reviews. Not that there were many places to eat in Yoder. There was the Carriage House Restaurant, the meatpacking plant that also served deli meats and cheeses, the Bull in Your Eye Diner, and the Sunflower Café.

Lottie finished the transaction and thanked the family as Sissy picked up one of the menus sitting by the register. It was clear plastic with red binding and only a couple of pages.

"Goodness," Lottie said. "We hardly use those." She nodded toward the menu Sissy held.

"Then how do people order?"

She pointed to the overhead letter board lined with meals and prices, then to the free-standing chalkboard just to the left of the kitchen entrance.

Daily Specials Chicken Fried Steak or Meatloaf $7.99.

Sissy blinked. "That's it?"

"Of course, you get mashed potatoes, gravy, choice of vegetable, and a yeast roll or cornbread."

That wasn't exactly what Sissy meant, but she had to admit, the food itself sounded amazing. Her stomach growled. She hadn't had anything to eat since she left Tulsa.

Lottie must have heard. She eyed her thoughtfully. "You eat yet?"

Before Sissy could respond, a large crash sounded, followed by a noise she couldn't readily identify and a cry of pain.

"Oh, no." Lottie turned and fled into the kitchen.

Sissy looked around, and since the café was empty, she followed the woman.

"I told you," Lottie was saying as Sissy entered the kitchen.

Bethel was sprawled on the floor, a large metal bowl beside her and scraps of lettuce, tomato, and purple cabbage all around.

"Are *you* going to run the place?" Bethel grumbled.

"Where's Josie?" Lottie sputtered and grabbed Bethel under one arm.

Sissy grabbed Bethel under the other, and together, they lifted the woman to her feet.

Bethel grunted in protest.

The woman was nothing if not stubborn.

"Smoking, I guess."

Sissy glanced around at the messy kitchen. It had the look of a place that was organized but cluttered, as if the person responsible normally put everything back in place. But times weren't exactly normal right then.

"Go sit down out front. I'll clean up this mess," Lottie said.

But Sissy had already grabbed a dustpan and a broom.

"Fine." But the one word was more of an exhale than an agreement. Bethel tucked the crutch under one arm and pinned Sissy with a hard, blue stare. "Sweep it up, but this doesn't mean you're staying."

Sissy had never swept a floor so slowly, but once Bethel and Lottie had gone back to the front of the café, she wanted to give them time to talk. If anyone could talk her aunt into allowing Sissy to help, she had a feeling it would be Lottie. Not even her cousin Lizzie had been able to get Bethel to agree. That was why they had tried such drastic tactics—Sissy driving all the way from Tulsa, unannounced and prepared to stay for as long as she was needed. Longer, even.

She sighed and dumped the last of the lettuce into the trash can.

A dark-headed woman picked that time to breeze in through the back door. She stopped when she caught sight of Sissy. "Who are you?" She was tall and thin and dark. Her hip-hugging jeans were name-brand, though they had seen better days, and the white ribbed tank top she wore could be picked up practically anywhere. Yet she wore them both regally, along with her black sneakers that Sissy supposed were of the nonslip variety. The force with which her long dark hair had been pulled back into a ponytail made her cheekbones seem even higher. Her accent was indistinguishable, though her tone was unmistakably hostile.

Sissy felt as if she had encroached on someone's sacred turf. "Uh . . . Sissy?" And just like that, her confidence was gone. She mentally scrambled to gather it back. "I'm Bethel's niece." The woman just continued to stare, her dark eyes penetrating and . . . shifty. Maybe. Sissy wasn't sure. But they were something.

"From Tulsa." Like that made a difference. And she remembered the conversation she'd witnessed between Lottie and her aunt. "You must be Josie." She stuck out a hand to shake.

Josie eyed it skeptically, then grunted and moved past her. Over to the sink to wash her hands. The smell of cigarette smoke lingered in her wake.

Sissy let her hand fall back to her side. "I've come to help out until Bethel gets back on her feet." She chuckled and waited for Josie to say something. Anything. But it seemed she was a woman of few words. And perhaps even fewer manners.

But Sissy wasn't going to let Josie's standoffish attitude bring her down. She had promised to come help, and come help she would. But for now . . .

She waited for Josie to dry her hands on a paper towel, toss it into the trash, and move toward the grill before she stepped up to the sink.

The large, stainless steel, double-sided sink was as big as a bathtub. An industrial-size dishwasher was set off to her right, while on her left, the sink flattened into a counter. Various utensils sat off to the side, waiting their turn to be washed, along with a bus tub half-full of dirty dishes. Sissy pulled a coffee mug from the mix, rinsed it out, and filled it with water before she headed toward the front of the café.

"Where are you going with that?" Bethel asked, the second after Sissy had pushed through the metal doors.

"To my car."

Bethel raised up to get a better look into the cup. "Water?" she asked.

"My dog's out there," Sissy explained.

"Your dog?" Bethel asked with an incredulous blink.

"Land sakes, girl," Lottie admonished. "Bring him in. He can't be out there in the heat like this."

"She cannot bring a dog in here, no matter how hot it is outside."

"It's closing time, anyway," Lottie countered.

Sissy shook her head. Truth be known, it wasn't that hot, and Sissy's little convertible had keyless entry, so she had left it running, with the top up, of course. "I'm sure Duke is fine," she said. "But I wanted to take him a drink and let him walk for a bit. I hate to have him confined in the car for long periods of time."

Lottie nodded understandingly, but Bethel just glared. "You think you're staying."

"I came with that intention." She stiffened her shoulders.

"I don't need your help."

"You need someone's," Sissy countered.

"Hear, hear," Lottie said with a chortle.

"Hush." Bethel turned her glare to her.

"I'll just—" Sissy inched toward the door. She needed to get out of there for a minute, reevaluate, figure out what she was going to do. She hadn't expected Bethel to welcome her with open arms, nor had she expected her to be so hostile. But one thing was absolutely certain: She was not going home. There was nothing to go home to.

"That's not a dog." The gruff voice sounded behind her.

Sissy didn't need to look to know who it was. "My vet begs to differ."

Bethel hobbled up next to her and studied Sissy's beloved pooch. "I've thrown back fish bigger than that."

"I suppose." Sissy looked down at the tiny black and tan dog on the leash. Duke of York, her Yorkshire terrier, lapped up the water she had brought out and otherwise ignored the humans and their less-than-flattering words. "But he's mine, and I love him."

A little of her bravado had leaked out after she had made her way outside. She had wanted to present herself as strong and capable. But under Bethel's harsh words and scrutiny, her confidence had taken a nosedive. Now all she wanted to do was find someplace to spend the night and regroup for tomorrow's battle. Except she didn't have a place to spend the night, and today's battle was far from over.

Bethel turned her attention to the contents of Sissy's car. It was her only indulgence. A Fiat 500 Cabriolet. Red, shiny, Italian, convertible. She had told herself that she deserved a great car when she first went to work at the paper, and the little import was good on gas and still easy enough on the pocketbook. Still, it seemed indulgent, and even though her column was wildly successful now, she wasn't about to get ahead of herself. The reading public could be fickle. And though Aunt Bess's writing was currently on the rise, that didn't mean it would always be that way.

"Why do you have your dog with you, Sissy Yoder?" Bethel asked.

"I take him everywhere," Sissy answered simply, truthfully. "He's my faithful companion." Especially since Colt had flaked out.

It wasn't that Colt was a bad guy; he just wanted different things than she did. Like buckle bunnies and one-night stands. While Sissy was looking more toward the future. Marriage, kids, that sort of thing.

Never trust a rodeo man, Aunt Bess always said. Too bad Sissy hadn't taken her own advice. Even country songs warned about it. She should have listened to country music more. Lesson learned.

"Why do you want to come here?" Bethel asked. "This is my home. It's where God put me, but you . . ."

"I live where my parents settled," she said. "Tulsa is home, but—" How did a person say *There's nothing left for me there* without sounding like a hopeless failure? And she wasn't a failure. She was strong and inventive, imaginative, and . . . worthy . . . and what was the other one?

"It's time for something new," she concluded. Whether

she was ready or not, the future was now, as Aunt Bess would say. And something new was on Sissy's agenda for the day.

So she had lost her boyfriend and her apartment in so many weeks. Coming to Yoder to help her aunt was a last-ditch effort at exerting some measure of control over her life. She was taking that back now.

Aunt Bess would tell her that she had been in control the whole time. Sissy had been the one to break up with Colt, and seeing as how his sister was her roommate . . . well, Sissy thought it best to move out before things got weird. Stephanie was her best friend in the world. But nothing ruins a friendship faster than dating a BFF's brother. Another lesson chalked up in the Should Have Already Learned Long Ago tally.

"Did Mary really send you?"

"Yes, ma'am."

Bethel frowned. Or maybe she was just thinking. Hard to tell, since the woman had done nothing but frown since Sissy had first laid eyes on her. "How did she know I needed help?"

Sissy shrugged. "Someone here, I guess." No way was she throwing her cousin under the bus.

"Why didn't she call and tell me you were on your way?" Bethel shifted, and Sissy had a feeling she was more uncomfortable than she let anyone know. Sissy herself had broken an arm once, and the cast had been unbelievably heavy. Of course, she'd been ten at the time and skinny as a rail, but she could imagine how the cast on Bethel's leg felt, lugging it around all day.

"I suppose because she knew you wouldn't accept the help when it was offered to you."

Sissy's parents had both grown up in the small Amish

community of Yoder, Kansas. But even with Yoder's less-conservative Old Order ways, they found the life too confining. They left the church and moved their family to Tulsa, much to the distress of their Kansas relatives. But Mary and James Yoder had kept in touch with their family. Shunning definitely wasn't what it used to be.

"I'm not turning the café over to you."

"I don't expect you to." Plus, she would need someone there to show her what to do. She had never worked at a café in her life, just the order counter at Whataburger.

"Lottie's a big help, but she has a new grandbaby. And everyone else . . ." Bethel heaved a sigh, but her expression didn't change. Sissy understood. Everyone else had a life of their own. Sure, the Amish were known for helping one another when times got tough. But Sissy supposed it was a whole 'nother ballgame when they started talking about working shifts at a busy café. It wasn't like people could come by and help after work. While they were working their regular jobs, the café was open and needed help of its own.

"That's why I'm here." Some of her confidence returned. She wasn't going to leave. This was her chance to regroup, to get herself together. To think about what she wanted, so when she went back to Tulsa, she would be able to start fresh, with a new life that she had control over.

Powerful. That was the word. She was strong, inventive, imaginative, worthy, and powerful.

"Fine," Bethel said, leaning heavily on her single crutch. "You can stay, but only until I get out of this." She knocked her knuckles against the side of her cast. Then she nodded sternly and started back toward the café.

Sissy managed to hide her smile until Bethel had

turned away. Then she scooped Duke into her arms and kissed the top of his head. She received several sweet doggie kisses in return.

"We did it, Duke," she whispered, for his silky ears alone. Now she just needed to find a place to stay. One down, one to go.

CHAPTER TWO

*A woman cannot survive on wine alone. She also
needs to have a dog.*
—Aunt Bess

Bethel was halfway back to the restaurant when she
stopped and turned. "You eat?" she asked.

Sissy shook her head, still nuzzling close to her sweet
pup. Her stomach rumbled.

Her aunt's eyes narrowed. "You got a place to stay?"

She shook her head again.

Bethel pressed her lips together. "Come on in and get a
plate," she said. "You can stay with me as long as you
like."

The words were so grudgingly spoken that Sissy wasn't
sure she meant to say them at all. What was it that made
her aunt so . . . grouchy?

Sissy put Duke back into the cool car with a promise
of a long walk later. As she trailed behind her aunt, she

went over all the things that her mom had said about Bethel.

Sissy's father, James, was quite a bit younger than Bethel, thirteen or so years. If Sissy was remembering it all correctly, Bethel was the oldest of the Yoder children. She had married Chris Yoder when James and Mary had still been in school. Sissy had thought it funny that they both had the same last name and weren't related. Her mother had explained how there were a great many Yoders in all the Amish communities, but perhaps none so many as the one in Yoder. And then their first names—Bethel and Chris—that sounded like they were part of the Nativity story. Bethlehem and Christmas Day. When Sissy had said as much, her mother had smiled and shook her head.

Sissy studied Bethel's back as she walked just ahead of her. Her aunt was slightly stooped, but Sissy couldn't tell if it was because of her natural posture or the crutch and her cast.

"How'd you break your leg?" she asked just as her aunt reached the door of the café.

Bethel's expression never wavered. "Ice skating on a cruise ship."

After what was certainly the best meal that Sissy had had in a long time, Bethel gave her the address to her house so she could get settled in. It was a short drive down the back dirt roads of the tiny town. She'd had to put the top all the way up to combat the clouds of dust. But she found the house without too much trouble. She pulled her car to a stop in front of a white clapboard two-story house. She had passed several like it on the way there, and she had a feeling it was something of an "Amish style." A detail she hadn't paid attention to as a young visitor.

This one was not much different—no electric lines leading up to it, a large front porch, and a tractor parked out front. There was also a carriage house. She wouldn't have known what it was had it not been open, exposing the shiny black buggy inside. The house itself looked normal enough, with a few sections that she could tell had been added on to the original structure.

Sissy put Duke on his lead and walked him up onto the porch and over to the front door. A note was pinned there. *Next door,* it said, with an arrow pointing to the right. Sissy looked at Duke, who merely wagged his tail and waited for whatever was next. "Let's go see," she told him.

They climbed down the steps, and Sissy led him in the direction the arrow was pointing. Sure enough, a door was there, complete with a storm door, which couldn't be seen from the front of the house.

Another note was pinned here. *Come in.*

Sissy looked to Duke, but once again, he had no answer. "I guess we'll go in, then."

She opened the door, poking her head in and cautiously calling "Hello?" The house was dark, of course, because no lanterns were lit. The only light came from the many windows all around.

"Back here," came the reply.

Sissy and Duke wound their way through the dim room and down the darkened hallway until they found the owner of that voice. Behind the last door on the left, she found a woman lying in bed, a book planted on her big, protruding stomach. She wore a simple cotton nightgown with a small pink bow at the neck and a calico kerchief wrapped around her dark hair.

"Lizzie?"

Her blue eyes lit with excitement. "Sissy?"

She almost melted with relief. "You shouldn't just let people in like that. Without the door locked." She gestured behind her as if it explained everything.

"Pah," Lizzie said, with a swipe of one hand. She sounded so much like a cheerful version of her mother that Sissy almost giggled. "This is Yoder. Nothing bad happens around here." She pushed herself up against her pillows. "When did you get in?"

"Just a little bit ago. I stopped by the café first." She shifted in place. "Your mom . . ." she started.

Her cousin waved away her need to finish that sentence. "Her bark is worse than her bite."

She bites? "How did she break her leg?"

Lizzie shook her head. "You'll have to ask her that."

"I did."

"Did she tell you that she fell out of a tree while rescuing a cat?"

Sissy chuckled. "No. Ice skating on a cruise ship."

Lizzie laughed so hard she snorted. She slapped one hand over her mouth, then motioned Sissy to come closer to the bed. "Sit. Sit. I'm so glad you're here."

Sissy smiled. "I'm glad I'm here, too." This was her chance for a fresh start, and she was claiming it with both hands. Cautiously, she eased down next to her cousin, careful not to jostle or bump her.

"Don't worry. I'm not going to break," Lizzie said, then she flung her arms around Sissy and hugged her as tight as her belly would allow.

Sissy absorbed the warmth of her embrace. After everything, all the people in her life who didn't want her—her boyfriend, her roommate, her aunt—it felt good to be cherished.

Having been ignored too long, Duke let out a sharp little bark, turning around in a circle on the rag rug next to the bed. He only succeeded in twisting himself up in his leash.

"Is that a dog?" Lizzie asked, finally letting Sissy go.

"Cousin Lizzie, meet Duke. Duke, Cousin Lizzie." She lifted Duke onto the bed so Lizzie could get a better look.

"He's so tiny," her cousin exclaimed. "Are you sure he's a dog?"

"What is it with everybody and my dog?"

Lizzie lifted Duke onto her large bump of a belly and scratched him behind one ear. He collapsed in sheer joy. Finally . . . the attention he had been craving all day. "Who said something about this sweet little guy?" Lizzie asked in mock anger.

Sissy waved a hand as if it were of no importance. She supposed in the big scheme of things, it wasn't.

"It's been so long," Lizzie mused.

Duke slid off Lizzie's belly and snuggled down next to her, knowing a good thing when he found it.

"Fifteen years." Sissy nodded. "That's what I figured."

"Fifteen years," she murmured.

And Sissy knew what her cousin was thinking: How could so long have passed without them seeing one another? She didn't have an answer.

"Where are you staying?" Lizzie asked. "You *are* staying. Please tell me you're staying. At least for a little while."

"Of course. Your mother said I can stay here until I find a place of my own."

Lizzie eyes sparkled. "That's wonderful."

Sissy wasn't sure *wonderful* was the word she would have chosen, but she wasn't about to rain on her cousin's personal parade. "Tell me," she said, doing her best to change the subject, "when is the baby due?" It had to be soon, judging by the size of Lizzie's belly.

"Babies," Lizzie corrected.

Sissy's eyes grew wide. "Twins?"

Lizzie nodded. "*Jah.* Two of them. Can you believe it?"

"That's amazing." She was so very happy for her cousin. And maybe just a teeny-weeny bit jealous. So she had a few setbacks; that didn't mean her time for a husband and family was never going to happen. Not with her new and improved positive attitude. And she had Duke, so it wasn't like she was totally alone.

From the front of the house, she heard a door open and close, but no one called out a greeting.

"That must be Daniel," Lizzie said. "My husband. Go out there and introduce yourself," she urged. "I'll watch after this little guy. You're going to have such fun meeting everybody."

By the time supper rolled around, Sissy had lost count of how many new cousins she had met, along with aunts and uncles she hadn't known before. As time to eat neared, more and more people stopped by to check on Lizzie. They brought food—casseroles and cakes—and otherwise stayed only long enough to deliver their gifts and get back on the road.

Sissy expected her aunt to come home anytime now. The sign on the door of the café said they were open until two. But she supposed Bethel would have plenty more to do after the café closed for the day. And she wondered if she should have stayed to help.

"Can I help with dinner?" she asked, coming into the kitchen. She had expected to find one or two straggling cousins—female, of course—putting the final touches on whatever food had been brought over. Instead, she found Lizzie's husband Daniel at the helm. The sight stopped her in her tracks. An Amish man in the kitchen? It seemed the times they were a-changin'.

Daniel was standing with his back to the door. He turned as she entered and gave her a smile. Like the other married Amish men, Daniel had a beard that didn't include a mustache. The style was a bit perplexing to Sissy, but she figured to each their own.

"I think I got it," Daniel said.

Sissy breathed a small sigh of relief. After one good look at the oven, she had regretted her offer. It was a standard gas stove, but she hadn't imagined heating up food in it. She was more of a microwave kind of girl.

What had she expected? That they would throw it on a plate and nuke it? And it wasn't like she couldn't cook. She could. But she wouldn't consider herself an expert.

Maybe coming here to help out in a café wasn't her finest idea.

She pushed those thoughts away. They were negative, and she was having none of that in her life. If she didn't know now, she would learn. It was as simple as that.

"You're a guest," Daniel continued. "But I wouldn't mind if you kept me company for a while."

"Of course." Sissy eased down at the kitchen table and glanced around. Now that the crowd had cleared, she had the time and the space to study her cousin's house.

She supposed that for the most part, it looked like just about anyone else's house. The main difference was it didn't seem to be filled with as much clutter. Some would have said treasures, but without all of it scattered around, the place seemed clean and open. It put a whole new spin on things. The walls were painted a pale creamy color, too light to be called yellow, and only a few pictures were hanging there. Not pictures, really, since the Amish didn't believe in taking photographs of themselves. Instead, there was a wedding sampler that someone had done up in counted cross-stitch and a framed Bible verse: Proverbs 3:5-6. *Trust in the Lord with all your heart and lean not on your own understanding; in all your ways submit to Him, and He will make your paths straight.*

"What do you think so far?" Daniel asked.

For a moment, she thought he meant the verse, but then realized that would be a totally *Englisch* question. He was talking about Yoder.

"It's a cute town. What I've seen of it."

"You got here this afternoon?"

"Yes."

Daniel gave a small shake of his head. "Then you've seen most of it."

Sissy laughed. She liked her cousin's husband. Lizzie had chosen well for herself. "You work at the meatpacking plant, right?"

Daniel nodded, then turned away to open the oven door. He pulled out the disposable casserole pan and set it on the stove top. Another pot of something she couldn't see bubbled there.

"Hand me that tray over there, and we'll make Lizzie's first."

Sissy fetched the tray and handed it to Daniel. "What time will Bethel be home?"

Daniel looked to the clock hanging over the sink. It was already after six. "She'll be along any minute. Though she'll come in her own entrance."

"Her own?"

"Bethel lives in the *dawdihaus*," he explained as he filled the plate—green beans, a piece of cornbread, and a helping of a familiar-looking casserole.

Yummasetti. It had been one of Sissy's favorite dishes growing up, though since she had moved out on her own, it had fallen off her "choices for dinner" radar. Too many carbs in the land of egg noodles. And if this was how her family normally ate, she was really going to have to watch it, or she'd end up as big as a house.

"I guess *Englischers* would call it something like a mother-in-law's apartment," Daniel continued. "She lives there, and we live here."

"And the two houses are connected?" Just one more thing she didn't remember from her youth.

"*Jah*. That's how you came into the house. We figured that was a safer way, since Liz is here all by herself most days." He picked up the tray and nodded toward the glass of water on the counter. "Can you bring that?"

She picked it up and followed behind Daniel, marveling at how he picked his way down the dimly lit hallway. Motion sensor lights had been placed along the bottom of the wall every five feet or so. They gave off enough light to get them there—to the *dawdihaus*—though Sissy didn't know how the Amish could live in such darkness. When the sun went down in her apartment in Tulsa, every light in the place was turned on. Just one more thing she would have to adjust to while living in Yoder. But she could do it. She was strong, inventive, imaginative, worthy, and powerful.

Not necessarily in that order.

The hardest thing to get used to was the all-encompassing darkness. She knew that the Amish didn't use electricity (though she hadn't asked her aunt why she could have it at the café if she couldn't have it at the house), but she hadn't thought through all the implications of it. Lack of electricity, that was.

No lights. No curling iron. No TV, radio, or comput- ers. No dishwasher. But she hadn't thought about exactly what *no lights* entailed. She raised her hand in the thick blackness that surrounded her. She couldn't see it. Not even a little. Feeling her movements, Duke whimpered and snuggled a little closer to her.

"Little chicken," she whispered, affection coloring her voice. "I'm glad I didn't get you for protection."

A heavy puppy sigh was her only answer. He wasn't about to act too indignant. He was afraid of the dark, after all.

Sissy glanced around her once again. Like it did any good. Pitch. Black. Lizzie and Bethel both had explained that there was a motion light close to the door. If Sissy needed anything—like to go to the bathroom in the mid- dle of the night—once she got up and started moving around, the motion sensors would pick up her actions, and the light would come on, allowing her to see the way.

She looked around once again. Not happening. If she

needed to pee before sunrise, she would hold it. Unlike Duke, she might not be afraid of the dark, but with darkness like this, she might have to rescind that claim.

It had been a little nerve-racking for Sissy to pack up everything she could fit into her car and head four hours from home without so much as a place to stay the night. Her mother had assured her that someone would take her in. Yet after that first, *dark* night with Bethel, Sissy knew she needed a more permanent place. You know, with electricity and everything.

The following day, she found the Chicken Coop. Or rather, the Chicken Coop found her. Yes, yes, it was just what it sounded like, a converted chicken coop that had been made into a one room/one bathroom flat, as the British would say. The original tiny house. It was perfect. Open, airy, and all hers—and Duke's—for the next six months.

Sissy stopped at the middle booth and poured a refresh of coffee for the young man sitting there.

He looked up from his notebook and smiled his appreciation.

"I just wanted to say thanks for turning me on to the Chicken Coop," she said as he lifted the cup and took a tentative sip.

Gavin Wainwright nodded and returned the white earthenware mug to its matching saucer. "No problem. I take it everything worked out?"

"Moved in yesterday."

"And Vera?"

"You could have warned me." She propped one hand on her hip and shot him a mockingly chastising look.

She had served Gavin lunch on her first day working at the café, and they had immediately hit it off. Not in a romantic way. Sissy wasn't looking for that right now. Not that Gavin wasn't handsome or anything. Maybe cute was the word. Not in the Brad Pitt sort of way. More like—she pulled her own wayward thoughts under control.

It didn't matter how cute he was or in what way. She wasn't in the market for romance and wouldn't be for a very long time. She and Gavin merely had a lot in common. He was the reporter at the *Sunflower Express*, the local underground newspaper. But she couldn't afford to get too close to him. She wouldn't want him to find out who she really was—the antithesis of Clark Kent, seeing as how her alter ego wore support hose instead of sexy spandex.

Gavin chuckled. "My great-aunt plays cards with her on Thursday mornings. She's something else, huh?"

"Something else is right."

Sissy had talked a little to Vera Yoder, whose family had left the Amish so long ago nobody remembered exactly when it had been. Vera owned the Chicken Coop and, as a proud resident of the small town, knew a great deal about it. How just to the east, a large field of sunflowers was grown every year—after all, Kansas was the Sunflower State. September brought the Kansas State Fair, which was always a hit, the salt mine and museum were a definite must-see, and the Carriage House Restaurant had the best chocolate peanut butter pie in two states.

"No offense to your auntie, see," Vera had said. "But Carriage House for pie." She smacked her lips. "That's where it's at."

Sissy had smiled and told her no offense was taken. She hadn't even been at the café long enough to know if they even served chocolate peanut butter pie. She supposed they must, if Vera thought exception might be taken to her saying one was better, but she was about ninety and might be getting things mixed up. Her blue eyes sparkled with intelligence and mischief, so Sissy had the feeling she rarely got things confused.

"Well, thanks again," Sissy told Gavin. "I'm really glad to have a place of my own."

"Again, no problem. And if you ever decide to write for a paper again . . ." He trailed off.

"I'll let you know," she said. Then she headed back to the waitress station to return the coffeepot to its waiting burner.

Maybe she shouldn't have told him that she had been a reporter. Of course, she had used past tense, because writing an advice column wasn't exactly reporting. Even if it did pay the bills. Even if her readership was growing. That was something she should be proud of. And she was. Just not enough to tell the world that Aunt Bess was a twenty-nine-year-old semi-failure from Oklahoma, and the wisdom she spouted came straight from her ex-Amish mother's lips. Wisdom she herself didn't always put into play.

"See what's taking Josie so long with the milkman," Bethel grumbled.

"Yes, ma'am." Sissy started toward the back, but only made it partway through the kitchen before she slipped. She caught herself against the ice machine. Some nonslip shoes these were turning out to be.

She supposed that was what she got for purchasing them at Walmart. Or THE Walmart, as half of Kansas called it. She smiled at the memory, then checked the bottoms of her shoes. Maybe she could still return them.

Maybe, she thought, as she pulled a slip of fabric from the sole of one and shoved it into her pocket. She supposed she could always try. With the nonskid capacity of these shoes, she might be better off in plain ol' running shoes.

"Josie," she called, turning the corner between the ice machine and large industrial sink.

She stopped in her tracks, the scene at her feet nothing like anything she had ever seen before. It looked staged, fake, too real to be real at all.

The back door was open, the milk delivery truck parked just outside. Its engine was running and the door to its cargo space pulled up. Clouds of cold steam billowed around the stacks of blue plastic crates still inside.

Three days. She had been working at the Sunflower Café for three days. Three days of her aunt's grumpy attitude, backbreaking work, and going home smelling like chicken fried steak. At least Duke appreciated that last one. And now this.

Was he dead?

The milk delivery man lay half in and half out of the back door to the café. His dolly, with its stack of crates, was parked in front of him, like he had been wheeling it in when *this* happened. One hand rested on the wheel. A large kitchen knife stuck out from his back. One of *their* kitchen knives?

Where was Josie?

She looked left, then right. Josie was nowhere to be seen.

Maybe it was a prank.

She inched closer, then nudged him with the toe of her not-so nonskid shoes. He didn't jump up and yell "Surprise!"

And one thing became very certain: This was no prank. Was he dead?

"Girl, where are you?" Her aunt called from the front, but Sissy couldn't move. She could only stare at his wide back and watch his pale blue shirt to see if it moved. She was careful to keep her eyes away from the growing red stain.

Kevin. Wasn't his name Kevin? More importantly, was he breathing?

And where was Josie?

"Girl!" Bethel's voice was closer now.

Sissy jumped. "Back here," she called. Well, she tried to call. Her words were barely louder than a squeak.

Then the clomp of her aunt's crutch and the thump of her not-a-walking cast against the tile floor preceded her arrival. "You've got customers who want to be fed out here. Quit your lollygagging."

"I'm not—" She started to defend herself but changed her mind. What good would it do? It surely wouldn't help poor Kevin.

Sissy stepped to one side so her aunt could get the full view of Kevin the milkman, literally stabbed in the back and still lying on their floor. "I think we need to call the police."

The café was closed for the rest of the day while the police, forensics, and the coroner all did their jobs. They dusted for fingerprints, notified the next of kin, and generally cleaned up everything. All the while, Sissy, Bethel, and Josie gave statements and waited for someone to tell them that they could go home.

It seemed Josie had opened the door for Kevin, then stepped outside to have a cigarette. The two of them—Sissy and Josie—were the most likely suspects. Though she supposed someone—anyone, really—could have come up from outside. Anyone at all.

Sissy had witnessed similar scenes on television where the unlucky person who had stumbled upon the body sat with a blanket over their shoulders while they drank tea or some other steaming liquid to ward off the shock. She didn't know why, but she had always imagined that it was tea. But she wouldn't be able to find out. Not today. For no one had brought her a blanket or a mug of anything, steaming or otherwise. And she certainly hoped that this would be the last dead body she would ever encounter.

Josie was outside, pacing in front of the café, chain-smoking, while a uniformed police officer kept watch. She was a tall girl, thin and willowy. Her long dark hair was pulled back into a low ponytail. She had dark eyes that seemed full of secrets, and to Sissy, she seemed as exotic as a gypsy. Josie might have been the last one to have seen Kevin alive, and she was definitely agitated over his death.

Bethel sat next to Sissy in the small room off the kitchen, a storeroom/breakroom where she'd sit down when her feet started to ache. There was a couch, along with a small table, two chairs that looked as if they had been moved from the main dining area, and stacks of cardboard boxes filled with everything from to-go lids to paper towels. Now there was also a small bed, sur-rounded by a section of baby gate, to keep Duke in place.

Bethel wasn't too happy with her guest, but since he wasn't in the kitchen per se, she frowned and went about her way.

He had been an angel all morning, but once the police arrived, he had started to bark. Sissy had to cover the top and the front of the gates to keep him under control. Even then, he was a little out of sorts as the coroner's men wheeled the milkman past the room.

A low growl came from behind the wall of dish towels.

"I knew it was a bad idea to let him come here."

Sissy turned to her aunt. "Duke?"

"*Jah.*"

"What's he got to do with anything?" He surely wasn't the one who killed Kevin the milkman.

"I don't know." Her aunt's frown deepened.

"Do you hate dogs or something?"

"He's hardly a dog."

Sissy pressed her lips together. "He's a faithful companion." And she wanted nothing more than to scoop him into her arms and bury her nose in his silky fur and forget today ever happened. Of all the people in her life, Duke had never let her down. Okay, so he wasn't a *people*, but he was still the one creature she could depend on.

Both women turned as a knock sounded. A large man stood in the doorway, blocking everything else from view. Duke started to bark again.

"Earl Berry," he said by way of greeting. "Deputy Sheriff. Which one of you found the body?"

Sissy raised her hand.

Duke continued to bark.

"I need to talk to you." He turned and frowned at the towel-covered lump that was Duke's home away from home. "Can you shut him up?"

"He's a little rattled by all the commotion."

Bethel harrumphed.

Maybe if Sissy held him. Maybe if he could see that everything was okay, relatively speaking; then he wouldn't be so jumpy.

"Just a minute." Sissy rose from her place on the couch and plucked Duke from his makeshift kennel. He let out a bark and licked her face. Then he finally noticed Earl Berry, the local deputy assigned to Yoder, and started to growl. "Hush," she said and kissed the top of Duke's little head. Then she turned her attention to the police-man. He had his notebook out and pen at the ready.

"What time did you find the body?" he asked.

"Just after eight."

He raised his gaze to her, one eyebrow at a disbeliev-ing angle. "You're certain." It wasn't an actual question. More of a challenge.

"Yes." She nodded, as if that somehow would make him believe her. And she had already told all this to an-other officer. "The milkman always comes at eight."

"Every morning." Again with the accusing words.

"It's a restaurant," Sissy started.

"Café," Bethel said from behind her.

What's the difference?

Duke continued to growl.

"We go through a lot of milk," Sissy finished. At least in her short experience, they had.

"And how long have you worked here?" He pinned her with sharp eyes.

"Three days."

"Uh-huh." He licked the end of his pen and wrote something in his book. Then he turned to Bethel. "What about you?"

"I own the café and have for thirty years. But you already know that."

Sissy may have only worked there for three days, but she had seen Earl Berry parked at the counter each and every one of them. It seemed he came to the café regularly, but she supposed he had only asked in his "official capacity."

He cleared his throat. "I only ask in my official capacity."

She watched entirely too many cop shows.

"And does the milkman come every day at eight?" Berry continued.

"I never noticed. My daughter normally works with me. She's the one who sees to the deliveries," Bethel explained.

"And where is this daughter?"

Bethel made a face that, to Sissy, looked like a struggle not to roll her eyes at the question. "At home. On bed rest."

"I'll need to ask her about that," he said.

Sissy frowned. "Shouldn't you be looking for the killer?"

"Need to establish motive," he said, but he was looking around as if it could be found there in the storeroom.

Duke growled.

"Shush," Sissy murmured. But she agreed. There was something about Earl Berry, Deputy Sheriff, that didn't sit well with her.

"Yep," he continued, snapping his notebook shut and pulling on his gun belt. Sissy wondered if his pants were truly sliding down or if he wanted them to be aware that he had a gun within his reach. "Motive and opportunity. And we know who had the opportunity."

* * *

"What did he mean by that?" Sissy asked as they were finally allowed to lock up the café and leave.

To her, it seemed that Josie had more opportunity than she had, and Berry didn't cross-examine her with such intensity.

Bethel merely grunted a response as she double-checked the door.

"Who had opportunity? Surely he wasn't talking about me." And surely, if he had made it through the police training, even if he was assigned to a small town like Yoder, he had to have some degree of intelligence.

Bethel grunted again and turned toward her tractor. The Amish in Yoder were allowed to have tractors to work in the fields, but they also drove them around like cars. Every day but Sunday, she had been told.

"I mean, who does he think killed Kevin? Me? And then all his irrelevant questions—'How did you break your leg, Ms. Yoder?'" She rolled her eyes, and then, realizing that she had reverted back to negative thoughts, straightened her shoulders and did her best to calm her own mind. Was it any wonder her thoughts were a jumbly mess of negativity after all she had been through today? "I'm sorry," she said.

Bethel stopped. "Why? Because you killed Kevin?"

She hoped her aunt was joking, but with Bethel's perpetual frown, it was impossible to tell. "I didn't kill Kevin," Sissy said emphatically. "It's just that when I decided to move here—"

Bethel whipped her attention around. "You're staying?"

"At least until after Lizzie has her baby." Sissy had figured six months. Two months of bed rest and four months of maternity leave. Yeah, it was a lot, but six months sounded like a good amount of time to reinvent oneself. "Where was I? Oh, yeah. When I decided to move here, I promised myself that I wouldn't let negative thoughts get in my way of a happy life." *Lord knows it hasn't been that happy lately.* Hence the vow to remain positive, regardless of the situation.

"Bah." Bethel crossed her arms and looked down the street, first one way and then the other.

"Do you need a ride?"

Her aunt turned a dubious eye toward Sissy's little car. "In that?"

Sissy frowned. She had taken hits about her dog and her car, and she was accustomed to this from her brother, but still . . . for someone who usually drove around on a tractor to say anything . . . "Yes, in that." She waited a heartbeat to see if her aunt would protest further. When she didn't, Sissy continued. "Come on. You know you want to."

Bethel made her way to the car, all the while shaking her head. The strings of her prayer covering swayed with the motion.

That was something different, Sissy thought, as Bethel slipped into the passenger's seat. Her aunt was wearing a *kapp* instead of a bandana. Which meant that she didn't feel the need to protect it. Amish women took great care in their prayer coverings. Her mother had told her stories about buying a new one because the one she had got wet or dirty somehow. Mary Yoder had also tried to explain how they were near-sacred to Amish women, but Sissy couldn't quite grasp the concept. She did understand that Bethel in a *kapp* instead of a bandana meant that she hadn't planned on being in the kitchen. Which meant she was starting to trust Sissy. And that was a great positive thought.

She shifted Duke, then handed him over to her aunt. "Hold him."

Her aunt blustered but took the dog. Sissy settled into the driver's seat and lowered the top. Duke barked his approval; for a moment, Sissy thought Bethel might bark in protest, but she didn't. She simply held onto Duke with one hand and her prayer covering with the other. And Sissy smiled a bit to herself.

They drove the short distance to Bethel's house, and after a brief visit with Lizzie, a refusal of an invitation to stay for supper, and one dog treat later, she and Duke were back on their way.

"You know what?" she asked Duke as she backed out of the drive. "I know she frowns and fusses all the time, but I think she likes us." And that was the best positive thought of all.

CHAPTER THREE

It's not always necessary to make the right decision. But you must always make the decision right.
—Aunt Bess

Sissy looked around and smiled. How do you know you've made the right decision? Everything falls into place. And—dead body aside—everything about her move to Yoder had fallen into place.

She looked over to where Duke lay on the bright coral and pink paisley duvet covering the bed. He loved it here, too. For now, it was home, a place of rest and sanctuary. Actually, it had been so easy to settle into the Chicken Coop and get comfortable. And he did look comfortable. So much so that she almost hated waking him, but it was Sunday, the café had been closed for two days, and she was going a bit stir crazy in the tiny, tiny house.

The first day that she had been without café work had been something of a godsend. She hadn't known exactly what she would need for her stay, and consequently, hadn't packed everything she owned, storing some of it at her parents' house in Tulsa. What she hadn't brought with her, she bought in neighboring Hutchinson, figuring she would spend more on gas than items if she drove home to Tulsa, then all the way back to Yoder. Dishes, a few towels for the kitchen, a Keurig from Walmart, and she was ready to move in.

Plus, that had given her time to write her column, answering a letter from a young woman who was having dating troubles. Oh, sister, get in line.

Not that the advice she had given Depressed in Denver in any way resembled her true thoughts. *There are more fish in the sea*, she had written, *which is great if you're a fish. Since you're not, be patient and open, and a man will come along. And when he does, and he gets on your last nerve, remember this letter. Then pick up his dirty underwear, put the toilet seat back down, and thank your lucky stars you found love.*

But today . . .

She walked over to the bed. "Come on, lazy bones."

Duke opened his eyes but didn't lift his head. He just breathed out a doggie sigh, as if he couldn't bear it.

"Wanna go bye-bye?"

That got his attention. He was immediately on his feet. He trotted to the edge of the bed, but Sissy scooped him up before he could make the plunge to the floor. He really was fearless. And he certainly didn't understand that he only weighed three and a half pounds and could hurt himself if he dove off the side of the bed. Even a bed as low as the one their new home boasted.

She set him on the floor, and he scampered to the door, bracing his paws on the trim as he waited impatiently for her to let him out.

"Just a second." She grabbed her sunglasses, her purse, and her keys, then snatched his leash off the hook by the door. Most cities had a leash law these days, though so many people simply disregarded it. She had no idea how strict Yoder would be about such matters, but after her encounter with Deputy Sheriff Earl Berry, she didn't want to take any chances.

She hooked the thin green leash to Duke's matching collar, then stepped out into the beautiful Kansas sunshine. "Wanna go with the top down?" she asked as she let them into the car.

Duke barked.

Like there was any question.

She wrapped his leash around the gearshift and pressed the necessary buttons to lower the ragtop. Sissy had bought the car when her Aunt Bess column took off. It had been her one extravagance from her success. A convertible. She loved to feel the wind on her face and the sense of freedom when she drove it. Duke liked it, too, running from one side to the other of his box-like car seat, loving that he could see more things and therefore had more things to bark at. But she always kept him securely tethered, in case his adventuresome nature got the better of him.

The one drawback was her fair skin, so prone to burn. She had so many freckles already, she figured if she got a few more, they would simply join together and become a tan. Still, she slathered on sunscreen and kept a baseball hat at the ready.

So, with her long copper hair pulled back into a ponytail and the address of the Chicken Coop in her GPS so she could easily get back, Sissy set off.

Most of the stores on Main were closed since it was

Sunday, but that was all right. Sissy wasn't really in the mood for shopping.

Visiting the salt mine sounded like a very interesting thing to do, but she wasn't sure she wanted to go over six hundred feet underground . . . alone—even if she would be with a bunch of strangers—and what would Duke do while she was down below?

With the blue sky above and the green grass all around, the day was perfect. Murder at work aside, she was beginning to enjoy her time in Yoder.

She had talked to her aunt and found out that today was not a church Sunday for them, and Bethel had plans to sit with Lizzie and help relieve some of the boredom of bed rest. Sissy just wanted to explore.

Most of the side streets in Yoder were dirt and gravel, which was fine until someone came from the other direction. With a convertible, the entire car filled with dust. If she rolled up her window when she saw another car, it wasn't as bad, yet a car detail was definitely in her future.

Sissy slowed as she neared the place where she had been told the school was. A line of trees separated it from the road, but she could still plainly see the long white building. It was actually two buildings, complete with a playground and a makeshift baseball field. Lizzie had told her that not all the Amish children attended the "one-room" schoolhouse. Some went to the "regular" school with the *Englisch*, or non-Amish kids. Once they completed the eighth grade, the *Englisch* kids went on to high school in neighboring Hutchinson, and the Amish kids were done.

She turned around in the drive, wondering what it would be like to go to such a small school. Her graduating class had a little more than three hundred. She couldn't imagine twenty or so kids in the entire school. Nor could she imagine not having a high school education. Or a college one, for that matter.

That wasn't the kind of life James and Mary Yoder had wanted for their children, and so they had moved.

Sissy continued down as many of the backroads she could find, sometimes traveling in one direction to turn around fifteen minutes later and find herself going the opposite way.

Duke loved it. Sissy had ordered him a car seat off the Internet so he could better see out the window. Still, she would have been nervous had he not been securely fastened on his leash and harness.

As they drove along, she slowed and checked out the signs, looking for hometown bakeries and candy shops. Nothing better than buying muffins out of someone's shed. Most would be closed today, but she'd make a note of places to come back to.

She eased off the gas as a deep brown sign came into view. Scrolling white letters declared YODER HORSE FARM: BOARDING, TRAINING, BREEDING.

It was like a postcard: the rolling green grass, the dark boards of the fence, and the blue sky behind. Sissy's breath hitched when she caught sight of the horses. She hadn't seen anything so beautiful in all her life. Shiny coats, waving manes, and rippling muscles. Chestnut, black, and a white roan. Absolutely amazing.

She pulled her car to the side of the road and watched the horses move around the pasture. Most were grazing on the grass and enjoying the day. Duke barked and growled, scampering from side to side of his box seat, as if those few inches would make a difference to the great beasts. Of course, they paid him no mind.

But they were simply too magnificent for her to just sit in her car and watch. She wanted to be closer to them, even if it was mere feet from where she sat to the fence. She turned off the motor, gathered Duke's leash, and got out. The horses ignored her as they continued about their easy munching, but Sissy knew that they knew she was watching them. And they loved the attention. She could tell with each shining swell of muscle as they continued to pretend that she wasn't there. Duke danced and barked, wagging his little stumpy tail as if he were about to meet a new friend. A friend that weighs in at nearly a ton.

"Hello!"

She turned as a man started across the edge of the pasture. He waved, and she returned the gesture, turning her full attention from the horses to him as he came near. He wore a chambray shirt, worn jeans, and a hat that looked somewhere between cowboy and Indiana Jones.

"I hope you don't mind my stopping," she said, then gestured toward the horses. "I had to get a closer look."

"Not at all." He smiled, revealing straight white teeth in a charmingly crooked smile. "Evan Yoder." He reached out a hand, his strong, tanned forearm revealed by the up-turned cuff.

"Sissy Yoder," she returned after shaking with him.

"No relation, I suppose."

"In this town, who knows?"

Evan Yoder was at least a decade older than her. A handsome man with dark hair, deep green eyes, and just the right number of sun lines creasing his face. "You like horses?" he asked.

She shrugged. "I like all animals, I suppose. Just never spent much time around horses, though."

"They are something, aren't they?" It seemed as if he

were talking about the horses, but his gaze never left her. She couldn't decide if it was flattering or creepy. One thing she knew for certain: Evan Yoder was intense.

"You work here?" she asked, searching for something to say before the atmosphere got weird.

"My family owns the farm, so I guess you could say that. Yeah."

Yoder Horse Farm, duh. Sometimes it was so hard to tell, since there were so many Yoders running around Yoder. Another duh.

"Of course," she murmured, hoping she sounded at least halfway intelligent. "Riding lessons, that sort of thing."

He smiled indulgently. A curve of the lips that told her he had answered the question too many times to count and found it on the whole to be tedious. "Boarding, breeding, training, that sort of thing."

Just like the sign said.

Duke picked that moment to grow tired of being ignored. He rushed toward Evan and propped his paws on the man's leg as he barked for attention.

"Sorry." Sissy tried to pull him away.

Evan, that same smile firmly in place, reached down and allowed Duke to smell his hand before scratching him behind one ear. The look on his face—Evan's, not Duke's—was one of masked . . . something. Sissy couldn't tell exactly what he was hiding, though she had a feeling he was uncomfortable.

She tugged on the leash once again. "Come on, Duke."

Sensing that his moment of attention from the stranger was over, Duke trotted back to her side.

"You're new in town, huh?" he asked, his gaze on her car.

A convertible was something of a novelty in a small

town, and in a town the size of Yoder, there couldn't be many. She was bound to be noticed—if not for her flaming hair, then definitely for her topless car.

"Yeah," she answered. "I came up to help my aunt. At the Sunflower Café."

He nodded. "Good food."

"Yes." What else could she say?

"Shame what happened."

She nodded. "Did you know him? Kevin?"

Evan's expression shifted, but the indifference remained firmly in place. "No."

Now, why did she feel like that was a lie? Maybe because there were barely eight hundred people in Yoder, including the Amish. She was pretty sure all the Amish people knew one another. Why not the *Englisch*?

And that was a prejudiced assumption. But still, the niggling doubt remained.

"He seemed like a nice guy," she said. Not that she had gotten to know him all that well. She had only been in Yoder three days when he had been murdered.

"A shame," Evan said again.

"What's that?" she asked, pointing to a sign across the road. The white paint and blue lettering had started to chip around the edges. BRUBACHER DAIRY. She needed to change the subject, and Evan's closest neighbor was as good a shift as any.

"Local dairy," he said with a dismissive wave. "Raw milk and cheese. That sort of thing."

"Raw milk?" she asked. The milk they received at the café came from a place out of Hutchinson. And though she hadn't looked that closely at it, she assumed it was just regular old milk.

Evan shrugged. "Not homogenized."

"It's okay to sell raw milk in Kansas?"

He gave her a perplexed look.

"I'm from Tulsa," she explained.

"Yeah. I guess it's okay. Never really thought that much about it. Guess they wouldn't have such an open business if it was illegal."

"Good point." She scooped up Duke and bowed her head to avoid his overzealous puppy kisses. "Thanks for letting me look at the horses," she said, then turned back toward her car.

"Anytime," Evan replied. Though she had a feeling he didn't mean that at all.

"Knock, knock."

Sissy turned from her place at the grill and checked the clock over the soda machine. Nine-twenty. The new milkman. Had to be. And late. She looked back to the almost-done bacon. If she left it now, it would burn. Things had been a little shaken up since the m-u-r-d-e-r. "Just a minute," she called.

She only worked behind the grill in times of need. That was usually Josie or Bethel. But Josie had an appointment, and Lottie was out front. Not that Lottie was much of a short-order cook. She would rather fill everyone's drinks and make sure they had enough napkins.

Sissy glanced back over her shoulder. Kevin had always let himself in, dropped the delivery, and waited for someone to check it and sign off.

Maybe the new guy was uncomfortable coming in on his first visit.

"Come in," Sissy called as she scooped up the bacon and deposited it on the waiting plate. Two steps over to slide it through the window. Then turned to find—"Argh!"

The milkman was standing directly behind her. He hadn't made a sound, at least none that she heard. Quiet shoes, quiet keys, no slamming door.

"Sorry. Did I scare you?" He smiled in such a way that Sissy got the feeling he wasn't the least bit remorseful for taking years off her life. In fact, she was beginning to wonder if he had done it on purpose. Or maybe she was still a little jumpy. It had only been a few days since she had found the bo—*him*, and she was still a bit rattled.

"A little, yes." She pressed a hand to her heart. "So you're taking over Kevin's route?" She looked at the name sewn into the blue industrial shirt he wore. "Mike?"

"Nah." He waved a hand as if the idea were ludicrous. "We just split up his stops for now."

Sissy nodded and reached for the invoice he still held.

Mike straightened and handed it over.

She glanced behind her as she moved to the large cooler where they kept the perishables. Look at the paper, check the cartons. "Do you have a pen?"

Mike patted his pockets as if searching, but Sissy knew it was all for show. "Sorry. And don't tell me . . . Kevin always had one."

Sissy didn't comment, but she wanted to say, "As a matter of fact, he did." "Just a minute," she said instead, and made her way to the front with the invoice.

Normally, at this time of morning, the café would be hopping. But today, not so much. The dining area contained only two of the regulars, none of the sporadic, and a couple of new faces that must have been from out of town and hadn't heard that a murder had taken place just yards from where they now sat.

Bethel shot Sissy a questioning frown but didn't comment as she signed the paper and took it back to the kitchen.

"Shame what happened," Mike said. Sissy didn't think he sounded like it was a shame. More like he was glad that it happened. Smug, even.

"Yes," she said and handed him the invoice.

He tore off the pink copy and shoved the rest into his shirt pocket. "Yeah. The company softball team just won't be the same without him."

Positive, she thought. *Be positive*. But a man was dead, and all Mike was worried about was the softball team? "He seemed like a really nice man."

"There's where it lies." Mike shook his head. "He *seemed* like a good man."

"You mean he wasn't?"

Mike shifted his gaze from one side to the other, as if checking to see if anyone was close enough to hear what he was about to say next. "You didn't hear this from me, but I heard that he was into some pretty shady gambling deals."

"Shady gambling?"

"Definitely not in the Indian casinos, if you know what I mean."

Sissy shook her head.

"More like under the table, bookie kind of thing. And he ended up owing the wrong people a lot of money."

She supposed that could happen to anybody—fall into debt, do something drastic to get out of it—but having it cost him his life?

"And you think those people were responsible for his death?"

Mike shrugged.

"But now that they've killed him, they'll never get their money."

"Who said the Mafia was logical?"

Wait. "The Mafia? *The* Mafia?" There was no Mafia in Kansas. Was there? She opened her mouth to say something, then realized. "You're pulling my leg."

"You got me." Mike laughed.

Sissy chuckled along with him, though not with the same gusto.

"Seriously, though, do you know why he was killed?" Mike asked.

"No. Why?" Sissy shook her head. She had been in Kansas exactly seventy-two hours when Kevin had died. How was she supposed to know who had a beef with him?

"I was hoping you'd tell me." He pointed a *gotcha* finger in her direction, his mouth open in mock surprise.

Sissy chuckled again, but this time, she couldn't make it sound natural. She held up the invoice. "Nice to meet you, Mike."

It was the biggest lie she had told in a long, long time.

"Girl," Bethel called from the front. She had finally stopped coming back into the kitchen, standing in the entrance for a moment, then retreating back to the dining area. Lottie had given her a chair and a stool to rest her casted foot on, and she had settled down into taking orders and ringing people out.

Now if Sissy could just get her to call her by name.

Keep positive.

She wiped her hands on a towel and headed out front.

"Chief is here." She nodded toward Earl Berry.

"Deputy Sheriff," he corrected.

Bethel grunted.

Sissy had the feeling the slip was intentional. Maybe there was more to her aunt than she realized. She hid her smile and turned her attention to the deputy. "Can I help you?"

"Yes, ma'am. I have a few more questions to ask you."

"Okay."

"Down at the station."

"In Hutchinson?" Bethel asked.

"Yup," Earl Berry replied.

Sissy opened her mouth to respond but found no words. Could she refuse? She looked behind her to the kitchen, then back to the deputy. Kitchen. Deputy. "I—"

"I can't spare her right now," Bethel said.

"It's a fifteen-minute drive," Berry pointed out.

"Can't spare her," Bethel repeated. "So unless you have enough evidence to arrest her, you can use a booth until a customer comes in. Then she cooks."

She didn't know whether to laugh or cry. Bethel was one tough cookie. "Where did you learn so much about the law?"

"You know." Her aunt shrugged, and her expression remained the same. "We have a cabin at the lake," she said, and gave another one of those jerky shrugs. "What happens at the lake stays at the lake." Then she winked.

Wait.

She winked at Sissy?

"If you know what I mean," Bethel finished.

Sissy wasn't sure, but she thought her aunt was talking

about television. As in, watching television at the lake cabin. But that couldn't be. The Amish didn't use electricity, and they surely didn't watch television. Cop shows. *Law & Order*.

But the thought of her aunt using electricity wasn't nearly as shocking as the fact that she had winked at Sissy.

At least, Sissy thought she had.

Sissy slid into the booth opposite the deputy and folded her hands on the table. She figured she should offer him a drink, but a mean-spirited part of her refused. Being positive all the time definitely had its drawbacks.

"So tell me, Ms. Yoder, what time did you arrive in town?"

How many times was she going to have to answer this one? "I got here at two o'clock-ish."

"And what day?"

"Tuesday. Are you going to write this down?" Come tomorrow, she would have been in Yoder for a whole week.

He shot her a cold smile that seemed to relay that he was the one asking the questions, and she should sit there and answer them.

I'm a jerk; what's your superpower?

Her lips twitched as she fought back a smile. Not the most positive thought for the day, but it cheered her up, anyhow.

"And where did you spend the night?"

Positive. Be positive.

"I stayed with my aunt and cousin."

"And since then?" he asked.

I'm positive he's a jerk.

"Miss?" he prompted.

Really. They had gone over all this the day Kevin was killed and the day after. She had told the deputy *and* his partner. How many times did they need to hear the same information?

"Wait a minute." Sissy sat back in her seat and crossed her arms. "You're trying to catch me in a lie."

There came that smile again. "And when did you first meet Kevin Saunders?"

"Wednesday."

"And he was killed on Friday."

She nodded. "See? Why would I know a man for three days, then . . . ?" She trailed off, unable to say the words. Well, she didn't want to say them. She didn't want to say anything out loud that had her name and *murder* in the same sentence.

"We're just keeping all avenues open, Miss Yoder. As of right now, you aren't a suspect. But as for killing a man after claiming to only know him for three days . . . well, stranger things have happened."

Sissy resisted the urge to roll her eyes. He didn't seem to be the sharpest knife in the chopping block, but he was still law enforcement and could arrest her if he so chose.

"Did you or did you not have an altercation with Mr. Saunders three days ago?"

"An altercation?" Sissy sputtered. "I mean, he yelled at me because I didn't unlock the back door for him." Which she hadn't known she was supposed to do.

"And did you yell back?"

"Maybe a little." She was a redhead, after all. Supposedly, they were known for having a fiery temperament. But that didn't make her a killer. "It was nothing, really."

Berry grimaced. Or maybe that was his smile. "I'll be the judge of that."

"I didn't know I was supposed to unlock the door for him, and he was angry that I hadn't. But I didn't know. So I didn't think it fair for him to yell for something I didn't know about, so I yelled back. End of story." Not really. It seemed the story hadn't really ended yet at all. Not if she was still being questioned by the police.

The deputy clicked his pen, gathered his notebook, then stood. "Thank you, Miss Yoder. We'll be back in touch as necessary."

CHAPTER FOUR

Fair is where you get cotton candy.
—Aunt Bess

We'll be back in touch as necessary. Sissy grumbled for the rest of the afternoon. It was just bad timing—or perhaps bad luck on her part—that she was the one who had found Kevin. Josie was the one who had let Kevin into the back. She was the one who had unlocked the door for him to come in that morning, not Sissy. She was the one who hadn't waited for him check the order. Like she was supposed to do.

But it seemed that Earl Berry, Deputy Sheriff, felt that since Sissy had found Kevin, that in turn made her guilty of his murder. Circumstantial evidence. But she knew people had gone to prison on less evidence than that. Or maybe she should stop watching investigative television.

"I just don't understand it," she said to Lottie. They were alone in the kitchen; Sissy was chopping cabbage for coleslaw while Lottie gathered up supplies to stock the front—napkins, to-go cups and lids, straws, and anything else they might need. Josie was on yet another smoke break, and Bethel was watching the front.

Lottie paused and studied Sissy for a moment. "You don't know then."

"I suppose not," Sissy returned. What was that saying? She couldn't know what she didn't know until she knew it. Or something like that.

"Earl Berry had a thing for your mom."

"Ew." Sissy made a face. "A thing?"

Lottie shrugged one shoulder. "You know, he liked her. A lot. Or so it would seem. It also seems like he never got over her."

"What's that got to do with me?" Sissy ran another wedge of cabbage through the shredder, then turned to face Lottie directly.

She liked Lottie. The woman was positive and supportive, and she gave the absolute best hugs.

"Well," Lottie started, "I think he might be picking on you because of that crush he had."

"On my mother?" It was weird to think about her parents doing something other than being her parents. "Did they date?" She'd never heard her mother talk about anything like that, and suddenly she wished she'd paid more attention to all of her mother's ramblings about her life in Yoder.

"I suppose," Lottie started again, "and this is just me talking here, but your mom left the Amish and became *Englisch*."

"Yes."

"That would have been the one thing that kept her from dating Earl Berry to begin with."

Sissy mulled that over. It made sense. She did know from her mother that she and her father had joined the church before deciding that life in the Amish community was just too difficult. And imagine! That was before cell phones and the Internet. "So you're saying that she probably told him, Earl, that she couldn't date him because he wasn't Amish, then she jumped ship and left the Amish with my dad."

Lottie shrugged that one shoulder again. "I have no evidence, but it seems to me. And most call it jumping the fence."

Sissy dropped another chunk of cabbage into the shredder, then propped her hands on her hips. "That just makes me mad. I didn't do anything. I wasn't even born yet."

"Who said matters of the heart brought about fairness?" Lottie asked.

Fair is where you get cotton candy, Aunt Bess would say.

Sissy pulled a head of purple cabbage from the bin next to the sink and started chopping it into chunks, perhaps a little more forcefully than necessary. "If you ask me, he should be looking at Josie, if he wants to blame someone at the café."

"Josie is as innocent as you are," Lottie said.

Sissy seriously doubted that.

"I've known that girl her whole life," Lottie continued.

"I suppose," Sissy mumbled. People changed. Life changed people. People hid the truth from those around them. Just because Lottie thought she knew Josie didn't mean she really did.

"She's lived here since she was born," Lottie added. "Except for her four years at Mizzou."

Sissy tossed a chunk of purple cabbage into the chute and waited for the grinder to stop before she replied. "Shouldn't that be a strike against her? Mizzou?"

Lottie just smiled. "You'll just have to trust me on this one."

"I suppose," Sissy mumbled, and chucked another wedge of cabbage into the shredder. Perhaps the rivalry between Mizzou and Kansas wasn't as hardcore as the one between OU and OSU. "What about the Mafia?" Sissy asked.

Lottie frowned. "What about it?"

"Is it still big?" Sissy asked.

"Lord, girl, how would I know something like that?" She gathered up the rest of the supplies and made her way back through the swinging aluminum doors to the front of the café.

Sissy sighed and turned back to her task. She knew the East Coast mob, the ones in Vegas, and even those in Chicago were not what they used to be. But whatever happened to the Mafia in Kansas City? It used to be pretty powerful. Was it still? And was that who Mike had been talking about when he tossed around the idea that Kevin might have owed some unsavory characters a large sum of money?

Sissy started peeling carrots. She had no answers to any of these questions, just like she had no answer to what Josie was doing with a bachelor's degree—assuming she had graduated after four years of study—and working in a tiny café in the middle of nowhere. Was the workforce so spent in Josie's major that she was resigned to working as a short-order cook?

Then again, so had she. But her situation was different.

And to Sissy's knowledge, Bethel hadn't even run a background check on Josie before she hired her. Years away could change a person; Sissy herself was testament to that.

Josie picked that moment to sweep back into the café. A trail of cigarette smoke followed behind her.

Sissy pretended to be concentrating on the vegetables in front of her but watched Josie from the corner of her eye. Pretty much all she could see was that crazy-looking Pegasus tattoo that wrapped around her upper arm and onto the back of her right shoulder blade.

And that was another thing. How come Josie got to wear whatever she wanted to work, aka white wifebeater tank tops, when the rest of them were supposed to wear the Sunflower Café T-shirts? Well, all except Bethel. She didn't have to wear one because . . . well, she was Amish and the owner, but she did spend a lot of time with the sunflower-printed kerchief tied around her head instead of a traditional white prayer covering. Sissy supposed that counted.

But why was it that the rules didn't seem to apply to Josie? And did "the rules" include felonies—like murder?

Sissy reined in her thoughts as Josie nudged her aside to wash her hands. Scooching as far over as she could without completely abandoning her post, Sissy waited for Josie to finish. Then it was back to coleslaw.

Was it just her, or was Josie taking an extra long time to get her hands clean?

Josie graced her with a tight, almost apologetic smile. Sissy had the feeling that perhaps Josie had overheard some of her conversation with Lottie. And if that were the case . . .

And Josie really was the murderer . . .

Sissy held her breath as Josie grabbed a couple of paper towels, then methodically dried her hands. With the precision of an NBA star, she tossed the wadded-up paper towels into the trash; then she picked up the knife sitting on the counter next to Sissy.

Sissy's heart stopped, her breath stranded somewhere between her nose and her lungs. Was this it? "I was using that."

Perhaps the dumbest phrase in protest of one's own murder ever uttered.

Josie ran a thumb over the edge of the blade. "It's dull."

"It seemed fine to me." Sissy winced. Not exactly a plea for one's life.

Josie continued to pluck a thumb across the blade. "I could hear you chopping all the way outside."

"Uh-huh." *Say something. Say anything to keep her from hurting you. Because if she could hear you chopping while she was on her smoke break, then she surely heard what you said to Lottie.* "I like it that way."

Stupid, Sissy.

Josie shrugged and handed the knife back to Sissy. The proper way, too; handle first, even. "Let me know when it's bothersome, and I'll sharpen it for you. I like my knives really sharp."

"Go on. Tell her." Lottie nudged Bethel in the side as they were preparing to leave the café. Sissy was pretty sure that today had been the longest day of her life. Time dragged by, and she was constantly on edge, as if she were fearing for her life. Every time she turned around, it seemed as if Josie was taunting her, or perhaps it was her own writer's imagination getting the better of her. It wasn't like she could ask Josie or anything. So she braced herself for the worst and said a little prayer for safety in case God was listening. She really didn't want to drag Him into this mess, but like Aunt Bess always said, *No good deed goes unpunished*.

Sissy had come to Yoder to help out; now, she was worried she was next in line for this murderer on the loose, and the local deputy was out to frame her for the killing. No good deed, indeed . . .

"Tell me what?" she asked, jumping on the chance to escape her own thoughts.

Bethel harrumphed. "We're not having a dinner on Friday night this week," she said.

"We're not?" Sissy asked. In all the excitement of the murder and being questioned within an inch of her life, she'd forgotten all about the Friday night family supper. Of course, it wasn't the first thing on her mind, since it was only Monday. "Why not?"

"Daniel's got a meeting," Bethel replied.

Sissy supposed it wouldn't be a family dinner without Daniel there. And she liked Lizzie's husband. "Oh. Okay, then."

Lottie cleared her throat.

Bethel stared at her for a moment; then she jerked a bit, and Sissy had a feeling that Lottie might've pinched her. The relationship between these two was truly amazing. If she were a psychologist, she could have a field day with it.

"We've moved it to tonight. And Lizzie wanted me to tell you so that you could come."

It was so thoughtful and sweet of her cousin to want to

include her, but Sissy wasn't sure she was up for a family dinner tonight. She was still a little frazzled and was starting to get a headache from clenching her jaw, something she did every time Josie passed behind her. Which seemed to be more often than usual. Or maybe it was her imagination again. "That's really nice of her," Sissy said. "But I think I'm gonna pass. I'm very tired. Exhausted." She faked a yawn, as if to add more weight to her excuse.

And she *was* tired. Plum worn out, as her mom would say. She really wanted nothing more than to go back to the Chicken Coop and sleep until she had to get up for her shift tomorrow.

Bethel grunted in that special way of hers and turned off the lights, as they started for the door.

Her aunt slipped the keys into her purse, and the three of them made their way around the side of the building back to where their cars were parked. Josie, of course, had gotten off early—again.

Sissy couldn't help but wonder where she went all the time. It seemed as if she was on a smoke break more than she was actually cooking, and she asked for more days off than Sissy had even worked so far. But Bethel seemed to take it all in stride, and Sissy figured it wasn't her business to question. She had come to help out, and scrutinizing her aunt's every move surely wouldn't be helpful.

Lottie chatted about the weather as they went to their respective cars.

"Do you need a ride?" Sissy asked. Her aunt had weeks to go until her cast was removed, and therefore, weeks to go before she could drive her tractor again.

Bethel shot a dubious look at Sissy's little import. "Not again in this lifetime."

Lottie shook her head. "What she means to say is that I had already planned to take her home."

"I don't mind," Sissy said.

Bethel planted her fists on her hips. "I thought you were tired."

Sissy shrugged. "Suit yourself." Though she felt her car was a lot more fun to ride in than Lottie's sedan.

Again, not her business. Not her problem. She was only here to help. She unlocked her car and slipped inside, immediately rolling down the top.

Her aunt looked over and shook her head. "You'll wear out that motor if you keep driving every day with the top off like that."

Sissy just smiled. "I didn't buy a convertible to drive around with the top up. See you tomorrow." She waved at them both, slipped on her sunglasses, and backed out of the parking lot.

Her car was the one thing that she enjoyed in that decadent way of triple chocolate cheesecake and margaritas before five. And she loved it, she thought as she drove home. Just as she was going to enjoy rest, relaxation, and an early night.

But after two hours of her own company, she decided maybe going out to her aunt's house was a good idea. Or maybe not a *bad* idea. Yeah, that was it. So she loaded up Duke, and off they went.

Sissy wasn't one hundred percent certain that the invitation included her dog, but she couldn't leave Duke behind. One reason was that Lizzie loved him, and she was cooped up all day just as he was. That first week Sissy had been in Yoder, she had gone to the hardware store and bought the biggest kennel they had. It broke her heart to

leave her dog in it when she went to work, but having him
at the Sunflower was too much. Especially after all the
mess with Kevin and the police.

"Knock, knock," she said, going in the back way like
she had the first visit with Lizzie.

"Come in, come in," her cousin gushed. "Mamm said
you weren't coming."

Sissy unhooked the leash from Duke's collar and lifted
him up onto the bed. It was quite a jump for a little dog,
and Sissy knew he would want to give Lizzie a few sweet
hello kisses. "I changed my mind," she said.

"Hello, precious." Lizzie scratched Duke behind the
ears, and he let out dramatic puppy sigh. Then he flopped
down next to her and snuggled in close, basking in the attention of someone other than his "mom." "I'm glad you
came," Lizzie continued.

Sissy was glad, too.

"Sit. Sit," Lizzie commanded, waving one hand in the
direction of the chair pulled up next to the bed. It looked
like one of the dining room chairs, and Sissy supposed
that someone had dragged it in here to be comfortable
while they visited with Lizzie. Sissy herself had never
been pregnant, or injured badly, or anything where she
had to stay in bed for an extended amount of time, and
she could only imagine how bored her cousin got.

"I should go see if anybody needs help with supper,"
Sissy protested. But only halfheartedly.

"You must visit with me first." Lizzie smiled. "House
rules."

"I can't argue with that." Sissy settled down in the
chair. "But only for a moment."

"I'll take whatever I can get."

"So," Sissy started, as casually as she could. "How

well do you know Josie?" A wave of guilt washed over her as the words came out of her mouth. They had been hovering around the edges of her mind ever since this afternoon, when she'd told herself the next time she saw her cousin, she would ask her in a nonchalant, nonthreatening way. She had not succeeded on any of those fronts.

Lizzie frowned, even as she continued to scratch Duke's ears. "We've known each other our whole lives."

"And you went to school together?"

Lizzie shook her head. "I went to the Amish school. Josie went to the charter school."

Sissy had heard that the students at the charter school were a mixed lot, some Amish, some not, but she had never thought to ask her cousin about it. It was an interesting concept. Then add in the fact that the Amish only went to school until the eighth grade, and it was a noteworthy notion, indeed.

"So you don't know her well at all."

"What's this about?" Lizzie was nothing if not sharp.

"Nothing, really," Sissy said. "It's just . . . she seems a little extreme." Even as she said the word, it wasn't what she wanted. *Threatening* was more like it. *Extreme* just brought to mind someone who was over the top. Not necessarily a murderer.

"She's been through a lot," Lizzie explained, though the sentence was no explanation at all. Everyone had been through something or another. But still, the guilt hung around. Sissy had come to visit her cousin and have a good evening, not quiz her on how well Lizzie knew the short-order cook at the café. It was just . . . well, Sissy had this terrible feeling that if she didn't figure out who killed Kevin the milkman, she might be sent away for the crime. She had seen enough shows about the Innocence

Project on Netflix to know that it was very possible to serve life in prison for a crime she didn't commit. Especially when there was a police officer who wanted her to be guilty. Cough. Earl Berry.

"That's what they tell me," Sissy said, referring back to Josie's past.

"Her brother's in prison, you know."

Sissy frowned. "No, I didn't know that." Although she had wondered if Josie might have done time. She was tough around the edges like that.

"I know it's got to be hard on her," Lizzie said. "Though she never mentioned it when we were working together."

Sissy nodded. "She just comes across a little scary. And then the whole Kevin thing."

"You don't think she had anything to do with Kevin's death?" Lizzie pushed up a little straighter in the bed.

"I don't know," Sissy said, shifting uncomfortably herself. She took a deep breath and finally admitted the truth to someone. "There was only the two of us back there. Me and Josie. And I know I didn't kill Kevin."

Lizzie nodded. "I understand what you're saying, and it makes logical sense. But I don't think Josie is capable of murder." She laughed. "What am I saying? Of course she's not capable of murder. I just can't fathom that."

And that was the problem with being close to someone, Sissy thought. You couldn't see the truth about them because you were blinded. You were too close to the action, too close to the emotion to see what was right in front of your face.

She should've never brought it up.

Sissy stood, brushed her hands down the front of her jeans. "I'll go see if your *mamm* needs any help."

"Will you leave this little sweetheart with me?" Lizzie

continued to rub the space between Duke's eyes, which were closed in blissful happiness. "I could use the company."

Sissy nodded, unable to get words past the lump that had suddenly formed in her throat. She hadn't meant to cause offense. Even though Lizzie was smiling and still petting Duke like nothing had happened, Sissy still felt an uncomfortable vibe between the two of them. And she hated it. "Of course," she replied, before ducking out of the room and heading toward the kitchen.

But instead of Bethel Yoder at the helm, Lizzie's husband Daniel was there once again, cooking something that smelled delicious.

Daniel turned when she came into the room. "Sissy," he greeted with a smile. "I didn't expect to see you today. Bethel said—"

Sissy shoved her hands into the pockets of her jeans and shrugged. "I changed my mind."

"I'm glad you did."

From the doorway that led from the kitchen to the living room came a harrumph. Bethel stomped into the kitchen, her crutch and cast making quite a bit of noise as she maneuvered around the small space.

"Who else is here?" Sissy asked, peering around her aunt as if others would start spilling into the kitchen.

"It's just us," Bethel said with a small frown. She propped her crutch up against the counter and began pulling down plates.

"Let me do that." Sissy started to move toward her, but Bethel shooed her away with the flick of one wrist.

Sissy stopped in her tracks. She wasn't sure why Bethel didn't like her, but she didn't need a road map to see the truth. Sissy could hope that it was because Bethel was so fiercely independent and didn't want to need help, even though she did. Yeah, that made things seem a little bit brighter.

"I've got a broken leg," Bethel grumbled. "I'm not helpless."

"Of course not," Sissy said. She opened her mouth to continue but stopped. She had almost asked where everyone was if this was to be this week's family dinner, but she had a feeling that the family dinner was canceled and Lizzie had made Bethel invite her anyway. Whatever the case, she was going to remain happy to be among family and count it all as a blessing, regardless of Bethel's surly attitude.

Unfortunately, Sissy was accustomed to dealing with coming in second. Her brother, Owen, was perfect. He was in medical school, killing it all the way, and she was . . . well, she wasn't.

She might have a widely read column in the major regional newspapers. Her parents might say that they were proud, but when you went to a party and couldn't tell everyone that you wrote the self-help column in the Sunday paper, did it really count as success? And now this. She was fixing to be arrested for murder.

They could say whatever they wanted, but she knew the truth. Earl Berry was going to do whatever he could to dig up evidence against her, and there was nothing she could do about it except come up with her own evidence, evidence that cleared her name. That was what Columbo would do. Or even Quincy.

Okay, so she had watched way too many '70s crime show reruns on late-night television. But still . . .

"Auntie," Sissy started.

"Don't call me that."

Right. The Amish didn't use such titles for their relations. Sissy took a deep breath to start again. "Bethel," she said, pausing in case her aunt had another interjection or comment about that greeting. When she said nothing, Sissy plowed ahead. "You know the help fund jar we have at the counter? The one for Darcy," Sissy continued when Bethel didn't respond. "Kevin's widow."

Bethel let out a short grunt, and Sissy considered that to be enough encouragement to continue.

"Well, I would like to take that to her." For two reasons, really. One was a measure of good faith in the community, and she wanted something positive out of the situation. And two, and maybe more importantly, it would give her an opportunity to talk to Darcy, maybe find out a little more about Kevin—who he was, and who would want to kill him. Because like it or not, someone had wanted him dead.

Bethel shook her head. "It ain't been there that long."

"No, it hasn't," Sissy said. "But it's got at least three or four hundred dollars in it already." Yoder was small but generous. "I'm sure she could use that for groceries." After all, she had ten kids to feed. They probably went through hundreds of dollars' worth of food every day. Sissy could only imagine. Her brother Owen just about ate their parents out of house and home when he was a teenager. There was no telling how much grub the Saunders family went through.

Bethel grunted again. "I suppose," she said.

"It's not like we have to take it down completely. We can take her what's in it and collect some more for later. She's gonna need assistance until the insurance pays out." Assuming that Kevin had insurance. Surely he had some sort or another through his company.

"If that's what you want to do," Bethel grumbled.

Sissy looked to Daniel to see his take on the situation, but his expression was impassive as he continued to stir the wonderful-smelling food in the pot that bubbled on the stove.

"It's settled, then," Sissy said, though strangely enough, she didn't feel a sense of relief. And she wanted to. It seemed like every step she'd made since coming to Yoder had been a battle, and she wanted to feel accomplished. Maybe that would come when she found out who killed Kevin. And she was going to. That much was certain.

CHAPTER FIVE

No good deed goes unpunished.
—Aunt Bess

Tuesday dawned like any other in Yoder, but for Sissy, this one was different. She had never been an early riser, but since coming to Yoder and working at a restaurant—excuse her, *café*—that was only open for breakfast and lunch, she had been forced out of bed at a horrendous hour each day, and slowly but surely, her body was becoming used to such abuse. But today was definitely different.

Because today, she had a higher purpose than simply cooking up eggs for the good citizens of Yoder, who had the audacity to be up, dressed, and out of the house by six a.m. Today, she was going to talk to Darcy, Kevin's widow. And talking to Darcy was going to help her figure out who killed Kevin, and that would get Earl Berry off

her case. Then she could go about her life without the big
cloud of possible arrest hanging over her.

She had showered and washed her hair last night, after
she had returned back from the family dinner with Bethel,
Daniel, and Lizzie. She hadn't brought up Josie again,
but every so often, she could feel Lizzie's gaze flick to
her and flutter away, as if she wasn't comfortable looking
at her for too long.

Okay, that was patently ridiculous. But Sissy couldn't
help the way she felt. And if she could talk to Darcy for
just a bit, perhaps she could figure out the connection between Kevin and Josie. There had to be something there.
There just had to be.

She dressed in her jeans, her running shoes (something
of a joke, seeing as how the fastest they had ever gone
was a brisk walk to the bathroom after too much lemon-
ade), and her Sunflower Café T-shirt. She gave Duke an
apologetic kiss on the head and kenneled him up for the
workday. Then she switched off the lights and turned on
the radio so he would have company while she was gone.

It was a new day. It had a new purpose that she was
anxious to see through. But of course, things were hopping when she got to the Sunflower Café. She looked
around at all the many faces that she'd seen practically
every day since coming to work here, and she had to
wonder if the good citizens of Yoder ever cooked breakfast for themselves. Not that she wasn't grateful for the
business. Tips were decent, and these hungry people provided her with a nice cover job for her 'day job.' That's
all that mattered. Still, she couldn't wait until the afternoon, when she could take the help fund over to Darcy
and ever-so-gently quiz the young widow about Josie.

By nine o'clock, the breakfast crowd had wound down

to almost nothing, though a few scraggly diners still remained. Several tables needed bussed, and Sissy grabbed one of the large gray plastic tubs and made her way over to the row of booths, where only one remained occupied. Three ladies sat there, lingering over their dirty plates and nursing their coffees. Sissy had heard Bethel call their names, but she couldn't remember them. Just too many faces and too many monikers in such a short period of time. But she had seen the ladies in the café before.

She nodded and smiled at them as she took up their dirty dishes. "Can I get you anything else?" she asked.

The women shook their heads, and Sissy continued on to bus the table behind them.

"I, for one, think it's wonderful," one of the women said.

Sissy hadn't been purposefully paying attention. The ladies weren't hard to overhear, seeing as how close she was to them. She hadn't meant to be eavesdropping, not really. Not at all. It was just . . . well, a reporter tended to overhear any conversation around them. It was something inherent to being a reporter. Okay, okay, so she was a columnist . . . that was still her story, and she was sticking to it.

"Of course it's wonderful," another of the ladies said.

This time, Sissy had been paying attention to who was speaking. Of the three women, she was the only one who faced Sissy. She was middle-aged with chocolate brown hair streaked with gray and cut into a stylish bob that reached just below her chin. Carol, she thought her name was. Carol something that began with the letter D, and maybe she worked at the school—the charter school, of course. Not the Amish one.

Sissy remembered hearing something about the school

being out today for administrative meetings. Which probably meant the other two ladies worked at the school, as well.

"After all they've been through," the third lady said.

By now, Sissy was doing everything in her power to look as if she was busy bussing the table, while she mentally took notes on the conversation. One day she would work as a reporter again. And it was a good idea to hone her skills whenever she had the chance.

That's what she told herself, anyway. And she believed it. Every word.

The third woman was blond, though her hair was a color so pale, Sissy wasn't sure it occurred anywhere in nature. She was tall, or she sat up straighter than the rest, and was thin. Sissy couldn't see her face from where she stood.

"But a baby at their age." The first woman shook her head.

"What are you talking about, Kathy?" Carol asked. "We're the same age."

Kathy, the blonde, nodded. "Exactly what I'm talking about. I have grandkids coming. I can't imagine having a newborn, as well."

The lady shook her head. Like Kathy, she faced away from Sissy. She had short brown hair that curled around her collar, and given the breadth of her shoulders, Sissy figured her face to be round and chubby like an overgrown cherub. "It's a miracle," this woman said. "Anyway you look at it."

Sissy cleaned the table as slowly as she could. She straightened the napkins, wiped down the salt and pepper shakers, reorganized the little caddy of sweeteners. Anything and everything she could think to do in order to stay close to these three ladies as they talked. Now that everything was clean—and she meant everything—she had no excuse not to move to the next table, away from them and out of earshot.

But she wanted to ask who they were talking about. It seemed that someone in Yoder was going to have a baby who was older—the couple, not the baby—and that it was a miracle. Since they had been through so much. Whatever that meant, exactly.

Kathy, Carol, and the other woman slid from the booth, waved to Lottie, and headed out the door. For the first time since Sissy had walked in that morning, the Sunflower Café was empty of diners.

She hoisted the heavy tub, bracing it against her midsection as she carried it to the back of the café. She set it down on the countertop attached to the sink and began unloading it.

"Who were they talking about?" she asked, directing her attention to Lottie, who had followed behind her.

"Who was who talking about?" Lottie asked.

They were the only two in the kitchen. Josie was evidently on another smoke break, and Bethel was in the office, working on orders. Which left Lottie and Sissy to take care of the front.

"The three ladies who were just here. They were talking about somebody having a baby," Sissy replied.

Lottie nodded. "Probably Abby and English Ben."

"English Ben?" Sissy began to spray the dishes and place them into the tray to be sterilized.

Lottie nodded. "There's an English Ben Yoder, and then there's an Amish Ben Yoder. We say their religion in front so we can tell them apart when we're talking about them."

"How terribly PC of you," Sissy quipped.

Lottie waved a hand, as if her comment were the funniest thing she had ever heard. "We don't worry about stuff like that when it comes to our people, I guess. As long as I've known them, they've been English Ben and Amish Ben."

"Are they kin?" Sissy asked.

Lottie shrugged. "I guess if you go far enough back, you'll find an ancestor or two that all the Yoders have in common. But these two aren't close, if they're kin at all."

"So English Ben and his wife, Abby, are going to have a baby. And they're middle-aged?"

Lottie held up one finger. "Let me check the front." She disappeared into the dining area.

Sissy dried her hands on a dish towel and followed behind. The dishes could wait. She had gossip to catch up on.

"Well," Lottie started, propping one ample hip against the counter where the cash register sat. "It's like this: English Ben and Abby have wanted a baby for as long as anyone can remember."

"That's understandable," Sissy said. Though she hadn't made it to that point yet, she knew that many women felt very strongly about the ability to have children. Sissy was sure one day she would want to have a child of her own. Right now, she was concentrating on her career. And helping her aunt. And the whole getting her life back on track thing.

"So they went through all these treatments and I don't know what all. They pretty much spent every dime they had trying to have a baby. And it seems this last time worked. Abby's pregnant."

"That's fantastic. We should do something for them."

"Danielle—that's Abby's sister—is planning a baby shower for her soon. But I don't have all the details."

Sissy waved a hand toward the help fund jar that sat next to where they stood. "Maybe next time we can take up a collection for them, too. I mean, if they spent all this money on fertility treatments, they might need a little extra when the baby comes."

"That's so sweet of you," Lottie gushed. She reached out and patted Sissy's freckled cheek.

Sissy shrugged. When in Rome, and all that. But she was enjoying being a part of such a small community. She would've never thought that possible. Tulsa was about the biggest small town around; it seemed that no matter where she went, she ran into somebody she knew. And sometimes it was annoying. But in Yoder, it was different; she couldn't put her finger on why. It simply was.

"Speaking of," she started, gesturing toward the jar that had been set out to collect donations for Kevin's widow. "I thought I might take that over to Darcy this afternoon."

Lottie shook her head, but in the most positive way. Her lips were pressed together as if in disbelief. "You have to be the sweetest thing."

Sissy was certain her cheeks were bright pink. She could feel the heat coming off them. Another tragedy of being fair-skinned, red-haired, and freckled. She tended to blush brighter than a stoplight. And Lottie's compliments were just too much. No, she wasn't really being sweet; she was serving her own purpose. But she couldn't exactly say that to the other woman, now, could she?

"Thank you," she said, falling back on her mother's strict instructions, instructions Aunt Bess backed up one hundred and ten percent: *When someone pays you a com-*

pliment, say thanks. Nothing else is necessary. Thank you is enough. But thankfully she was saved from having to say anything else, as the door opened, and Earl Berry stepped inside.

"That's my cue to exit," Sissy said.

"Yep," Lottie agreed. "You better get back to finish the dishes up before Bethel sees you out here gabbing."

Sissy spun on her heel, pretending Earl Berry wasn't there, and headed back to the kitchen. Let him make what he would of that.

It was after three before Sissy could make her escape. And she was more than a little guilt-ridden as she clutched the jar and headed up the steps that led to Darcy Saunders's house.

And not just because she was trying to find some connection between Josie and Kevin, but because poor Duke was shut up in his kennel at the Chicken Coop.

She debated about whether to go home and let him out for a bit, but she would have to crate him back up when she visited with Darcy. It seemed kinder to merely leave him where he was instead of breaking his heart twice in one day.

Next paycheck, she was going to get one of those cameras, like a nanny cam. She could set it up facing the kennel and check on Duke during the day. That way, she would know that he was fine and dandy, even when she was at work. Or if something like this came up again and she couldn't go straight home.

Several cars were parked along the street where Darcy lived, and Sissy had to park a ways down and walk up to the house. Not that it took long to get there, but it sure seemed that way. She shifted the plastic jug that she was certain once contained mayonnaise to her left hip and raised her right hand to knock. She wasn't sure if she should knock or ring the doorbell, so she did both.

At the summons, chaos exploded behind the thick wooden door. Someone squealed, as if they had been goosed and were now losing a tickle fight. A dog started to bark. She heard footsteps, some running and some not. Sissy hadn't thought coming by would create such havoc. But if it were true that Darcy had ten children—and Sissy saw no reason it shouldn't be—she was certain chaos was a normal state of affairs.

She raised her hand and knocked again.

The door opened. A young woman stood there. She had shoulder-length dishwater-blond hair and Kevin's eyes. "Can I help you?"

There was something inherently childlike about the woman. Sissy couldn't put her finger on exactly what it was—something in the angle she held her head or the lilt of her voice. Or perhaps it was the straight-cut fringe of the bangs that bisected her forehead well above her *au naturel* eyebrows.

"Is . . . is your mother home?" It might've been easier if she had ever met Darcy Saunders, but one look at this girl, and anyone could tell that she was Kevin's child. Sissy had only seen the man three times, and she could see the resemblance.

The girl stood back and gestured for Sissy to come in. "Is she expecting you?" Her words were practiced and formal.

Sissy shook her head. "My name is Sissy. I work at the

café, and we've been collecting money for your mom. I would like to give it to her. I figured you could use some help right now."

The girl nodded importantly. "I think she will be very pleased to see you." She led the way down a hall and back to a room that Sissy was certain they referred to as the den.

Darcy was standing at the sliding-glass doors, one foot inside and one outside. She held a tiny dog, some sort of Chihuahua mix, cradled on one hip. The acrid stench of cigarette smoke floated about the room.

"Mommy, this woman is here to see you." The formality had leached from her voice. Her childlike demeanor led Sissy to believe that the young woman was somehow delayed developmentally.

Now Sissy was doubly glad that she had brought the money today instead of waiting. She might have her own motives, but if this young woman still lived at home, how many other Saunders children still remained in residence with their mother? Considering the scattered mess around them, Sissy couldn't be sure. But it looked like a great many.

Darcy dropped the cigarette butt to the planter just outside the door and waved a hand in front of her face. "Dani, how many times have I told you?"

Dani ducked her head, her straight blond hair a curtain that hid her face from each side. "A bunch."

Sissy wasn't sure what Darcy had told her. Not to interrupt her when she was smoking? Not to allow strangers to come into the house? Surely that was it.

Darcy waved a hand in the air in front of her face once again, then stepped into the house and shut the sliding-glass door behind her. She adjusted the dog into the crook of her arm and carefully eyed Sissy. "And you are?"

Sissy took a step forward, then one back. She held out the jar full of money that had been collected in the days since Kevin's murder. "My name is Sissy Yoder. I work at the Sunflower Café?" And why did that sound like a question? "We've been collecting money for your family since . . . everything happened, and I wanted to bring it to you. In case you needed groceries or something."

The lines around Darcy's mouth softened, and Sissy could tell that at one time, she had been a beauty. Her slender build showed only a few signs of the many children she had carried. The most obvious being the tiny, rounded paunch that had settled between her hipbones. Her blond hair was overdyed and a bit frizzy-looking but still styled in a way that said she cared about her appearance. Yet she seemed brittle around the edges, maybe a bit hardened. Or perhaps she was simply tired.

"It's nice to meet you, Sissy," Darcy said as she made her way to the couch. She gestured for Sissy to take a seat. There were two armchairs and a couple of beanbags scattered across the floor. Sissy sidestepped one and sat in the chair closest to the couch.

If she had to guess the official name of Darcy's decorating style, she would have called it Woman Worn Out. Clutter graced every surface, right down to the plethora of magazines that haphazardly covered the coffee table, and enough toys were scattered across the floor to stock the family's very own store had they chosen to pick them up and organize them.

A playpen sat near the kitchen bar, and Sissy could see dishes piled up in the sink. She wasn't trying to pass judgment on the woman. Darcy Saunders was obviously grieving, but surely someone had been by to help with such things. Didn't Darcy have family in town? Sissy would have to ask Lottie. And what about her children? Surely a few of them were old enough to help. The young woman who had opened the door, for instance.

"Did I hear the doorbell?" Another young woman came hustling down the staircase that Sissy hadn't noticed before. It was hidden on the other side of the fireplace and seemed to empty out right onto the couch. The woman could have been the twin of the young girl who had opened the door, except she had no bangs, and streaks of red and black colored her hair. Like her sister, she had her father's eyes. Sissy guessed her to be at least twenty-five, and definitely capable of picking up after herself and her siblings, for that matter.

"No one's here for you, April," Dani said. She crossed her arms and rounded on her sister as if somehow offended by the question.

"I'm expecting Brad," April said, crossing her arms in a similar fashion. "We have a gig tonight, so he's coming by early to get me."

Darcy sighed. "Another gig?"

"This one's supposed to pay." April smiled proudly. "A hundred dollars each."

Dani scoffed and turned to Sissy. "April thinks she's a rock star."

"You'll all be laughing when I am." April raised her chin to a haughty angle.

Darcy rubbed the dog's ears thoughtfully but didn't address either of the girls.

Sissy breathed in and out and wondered if she should say something or just pour the money out on the coffee table and leave. She wanted to ask Darcy about Kevin and Josie. But now that she was there, and she could see the sadness that hovered around Darcy like her own personal rain cloud, she couldn't do it.

"Mom, Kevin Junior and Joe won't let me play my video game in the playroom now, and it's my turn." Another young girl, young *woman*, came flouncing through the kitchen and into the den, a pout worthy of Paris Hilton on her lips. She was eighteen if a day, and yet seemed to be wholly dependent on her mother.

"Fiona, please," Darcy said, and for a moment, Sissy thought that might be all of the message. "Use the television in the dining room." Darcy pointed toward the room just off the kitchen. If Sissy was keeping up with the structure of the house correctly, it was also right next to the garage from where Fiona had just arrived.

"Mo-um." Fiona dragged out the name until it was a minimum of four syllables, something Sissy hadn't known was even possible. "I can't move around good in there. It's too cramped."

"She doesn't want to play a game," Dani said. "She's doing an exercise tape so she can lose weight."

It didn't look like the girl needed to lose any weight, but Sissy was staying out of this one. Big family issues were definitely not her forte.

"Mind your own business, Dani," Fiona snarled. But she didn't have the chance to say anything else before a wail came from the direction of the playpen.

"Great. You woke up Dakota." Dani moved toward the playpen to rescue her sister . . . or brother . . . Sissy wasn't sure, and the child was dressed androgynously enough that she couldn't tell. Green overalls, pale yellow shirt. And with a name like Dakota, who knew?

Dani bounced the baby on her hip, and Sissy was glad to see that she was helping her mother, who seemed like she wanted to stretch out on the couch and take a nap. After everything that Sissy had seen, she couldn't blame her.

"Mom!"

Two more Saunders children entered the fray. These girls were much younger than the three currently still arguing about rock-star gigs and video games versus exercise tapes. Each sister held opposite sides of the same book, doing everything in their power to pull it from the other's grasp as they lurched side by side into the room.

"Tell Jewel this is my book," the taller, and Sissy supposed the older of the pair, screeched, jerking the book toward her.

"Jewel, it's Madison's book," Darcy said tiredly.

But Jewel refused to let go. "Tell Madison she has to share." The last word was punctuated by her own hard tug that nearly pulled Madison off her feet.

"Madison, you need to share." Darcy continued to rub the dog's ears, and Sissy felt the urge to step in and bring some sort of order to the chaos. She tamped down that impulse. It was none of her concern, and yet . . .

She did a quick head count. Eight, including Kev Jr. and Joe. There were still two more children unaccounted for, and she could only imagine what the house was like with all of them in the same room. The Brady Bunch this was not.

"She can't even read it," Madison protested.

"You could read it to her." If Sissy had been standing, she would have kicked herself in the rear for getting involved. "You can read, right?" she continued. In for a penny, and all that.

"Of course I can. I'm eight." She said the words as if any fool should have been able to see that; then she stopped tugging at the book and crossed her arms.

With the lack of tension on the object, Jewel went sprawling across the floor.

"Mom," Jewel cried.

"Madison," Darcy groaned.

"You're okay, Jewel." Dakota still cradled on one hip, Dani marched over to her sister and helped her to her feet.

"But she's mean," Jewel protested, brushing imaginary dirt from her shorts and studying her elbow as if trying to find some sign of injury, anything to further her case. Finding none, she cautiously tucked the book beneath her arm. Sissy could tell that she was hoping against hope that her sister had forgotten about it.

"Wait a minute," Darcy said, for the first time looking halfway alert. "You're Sissy."

Sissy nodded. Hadn't she introduced herself when she came in? She thought she remembered, but so much had transpired since then, she was beginning to lose track.

"You found Kevin's—I mean, you worked with Kevin."

Sissy nodded. "That's right."

An awkward moment stretched between them, but then it was broken by Fiona's demand.

"Are you going to make Junior and Joe let me have the television?"

Darcy sighed. "No one can *have* the television, Fi."

The doorbell rang.

"That must be Brad." April let out a small squeal and clapped her hands.

Madison marched over to her sister and snatched at the

book. Jewel was ready for her, and the tug-of-war was on once again.

Sissy used that moment to slip a couple more twenties into the help fund jar. She didn't have a lot of extra money to be throwing around, but this family was definitely in need.

"I guess I should be going." Sissy stood and held the jar out to Darcy.

The front door slammed, and she supposed April and Brad were off to their possibly paying gig.

"Thank you." Darcy took the jar and plopped it onto the magazine-strewn coffee table. Then she picked up a pack of cigarettes from the mess and shook one out. Somehow she managed to light it while cradling the dog in one arm.

"Mom," Dani admonished. "You promised not to smoke in the house."

"I know. I know." Darcy waved one hand as if to dispel the smoke, but since it held the burning cigarette, it was a useless gesture.

"Mom," Dani protested once again.

"I'm going. I'm going." She gave Sissy a somewhat apologetic smile, then made her way back over to the sliding-glass door.

"I'll show you out," Dani said formally. Still holding the androgynous Dakota, Dani led the way to the front door.

As she left the living room, Sissy could hear the renewed efforts of Madison to take the book away from her sister and Fiona's loud groan before stomping off.

"Thank you for stopping by," Dani said, smiling sweetly at Sissy.

"Of course." Sissy had to bite her tongue to keep from

saying more. Like telling Dani that if she needed anything, to come by the café. It wasn't really any of her concern. None of Kevin's family's problems were any of her
concern. And taking them on would only serve to make
her look like she had a guilty conscience, something she
should have thought about before trekking out here with
the money jar.

Sissy stepped out onto the porch, and Dani closed the
door behind her. Sissy could hear her yelling at her siblings. Poor thing.

She looked both ways, hoping that Earl Berry hadn't
followed her. What would he make of her coming out to
Darcy's today? She turned back to the front, then did a
double take.

Realizing the motion looked even more suspicious
than merely staring, she ducked her head, as if she were
digging in her bag for something. But it wasn't Earl
Berry. It was the same man she had seen at the café earlier. He had sat down at the counter and looked around as
if casing the place. Then he'd ordered coffee and left a
ten-dollar bill. A person had a tendency to remember a tip
like that.

At the time, she had thought he looked out of place.
Shiny new suit and silk tie. No one in Yoder dressed like
that. And for a moment, she thought she saw a bulge
under one arm. At the time, she had dismissed it. At-
tributing her seeing things to Mike's talk about the Mafia.
But now, she was rethinking her suspicions and Mike's
not-so-candid revelation, for the same man was standing
at the end of the block, watching her.

CHAPTER SIX

*A girl who is going to do big things cannot let
small things get to her.*
—Aunt Bess

She couldn't see him well enough to determine if he
still had that lethal-looking bulge under one arm. And
she surely couldn't openly appraise him to see if it was
still there.

"Now where did I put my keys?" She said the words
overly loud and winced. She had wanted to make a play
at seeming preoccupied, not look like she was part of
some dreadful community theater.

The problem was she had to walk toward him in order
to get to her car. She didn't want him to think that she was
confronting him. And she didn't want him to think that
she knew he was following her. Or *if* he was following
her. Or something like that. Because it really looked like
he was following her.

Sissy reined in those thoughts. They were starting to

make her dizzy. She walked as slowly as possible toward her car while pretend-searching in her bag for the keys that were dangling out of her left hip pocket. Finally, she looked up, and the man was gone. Then she got a good look at where he'd been standing, and her mouth went dry. He had been right in front of her car.

The Sunflower Café was closed the following morning. It was Wednesday, and they were laying Kevin to rest.

Bethel had told her when she left the afternoon before that the café would be closed out of respect for Kevin and his family but would open again around noon. They would all be attending the funeral.

Sissy didn't really want to go to Kevin's funeral, but something in Bethel's tone suggested that she was expected to. So, Tuesday after she left Darcy Saunders's house and dodged the mob guy who was casing her car, she headed over into Hutchinson to Walmart to pick up something presentable. She didn't own many black clothes, just the obligatory little black dress and further obligatory black business suit, both of which were in storage. In Tulsa. Just waiting for her to get herself back together and come home. Until then, she needed something presentable for the funeral.

Thankfully, she found a black peasant dress that could be worn off the shoulder as well as up in place and might possibly double as something she might want to wear when she wasn't attending the funeral. Possibly, anyway. As a redhead, black wasn't really her color.

They all attended, every employee of the Sunflower

Café, from Bethel herself right on down to Freddie Howard, the young African American kid who came in on Saturday afternoons to help get everything spick-and-span,
since they were closed on Sunday. Sissy had never met
him before, but he seemed like a nice enough kid, seventeen, with a girlfriend and a letter jacket for basketball.
He had two jobs, Lottie had told her. He also worked at
the Quiki-Mart, which sat side by side with the flower
shop just before you got on the highway toward Haven.

Sissy sat as patiently as she could through the eulogies,
wondering how much of the information being spouted off
was true and how much were just fond memories of
someone who was no longer with them. She learned that
there was no bigger Iron Maiden fan than Kevin. She also
heard how he met his wife in high school and had somehow won her heart forever. How he was such a hard
worker, and it was nothing to see him driving down the
road, munching on a sandwich between stops. It went on
and on and on.

After she had heard all about his musical taste and
lunch habits, she couldn't help but look around at all the
funeralgoers. Chances were that the murderer was among
them. Wasn't that what all the TV murder mysteries said?
That the killer always came to the funeral? Well, they
didn't say it *exactly*, but that's the way it happened. They
buried the victim, and everyone, including the killer,
stood around wearing black while a man on a hill somewhere played "Amazing Grace" on the bagpipes. There
were no hills here, nor any bagpipe player, but she knew
the killer had to be standing there among them. Except
there were only a handful of people there whom she knew
by name. Lottie, Bethel, Freddie, Josie, Evan Yoder, and
Vera Yoder, her landlady.

Evan Yoder. What was *he* doing at the funeral of the man he claimed not to know?

As far as Sissy was concerned, that made him doubly suspicious. Even though she had known from the beginning that he'd been lying about not knowing Kevin Saunders.

She watched Evan for a bit, doing her best not to let him see that she was watching him. Then she allowed her gaze to wander around the crowd as she looked for possible suspects. As far as she could tell, no one looked like they didn't belong in Yoder. Like that man she had seen at the Saunders house the day before. He hadn't belonged in Yoder. That much was completely obvious. And though he had been watching the Saunders house at the time, he hadn't attended the funeral.

There were a few more mourners whose faces she knew but not their names. They had come into the café during her shifts. And there was Darcy Saunders. Wasn't the widow always a suspect? You know, for the insurance and all that.

Her gaze traveled a bit more, then snagged on a serious blue one. Earl Berry. Had he been watching her the entire time? Yes, he had. She could see it in his eyes. And she could also see that he was thinking the same thing she was. That the killer was right there among them, but unlike her, he thought *she* was the one responsible for Kevin's death.

Thankfully, the pastor took that time to wrap up the funeral sermon and asked them all to bow their heads and pray. She held Earl Berry's gaze until he finally closed his eyes and bowed his head. She wouldn't have called it a staring contest, but whatever it was between them, she had won this round. Like the victory would do her any good.

After the prayer, everyone stood and started to mingle. No one seemed to be in a hurry to leave. She supposed that's what happened when a small town buried one of their own.

"Are you going to stay for a bit?" Freddie asked. The young man appeared nervous, glancing around as if uncomfortable in his own skin. Now what was *that* all about?

She supposed that out of all the funeralgoers, he appeared the most suspicious, the most antsy, and yet he never came in contact with Kevin the milkman at the café. In fact, Freddie didn't even make the top twenty on her list of suspects. Well, her list didn't have twenty names on it, but if it did, Freddie wouldn't be among them.

He stuck right by her, chattering on and on about nothing, as she aimlessly, though purposefully, wound her way through the crowd of people at Kevin's funeral. Okay, so truthfully, she was looking for Evan Yoder.

"I know some people didn't like him," Freddie was saying. "But I know I'll miss him."

Sissy stopped trying to find Evan Yoder and turned back to Freddie. "Who?"

Freddie shook his head, as if he couldn't believe Sissy was being so obtuse. Still, his overall demeanor remained open and friendly. And anxious. Sissy supposed he must've known she wasn't listening. "Kevin."

"How do you know Kevin?" Dumb question. She'd forgotten her first rule of journalism. Never make assumptions until a suspect is cleared. Well, maybe that wasn't the *first* rule of journalism, but she had been taught the edict early on in her studies. Yet she had simply breezed over Freddie because of his age, nothing more.

"From the Quiki-Mart."

That's right. Freddie had two jobs, in addition to still being in high school. But him encountering Kevin at the Quiki-Mart would mean . . .

"I thought you were in school during the week."

Freddie grinned, his smile infectious like that of Michael Jackson during the early years. "Nah, I have it where I work during the day, then go to school during the afternoons."

"I see," Sissy murmured. She really had to get on top of her game if she was going to solve this and not end up in prison. "So you liked Kevin?"

"Almost everybody likes Kevin." His smile wilted on his face. "Liked," he corrected himself and that smile returned once again. "Except for old man Winston."

"Who's that?" Sissy hadn't met anybody with the first or last name of Winston since she'd been in Yoder. She was fairly certain she would remember a name like that. Especially with all the Yoders running around.

"You haven't met Winston Yoder?" Freddie laughed.

She had spoken too soon. "I suppose I haven't." She waited patiently for Freddie to continue.

"He's a Vietnam vet. Or maybe it was Korea." Freddie shook his head, as if that would make the memory clearer. "Anyway, he has one of those Jazzy scooters. Those motorized chair thingies. For some reason, he likes to drive it through the alley between the Quiki-Mart and the flower shop. You've been over, right? I mean, everybody has to come to the Quiki-Mart at some time or another."

Sissy nodded dumbly. She had been over; the Quiki-Mart was the only place in Yoder to buy gas. But she hadn't really noticed an alley between the two buildings. They sat side by side with the park right behind them, *park* being a very euphemistic word for large grassy area with a couple of picnic tables and a basketball hoop.

"So old man Winston—"

"Yoder?" Sissy interjected just to be sure. Was everybody in this town named Yoder?

Freddie nodded, a little taken aback that she had interrupted his flow. "That's right. So old man Winston *Yoder,*" he emphasized, "likes to go over to the Bull in Your Eye Diner and eat lunch every day, but I guess he eats lunch about the same time that Kevin would take his lunch. Kevin would park the milk truck in the alley between the Quiki-Mart and the flower shop, and he couldn't make it through."

"Winston?" Sissy asked.

Freddie nodded.

"Yoder?" she asked again.

"That's right," Freddie said. "And he would get mad as a hornet. Winston. Yoder," Freddie clarified, in case Sissy missed something along the way.

"So not everybody likes Kevin," Sissy deduced.

Freddie's expression fell from one of happy recap to something akin to horror. "Well, I guess not everybody. But I don't think Winston Yoder would—" He shook his head, as if unable to say the words that he didn't believe to be true. That Winston Yoder could be responsible for Kevin's untimely demise. "Plus, the man only has one leg."

"A handicap such as that didn't stop the one-armed man," Sissy quipped.

Freddie frowned. "What one-armed man?"

"Never mind." Classic TV references were lost on the younger generation. He probably hadn't even watched the Harrison Ford remake.

"He came into the Quiki-Mart at least once a week to complain," Freddie continued. "Surely he wouldn't have been so open about it if he had plans to . . ."

"So did they ever do anything about it?" Sissy asked.

"Who is they?" Freddie asked.

"The people who own the flower shop, or the owners of the Quiki-Mart?" Even as she said the words, she realized that the flower shop was most likely the one owned by English Ben Yoder and his wife, Abby.

"Nah." Freddie raised a hand as if to dismiss the question entirely. "Eddie—that's my boss—he said that the alleyway was meant for deliveries, and since Kevin was making a delivery and old man Winston wasn't, that Kevin had more of a right to park there than Winston had to cut through."

It made sense, Sissy supposed. It was such a small-town thing, complaining over someone parking between two buildings and trying to get to the park on the Jazzy scooter with one leg. Well, the man had one leg, not the Jazzy scooter. The whole scenario was just so quintessentially small-town.

She looked up and saw Evan Yoder in the crowd. Maybe she should ask him why he was there. If he didn't know Kevin Saunders, why would he come to his funeral? Sure, there wasn't much to do in Yoder, Kansas, but attending funerals of people you didn't know surely wouldn't make anyone's list of nothing-else-to-do entertainment.

"Excuse me," she said to Freddie, and started drifting toward the spot she had last seen Evan.

Freddie looked a bit crestfallen but nodded. "I guess I'll see you at work this weekend," he said.

"See you at work," Sissy returned. But even as she scanned the crowd for another sight of Evan, he seemed to be nowhere around. Then she thought she heard his name. Or maybe she was projecting her thoughts onto the crowd. Then she heard Darcy Saunders's name mixed in, and she tried to find who was talking. But everyone was talking and everyone was dressed in black and everyone was milling around and most everyone was a stranger, so she had trouble discerning from which person the name had come.

Of course people were talking about Darcy. She was the widow, and maybe Sissy had just thought she heard Evan Yoder's name in the same voice. But like Evan himself, the words were lost in the crowd.

Sissy never did find out what was being said about Evan Yoder, but of all the people at the funeral, he was the one acting most suspiciously. Freddie aside, that was. Or rather not. Evan was the one acting the *least* suspiciously, and as far as she was concerned, that made him doubly suspicious. She wondered why Earl Berry wasn't out talking to him. But of course, Earl Berry knew that Evan Yoder knew Kevin Saunders, and it seemed that maybe Evan hadn't lied to Earl Berry like he had lied to Sissy. So naturally, Earl Berry wasn't suspicious of the man. Or something like that.

When the funeral was over, and the café was once again open for business, Sissy wondered if the town had at least a little bit of closure, even if they didn't know who killed Kevin. Perhaps there was a little bit of that conclusion, seeing as how every seat at the café had a butt planted in it, and the funeral had been over less than an hour.

Another thing that seemed suspicious about Evan Yoder: Practically everyone had come through the doors of the Sunflower Café in the short time that she had worked there. Everyone but Evan Yoder.

Now that they had laid Kevin to rest, and the respect for the dead man, so to speak, had been placated, the café was busier than ever. In fact, Sissy regretted not taking the time to change her shoes before coming to work after the funeral. She supposed she just hadn't planned well enough. She brought her jeans and her Sunflower Café T-shirt to change into, but she hadn't thought about shoes. The ballet flats she had worn to the funeral didn't give her near the support she needed for the number of orders they were taking in. Still, she barely had time to breathe, much less go out to her car and dig around in her trunk, to see if she had left any random workout shoes in there. You know, from the time she planned to go to the gym and never quite made it. That was the great thing about Yoder. As far she could tell, there were no gyms, so no call to work out. Perfect.

Of course, talk among the customers was mainly of the funeral, all the things that people normally said when someone dies—how many people attended, and the attendees who'd surprised them; how beautiful the flowers were, and how natural the deceased appeared; and then there was the talk of the widow.

It seemed everyone was curious as to what Darcy was to do now, especially financially. She hadn't worked since April was born. April was the older girl whom Sissy had met when she'd taken the help fund over to Darcy. Talk speculated about whether Kevin had some sort of pension plan, though consensus seemed to be doubtful, or negligible if it existed at all. That was the problem with working for some of the smaller companies.

And then there was talk of moving on and the other news in the community. Like the fact that Abby and English Ben Yoder were pregnant.

Sissy laughed whenever she heard that; it was almost always corrected with, "Abby is pregnant, and Ben is simply ecstatic about the news." They had been through so much to finally be having a baby. That was surely one thing that would help the town heal from the devastating loss of one of their own.

And then, of course, there was Earl Berry. Just after the funeral, he parked himself on one of the stools at the serving counter at the Sunflower Café. Normally, he came for breakfast, and Sissy was curious to see what he ordered for lunch. Nothing special: coffee, BLT, and fries with no ketchup. Just another strike against him, as far as she was concerned.

Sissy tried to keep an eye on him to see whom he was keeping an eye on, but every time she looked up, he was looking at her. Of course. It seemed he didn't have anyone else on his guilt radar but her.

She delivered plates of chocolate pie to a group of four women, who were all merrily chatting about how happy they were about English Ben and Abby and their upcoming baby. All four women had been standing together at the funeral solemn, but dry-eyed.

Come to think of it, not many people were crying at the funeral. Strange for a funeral, especially one so well-attended. Or so it seemed to her. And despite the fact that Freddie claimed most everyone liked Kevin Saunders, she had a feeling the man had a few enemies in the town. Nothing concrete, mind you; just a feeling.

After all, Kevin had jumped all over her because she hadn't unlocked the door, and then Mike came around talking about the mob and how Kevin supposedly owed a lot of money. Perhaps that was how he cared for ten children all living at home and a wife who didn't work.

The wife. She appeared to be the only person at the funeral who was upset. Darcy. Yet somehow, Sissy got the impression that Darcy was more aggrieved over the fact that she had been left behind to take care of ten needy children than the fact that her husband was dead.

CHAPTER SEVEN

*If you can't say anything nice about someone,
come sit by me.*
—Aunt Bess

Sissy slid into the booth opposite Lottie and pulled a
stack of the napkins toward her. Of all the chores at
the Sunflower Café, rolling the silverware might be her
least favorite. Well, the actual chore might be at the top of
her *meh* list, but being able to sit down and maybe find
out a few things from Lottie was certainly something
worth looking forward to.

"It was a nice funeral," Lottie said as she expertly
rolled the flatware together—knife, fork, and spoon, all
nestled on top of one another and tightly wrapped in
clean white paper.

"I guess so," Sissy said. That was just another one of
those things people said at the end of the funeral. But it
was good that the person had a respectable send-off. As
far as Sissy was concerned, it could be the finest funeral

known to the human race, but the man was still dead. Even worse, she had the dreadful feeling that she was the one about to be arrested for the murder. And just because she found the dead body. *I mean, really.*

"Tell me about Evan Yoder," Sissy said.

Lottie stopped rolling; her nimble fingers cautiously stilled as she looked up at Sissy. "Evan Yoder? What do you want to know about him?"

Sissy placed the newly wrapped bundle of silverware next to the stack Lottie had created and shrugged, as if her question was of no consequence. "I don't know," she said nonchalantly, perhaps too nonchalantly. She created another stack of silverware to be rolled. Knife, fork, and spoon placed diagonally on the napkin. Fold up the bottom, fold over the side, and roll. Should have been simple, and yet Sissy could look at the finished products and tell which ones were Lottie's and which were hers. "He's lived here his whole life, right?"

Lottie paused for a moment, staring at Sissy as if trying to figure out why she was asking about Evan Yoder. Either she found something that satisfied her, or she gave up. At any rate, she turned her attention back to the silverware and started rolling once more. "That's right."

"So he had to know Kevin. I mean, they are—were—around the same age."

"Of course he knew Kevin." Lottie's cautiousness, or whatever it had been, evaporated like mist in the sun. And she found herself at home, in gossip. "See, Darcy had been dating Evan Yoder way back in high school."

"Darcy?" Sissy asked. "You mean Darcy Saunders?"

"Only Darcy in town," Lottie said. She went right on rolling the silverware while Sissy let it all sink in. "Of course, she was Darcy Andrews back then."

"So Evan was dating Darcy," Sissy repeated, just to make sure she had it all correct.

"That's right."

"But she married Kevin." Sissy did the math. Darcy's age minus April's age would mean . . . "Darcy had April right outside of high school."

"The next year." Lottie shook her head. "That girl . . ." She pressed her lips together, still shaking her head.

"What about her?"

Lottie playfully tapped Sissy's hand. "You didn't hear this from me," she started, "but Darcy had the world ahead of her. Everything. She'd just been named Miss Kansas. She was about to go into the Miss America Pageant, but had to give up her title, because she got married and she got pregnant—not necessarily in that order—and then baby, baby, baby."

That would explain a lot. Darcy's brittle beauty, her apparent resentment, and her downtrodden attitude. And Sissy couldn't help but feel just a little sorry for the girl. Not only because she had lost her husband, but she'd seemed to have lost her way, as well.

"And they really have ten kids?" How many had she counted when she had been at the house—seven? Eight? After that, what were a couple more?

"You would think they would know by now what caused that, huh?" Lottie chuckled. "I suppose Kevin had himself some really good swimmers."

Sissy gave a courtesy laugh. "I'll take that as a yes, then."

"That's a yes. It's funny how some people have so many babies, and then others only have one or two."

Her words brought to mind the florist and his wife. English Ben and Abby.

"What about the couple at the flower shop?" Sissy asked. "They're having a baby now, right? Isn't that what everybody's been talking about?"

"Now *there's* some happy news." Lottie gathered up her brilliant pyramid of stacked silverware and placed it in one of the gray bus tubs like those they used to clean the tables. This one had a strip of blue tape all the way around, signifying it was only to be used to store the silverware. But instead of standing and taking all of their hard work over to the waitress station, Lottie leaned back and crossed her arms in a satisfied manner. "There's some good news, indeed. It's so wonderful to see a couple finally have a baby after years of trying."

"But isn't she in her fifties?" Sissy asked. As far as she knew, any age past forty was high-risk. And if that were the case, it seemed everyone was celebrating a tad early.

"She's almost fifty," Lottie admitted. "And I suppose it is more dangerous the older a woman gets. There's more chance for birth defects and Down syndrome and things like that. But I think when you want a baby that bad and you want one for that long, those kinds of things aren't as important as you might have thought when you were twenty."

"I wouldn't know," Sissy murmured. Aunt Bess had had the chance a time or two to promote blended families and adoption, but she hadn't had any late-in-life pregnancies to advise. Maybe Sissy would feel differently if she were in the same situation, but from where she stood in that moment, it just seemed like too great a risk.

"So they went through a lot of tests and things like that?" Sissy asked.

"They went through everything you can imagine and some things you even can't. But nothing ever took. And then, earlier this year, they decided they were going to give it one last try." Lottie beamed as if somehow, she were single-handedly responsible for the fertilization. "And then here we go. Baby's on the way."

Sissy figured ten years ago, she could have chalked it up to lack of the cable TV out in the boonies. But seeing as how everything was in the cloud and streamed these days, there was no reason for the citizens of Yoder to be entirely enthralled in the lives of the other citizens of the town. But that was just how it worked here, she supposed. What your neighbor was doing was more important to these people than anything a TV producer could come up with. In some ways, it was kind of sweet. And she was certain that in other ways, it could be annoying. Just depended on which side of the gossip you ended up on.

"They even went as far as to go to St. Louis to a specialist," Lottie added. "But they never could conceive."

"Why not?" Sissy asked.

Lottie shook her head. "I don't know."

"What does he look like? English Ben?" Sissy asked, certain he had been at the funeral.

"He's kind of short with dark hair. He's bald on the top, and he's got a thick, thick mustache." Lottie stood and groaned a little as her knees cracked and popped. Then she picked up the tub full of silverware and started toward the waitress station.

Not willing to let the conversation end there, Sissy stood, as well, and followed behind her. "He was at the funeral? Right?" she asked. She seemed to remember a man fitting that description.

"Of course." Lottie slid the bus tub full of silverware into its usual spot at the waitress station. "They did all the flowers for the funeral. Word around town was that Ben, English Ben, wanted to do them himself, but Abby insisted that she do the bulk."

Even though she was pregnant and high-risk.

"So how did she know Kevin?" Sissy asked.

Lottie placed her hands on her hips and shook her head. "Land sakes, girl. You sure are asking a lot of questions today."

Sissy smiled. "In my last life, I was a reporter." It was better than divulging that in this life, aside from being a waitress-in-training and a budding short-order cook, she was also a columnist hiding behind the advice from her alter ego. Advice that she never managed to apply in her own topsy-turvy life.

"I seem to remember Bethel telling me that you were a writer."

"Bah," Bethel said, coming out of the back room. She had her crutch in one hand and her handbag in the other. "If y'all are done jawin', it's time to go home."

"That reminds me." Lottie turned her attention back to Sissy once again. "Lizzie called and said you're welcome to come out to supper tonight."

Bethel shook her head.

"That's sweet, but—"

"Lizzie is a sweet one," Lottie agreed. "She didn't think you would want to be alone and eating by yourself after a funeral."

Sissy supposed that could be the reason, but she had a feeling that her cousin needed the company as much as she thought Sissy might. Still, she couldn't run out there and eat every night. That just didn't seem quite right.

She loved visiting with her cousin, and she looked forward to it. Needed it, even. They both did. Lizzie needed

the distraction, and Sissy needed the connection, but
Sissy didn't want to be a burden. Plus, all the groceries
that she had bought were starting to go bad. You know, all
those tomatoes and lettuce and stuff for healthy eating,
because once again she had promised herself that she
would eat more salad. And there was no way Daniel and
Lizzie were eating salads. It was pasta and more pasta
with creamy sauce, gravy and meat, and green beans seasoned with bacon grease. Sissy needed to be eating at
home, but she didn't want to offend them by not coming
out. It was a conundrum. And green beans seasoned with
bacon grease were good. So there was that. But for now,
she was sticking to the plan.

"Tell Lizzie thanks," Sissy said, directing her words
toward Bethel. "But I need to be at home tonight." Which
wasn't exactly a lie; she really did need to be at home
tonight, eating salads instead of green beans seasoned
with bacon grease—no matter how delicious they were.

They all gathered their things and started for the door
of the café. Though Sissy wasn't much of a morning person, it was kind of fun getting off at three in the afternoon
and having the rest of the evening to herself to do the
things that she wanted to do. And maybe start that book
that she'd been saying she was going to write . . . But for
now, she would just settle for making a salad, even
though she would rather have a hamburger. And working
on Aunt Bess's column for the next edition. She stopped
before getting into her car.

"Lottie," she said. "I remember English Ben from the
funeral." He had been sitting across from her, and for
some reason, he had caught her eye. Maybe because, like
Lottie said, he had such an unusual mustache. "He was

sitting between two women." Both were about the same age.

"That's right," Lottie said. She had opened her car door and stood in the jamb waiting for Sissy's question. Bethel stood on the opposite side, waiting as well, though a bit impatiently.

"So which one is Abby?"

She thought about it a moment. "Abby was on the left." She seemed to think about it a minute more. "Yes, she was on the left. And Danielle, her sister, was on his right. Then Danielle's husband Clint."

The two women looked so much alike, Sissy didn't need to be told they were kin. There was one major difference in the pair, though. The woman on the left had been visibly upset, shaken, on the verge of tears. While the one on the right seemed normally sad for the funeral. Solemn, elegant, quiet. But not outwardly grieving.

"So did Abby and Kevin know each other?" Sissy asked. Must've been good friends for her to appear so upset at his funeral.

"This is Yoder," Bethel said, popping one hand on the top of Lottie's car. "Everyone here knows everyone."

Yes. She had forgotten about that. And yet . . .

"Abby is a tender soul," Lottie explained. "Between all the pregnancy hormones and I'm sure the exhaustion from getting all those flowers together, she was feeling a bit fragile." Lottie nodded at her own words and got into her car.

Sissy stood and watched as the pair of them started to drive away. Then Lottie rolled down her window and looked over to Sissy. "Are you staying in the parking lot all night?" she asked.

"No," Sissy said, spurring herself into action. "I'm going home now." And trying to figure out exactly how a funeral, the baby, and the KC mob had anything in common.

Salad. That was exactly what she needed to eat. A big, healthy salad with grilled chicken and lots of tomatoes. She did the best she could to pretend that it was a hamburger. But even her crazy imagination wasn't enough to pull that off.

Supper had seriously depleted her food supply. The lettuce had been going bad for days, and she barely salvaged enough of it to make a salad. She had used all the tomatoes, because they, too, were on their way out. The salad tasted okay, but man couldn't live on wilted vegetables alone. She was going to have to head over to Hutchinson to Walmart and grab a few things for her fridge.

But she had to fill up with gas before going to Hutchinson. So one thing just kept leading into another. Maybe it was a good thing that she hadn't gone over to her aunt's tonight. What had started off to be a quiet evening at home had turned into an evening of running multiple errands.

She grabbed Duke's leash from its hook by the door. "You ready to go bye-bye?" she asked the pup.

He barked from his customary place on top of the orange paisley cover on the bed and danced a little in place as he waited for her to scoop him up. He licked her face, and she laughed as she set him on the floor and hooked the leash to his collar. "All right, then, big guy. Let's go."

She secured Duke in the car, rolled the top down, and started off toward the Quiki-Mart. Sure enough, there was an alley between the two buildings—the Quiki-Mart and the florist shop—that was paved and wide enough for the milk truck but not much else. And the park. Once again, she thought this a generous name for a field of grass and a covered concrete slab with a couple of picnic tables underneath.

Sissy pulled up to the pumps and got out with her credit card, surprised to see that on the old-fashioned pumps, there wasn't a pay-outside option.

She looked from the door of the convenience store back to where her dog waited in the car. As she could see it, she had two choices: She could roll up the top and lock Duke inside, or unhook him for a moment—and pay her bill—and hurry back out. It seemed the more logical choice. Even if it meant taking her baby into an establishment where non-seeing eye dogs might not be welcome. Or something like that. But what choice did she have, really?

"Come on, then." She unhooked Duke and cradled him in the crook of her arm. Strangely enough, as many times as she had carried him this way, this time, he reminded her of Darcy Saunders and her little Chihuahua. And she wondered how many more layers there were to Darcy Saunders. She wasn't all that she seemed. Maybe not as confident, carrying the small dog around like a baby. Emotional support. Wasn't that what they called it? Sissy couldn't blame her. If she had lost her husband and was left with ten kids to raise by herself, she would need all the emotional support she could get.

Sissy hurried across to the doors of the convenience store and walked inside. A bell jangled overhead as the door closed behind her. "I'm sorry," she said to the girl behind the counter. She looked too young to be working alone in the convenience store, but Sissy had noticed lately that the older she got, the younger everybody else looked.

"He's so cute," the young girl said. Her voice sounded young, as well, and Sissy suspected that she wasn't much over fifteen, if even that. She had dark brown eyes that looked like liquid, and she wore a hijab covering her hair and neck.

"I'm sorry I had to bring him in, but with my car and the pumps . . ." She let the words trail off.

"It's okay," the young girl said.

Sissy smiled her thanks and ignored the rumble of her stomach as the smells of fried chicken and fried potatoes filled her senses. The Quiki-Mart was one of those great little stores that every town should have; where almost anything was for sale. Candy, bumper stickers, emergency tampons, antacids, and headache tablets, but also fried chicken and potato wedges.

Her stomach growled again.

She smelled fried foods all day long. A person would think she would get tired of it, but this was different. She was starving. Okay, she *thought* she was starving, but a salad was just a salad. And it really hadn't been that much salad, considering most of the head of lettuce had already turned rusty.

"How much on the gas?" the girl behind the counter asked.

"I'd like to fill it up, but then I'd have to come back in and sign."

The young girl nodded with a small frown. "Sorry about that. Dad's supposed to be updating everything, but until then . . ."

"Your dad? He owns this place?"

"Yeah, Eddie. He's my dad."

Which would explain why such a young girl was allowed to work at the store.

"I think it'll take twenty," Sissy said. "And then I would love to have some chicken and potatoes."

The young girl smiled. "The smell gets you every time, right?"

Sissy laughed. "Every time."

"How much chicken and potatoes?"

Sissy got a half pound each.

The girl ran the card. "I'm Lina, by the way," she said.

"Sissy." She shifted Duke to her other arm and reached out her right hand to shake. "It's nice to meet you."

"Sissy," Lina said. "You work at the Sunflower Café."

"That's right," Sissy said. She didn't think she would ever get used to how small Yoder really was. "And this is Duke," she said, indicating the pup she cradled in her arm.

"It's nice to meet you, Duke." Lina gave a small nod of her head. "Y'all come back in anytime."

With a smile like that, how could Sissy refuse? "Of course. Thanks for the chicken and taters." Then she said goodbye to Lina and started out the door. But she nearly stopped in her tracks and dropped both her dog and the food when she saw that a car had pulled up next to hers at the gas pumps. And right there stood Evan Yoder.

CHAPTER EIGHT

It isn't the ups and downs that make life difficult;
it's the jerks.
—Aunt Bess

She shouldn't have been so surprised. The man had to buy his gas somewhere. And as far as she knew, the Quiki-Mart was the only place in Yoder where he could do that.

Duke let out a low growl deep in his throat. Then he started barking.

"Hush, Duke," she said. They had met Evan before, and Duke hadn't set to such carrying on then. Well, not right off the bat.

She sent Evan a tentative smile, part greeting, part apology, then she hooked the dog back to his leash in the front seat of her car. He braced his paws on the driver's side door and continued to bark as if his life depended on it. With the look that Evan Yoder gave him, Sissy thought that it might actually be the case. She opened the door, scooched the dog over, and rolled up the window. Just in case.

"Copper hair and just like the proverbial bad penny."

"Evan Yoder. Good to see you, too." Sissy removed the nozzle and began to pump her gas, thankful to be on the other side of the pumps from him. He hadn't been inside yet, which meant he hadn't paid. He wasn't pumping gas yet. He was just standing there, almost daring her to ask the question that had been bothering her since she had seen him at Kevin's funeral. "Why didn't you tell me that you went to school with Kevin and Darcy?"

She could only see part of him through the dual gas pumps, but he was tall enough that she could definitely see his face, his eyes. Something in them changed at the mention of Darcy. Or was it Kevin's name that brought about the shift?

"I really don't see how that is any of your business."

Touché. Strangely enough, the words were spoken without malice or threat. As far as Evan was concerned, it was simply a fact. A fact she couldn't deny. Still, her red-haired temper rose to life inside her. She tamped it back down. *Easy, girl.* "Earl Berry's trying to pin this murder on me."

Those glorious green eyes got darker still. And then it was as if a door had been slammed down on his emotions, like one of those roll-top garage doors. Just *bam!* and his expression was clear, blank.

"Sucks to be the new girl in town." And with that, he turned on his heel and made his way into the Quiki-Mart, leaving Sissy staring after him.

*   *   *

Rattled. That was the best word. Her encounter with Evan Yoder had left her rattled. But she was not going to allow it to take over her night.

What had she expected? That she would confront Evan Yoder, and he would confess out of sheer good manners? That if he didn't, then she would surely be blamed for Kevin's murder?

She hadn't been ready for it, that was all. She would get herself together, though, and the next time she ran into him, things would go her way. She would ask the questions she needed to ask, and she wouldn't try to guilt him into a confession. Truth be known, she didn't have any reason to believe that Evan might have killed Kevin other than she didn't like him. Evan, she meant.

Okay, okay, there was the little matter of the fact that Kevin had taken Darcy away from Evan in high school. But that was high school. Didn't people let that stuff go after a couple years?

Of course they did. It was a silly question.

"What do you think, Duke?"

Upon hearing his name, her little dog barked.

If only she could speak Dog.

She pulled her car to the side of the road to stop for a minute and just take in the sights. Once again, she found herself out by the Brubacher Dairy. Surely it wasn't because she had Evan Yoder on the brain, and the Yoder Horse Farm was right across the road. It was simply because the air was so peaceful out here. This is what people talked about, poets citing rolling green hills and grassy knolls. Okay, so it was Kansas and about as flat as a pancake, but still, she felt the poetic-ness of the place. Then, add in her growing curiosity concerning raw milk . . .

They didn't have raw milk in Tulsa. At least, none that she knew about, and she couldn't help but wonder if it was any good. Could people really tell the difference?

Yeah, that's all it was: reporter's curiosity. Maybe she could do a freelance piece on the difference between raw milk and homogenized milk. It might make a good story.

She turned to her pup. "What you think, Duke? You want to give it a try?"

Duke barked three short yaps. She didn't have to get out her English-to-Dog dictionary to understand that was a resounding *yes*. Okay, so she spoke a little Dog.

"All righty, then." She put the car into drive once more. It was only a short distance to the driveway at the Brubacher Dairy, and they practically coasted there.

Sissy parked her car and got out. "You stay here," she told the dog. He was strapped in, or she would never be able to trust him on a strange farm with the top down.

An old yellow dog lay in the shade of an oak tree, up near a house that could have used a coat of paint. But it was a good house, solid, and she was reminded that the family who lived there was Amish. Two stories, white clapboard, wraparound porch. A row of crepe myrtles had been planted in a diagonal path between the porch and the large white barn that sat directly in front of her. Off to her left and just up a piece from the peeling sign that clearly indicated that she had come to the Brubacher Dairy was a small building, something akin to a large shed, with windows across the back and a screen door protecting the entrance. A small sign had been screwed to the outer wall of the building, just to the left of the door. HOURS OF OPERATION, it declared.

A store? That was unexpected. Truthfully, she didn't know why she had come out to the dairy, other than just curiosity, but now . . . now, she had to see what they had for sale.

"Can I help you?" A man came toward her, casually striding across the patchy grass that separated the house and the drive where she had just parked. He appeared to be in his late thirties, maybe early forties. He was handsome in a workaday way, with rusty hair and tanned forearms that declared he spent a lot of time in the sun. But he wasn't dressed Amish. Perhaps she could say partially Amish. He had on a blue button-down shirt and black suspenders, but he had paired them with jeans and black boots that could've belonged to any generation or religion. Except for maybe the Hare Krishnas. Weren't they usually barefoot?

Sissy pulled her thoughts back in. "I didn't realize you had a store here."

He nodded. "You're welcome to come in and browse around. Are you looking for anything special today?" He walked past her to the screen door and opened it, standing to one side as if to herd her in.

"Thank you," Sissy said. She took two steps toward the open door, feeling a bit foolish for just loitering in the man's yard. She had to wonder if he'd been sent out to make sure she didn't get lost between her car and the store.

In all fairness, she was certain all sorts of people came out this way, curious onlookers wanting to get a taste of the Amish life firsthand.

An oddly familiar whirring sound came from behind her, and she turned as a strange figure came into view.

She supposed *strange* wasn't the best word. Perhaps *unexpected*. For it was a sight she had seen often down on Riverside and other places in Tulsa: the silhouette of a serious biker. Cyclist, she corrected herself. Multispeed bike, spandex shorts, rash guard shirt, half-finger gloves, and one of those bike helmets that seemed space-age in its design.

As Sissy watched, the cyclist stopped, put down the kickstand on his bike, and pulled off his helmet.

"Gavin?" she exclaimed, as the reporter for the *Sunflower Express* grinned at her. His black-rimmed glasses had been replaced with goggles, and that flop of hair had been pushed back off his forehead and squashed down by his helmet.

"One and the same." He tucked that helmet under one arm and nodded to the man who stood behind Sissy. "Jonathan," Gavin said by way of greeting.

Jonathan returned it in the same manner.

"You ride a bicycle?" Sissy asked. If she hadn't been so surprised, she wouldn't have let that stupid question get past her lips, but there it was, out in the open for both men to hear.

"Yeah," he said. "It gets me around in my off time."

Sissy just stared at him, trying to think of something else to say that didn't sound quite as dumb as what she had said so far. She looked down the road and back the other direction, even though the house blocked one side of her view. "So you live close?"

Gavin turned a little pink, or perhaps that was just from the exertion of riding all the way here. There wasn't a house for miles, most of the land eaten up by the dairy and the horse farm across the road.

"I live close enough."

"You want your usual?" Jonathan asked.

Sissy turned toward the man. *Jonathan*, she thought. She did her best to commit both his face and name to memory. It was always good to know people in your neighborhood.

"Please," Gavin said, and started toward the store.

Still not knowing what to make of the situation, Sissy followed them inside.

The small building that served as a store for the Brubacher Dairy was just what it appeared to be from the outside—a simple shed. A modest yet sturdy wooden table held a cash register and a notepad and pencil, along with one of those little trays where people could place their extra pennies in case the next person in line might need one. There was no credit card machine, just a waste-paper basket underneath and a folding chair propped against the wall behind. Two sides of the shed were taken up by floor-to-ceiling coolers containing pint and quart jars of creamy white milk as well as half-gallon jugs like those traditionally seen in the grocery store. There were blocks of cheese, both yellow and white, some with herbs and other tasty additives already inside. There were also tubs of sour cream, packages of creamy cheeses, dips, drinks, and other tasty-looking add-ons.

"What's your usual?" Sissy asked in a low voice.

Gavin just smiled. "Half a gallon of milk, a quart of heavy cream, and a brick of cheddar cheese." Then he turned to Jonathan. "I'd like to add some of that basil and sun-dried tomato cheese. I've been having a craving for a grilled cheese."

Jonathan nodded and moved to the cooler where the cheeses were stored. He selected one and put it in the bag he'd been filling while Sissy had gawked at all the products available.

"And all this is made right here?" she asked, still a bit in awe.

Jonathan nodded as he moved behind the table where the cash register sat to ring up Gavin's purchases. "We make it in the barn."

"With the cows?" she asked.

"It's a big barn." Jonathan chuckled, and she was sure he had fielded this question hundreds of times. "Half of it is dedicated to the cows, and the other half is dedicated to making the cheeses. Everything's clean and inspected. We have a health department rating and all that, if you'd like to see it." He jerked his thumb over his shoulder, where a corkboard hung on the wall. The A rating from the health department was pinned there for all to see, though seemingly more as an afterthought than with great pride. And Sissy wondered if it meant anything to the Brubachers at all. They did what they did, and with a pride the health department couldn't report.

"They do tours and stuff," Gavin added. "You should take one sometime."

"I think I will," she said. "When I don't have Duke with me, that is."

"Good plan," Gavin said, and then he made his way to the door, his biking shoes clicking against the floor as he let himself out.

"So can I help you find something?" Jonathan asked.

"What about E. coli?" The question just slipped out before she could think twice about it. That reporter in her wanted to find out every bit of information possible before she made her purchase. Aunt Bess would say that it was both a blessing and a curse.

"The chances of you getting E. coli from raw milk, or what we would rather call *fresh milk*, are only slightly greater than what you get in pasteurized milk. About two percent more." He waved a hand around, as if he couldn't be bothered with all the details. "The US government regulates the cheese. It has to be held for sixty days if it's made in America with raw milk. All of our cheese meets these government standards, and really, at that point, it just becomes a matter of taste."

She nodded, allowing his words to sink in. Kevin was a milkman. Could it be that the raw milk industry wanted to bring down the milkmen of the world who delivered pasteurized products to the cafés across America?

Not hardly.

Then something Gavin had said struck with her. "You have cheese with basil and sun-dried tomatoes in it?"

Jonathan nodded. "My wife grows the basil and the tomatoes in our garden each year. We freeze-dry them. The basil we put in fresh, and it makes the best grilled cheese on sourdough bread you would ever want to eat."

That did sound good. Even better than the greasy fried chicken and potatoes she had scarfed down on the way over here. "Do you have a bakery of choice?"

Jonathan smiled, and she could tell he knew he had her on the hook. "I believe all the bakers in Yoder are worth their salt, so just take your pick on that one. But be sure to get some of our fresh milk butter."

"You got it." Sissy gathered up the things she wanted to try—the basil and sun-dried tomato cheese, a block of cheddar, a half-gallon of milk, and the butter that Jonathan had recommended. It was a good start. She set her purchases on the table, and Jonathan rang them up. "I gave you the new resident discount," he said. "Fifteen percent off."

She handed him his money and smiled. "How did you know I was a new resident?"

He shrugged and put her money into the cash register.

He counted out her change and shut the drawer, then pulled the receipt tab and handed it all to her. "Just a guess. Not many people who are just visiting run into someone they know at our little shop."

She nodded. "Sissy Yoder," she said.

"Jonathan Brubacher."

Well, there went that theory of him not being a Brubacher and perhaps a hired English hand. Her mother always said shunning wasn't what it used to be, and it definitely appeared that Jonathan had left the Amish, even though he still worked in the family business. Things were definitely changing in the Amish world.

"Thanks, Jonathan. And it's nice to meet you."

"You, too," he said.

With a small wave, she let herself out of the shop.

"Gavin," she called, more than a little surprised to see him still standing by her car. He was petting Duke, who in turn was licking his hand. "I figured you'd be long gone."

"I couldn't walk right by and not pet your dog."

"Gavin, meet Duke. Duke, Gavin."

Gavin grabbed one of Duke's furry little paws. He shook it as if shaking hands with a man, a playful smile on his lips. "It's nice to meet you, Duke."

Duke licked Gavin's hand once again.

See? Duke wasn't a hateful dog. He merely didn't like Evan Yoder. Still, to Sissy, that seemed a little strange. She didn't dislike Evan Yoder. She just hadn't found a good reason to *like* Evan Yoder. It seemed that Duke wasn't quite so particular. He had given the man a chance at their first encounter, and when he didn't make it up to scratch . . .

Gavin was a different matter altogether. And in this

light, he looked almost cute. Not at all as dorky as she had first thought. The skintight spandex should've made him look ridiculous. Instead, not so much. His shorts showed off the firm muscles of his thighs, and his muscular calves, as well. And the rash guard surely hid a set of six-pack abs not at all visible while he was wearing his standard work button-down. He was lean and toned, surely from riding that bike. Or perhaps he had a gym membership in Hutchinson.

Then again . . .

"You don't live all that close, do you?" Sissy asked.

Gavin settled the helmet on his head and slipped the chin strap into place. "Close enough I can bike over here." He grinned; then, with a jaunty wave, he kicked off and headed in the opposite direction that Sissy had to go to run her impulse purchases by the Chicken Coop. She supposed "close" was a relative term to someone who was a serious cyclist. And she had a feeling that Gavin was as serious as they came.

She got into her car and watched as he rode out of sight. Then she started for home, pausing just for a moment to look across at the rolling grassy hills of the Yoder Horse Farm. She wished she had an excuse to drop by there and check in with Evan. She supposed she could sign up for horseback riding lessons and see if she could discover what Evan Yoder knew about Darcy and Kevin Saunders. Then again, she was liable to break her neck on the back of the horse. She would just have to take her chances with Earl Berry.

CHAPTER NINE

Never miss a good chance to shut up.
—Aunt Bess

By Friday, business at the Sunflower Café was back to normal. Or normal as she knew it—aka, the first two days she was there before Kevin was murdered.

The mayor came in and ordered a hamburger and fries, as he was always prone to do on Fridays. Lottie had filled Sissy in on the details. Tom Daly had to watch his cholesterol, and if he did good all week, he treated himself to a hamburger for breakfast on Friday. Lottie also claimed that Tom was the only person Bethel would make an exception for, bending her rule of no lunch served before ten forty-five. Keisha and the girls from the Hair Joint took turns coming in on Friday for coffee and pie just around ten thirty. And Earl Berry, Deputy Sheriff, parked his keister on stool number three at the counter and ate three eggs over hard with half a side of bacon, half a side of sausage, one large slice of tomato, and a piece of toast with a little bit of gravy just to make things interesting.

Lottie assured Sissy that Earl Berry's frequent trips to the café were just proof of his bachelor status and not any indication that he was out to get her.

Sissy wanted to believe what Lottie was saying, but she couldn't. Mainly because Earl Berry had never done a single thing to make her believe that he wanted to arrest anyone other than her for Kevin's murder. She felt as if he was following her around just to see if she would slip up. Even last night, as she was coming home from the dairy, she passed him as she pulled into the neighborhood where the Chicken Coop was located.

Okay, so *neighborhood* was a very generous word for the little gathering of houses strung next to downtown Yoder. And *downtown* was a generous way to describe what basically consisted of a handful of miscellaneous shops, the hardware store, and the post office. Yet she was starting to like small-town life.

She would like it even more if she didn't have murder charges hanging over her head.

"You need a refill, Deputy?" she asked. It was hard to know how to handle him. She didn't want to be too nice and have him thinking that she was just buttering him up, and she didn't want to be too stern. She was still working for tips, you know. It was definitely a delicate balance.

She supposed the thing that bothered her most was the person Earl Berry should have been questioning further was standing in the kitchen while Earl himself watched every move Sissy made.

Sissy had to bite her tongue not to ask him why he wasn't back there questioning Josie. First of all, she couldn't throw Josie under the bus like that, and second of all, she was afraid it would just make her look that much guiltier.

Earl harassed her for a time, until Lottie told him that Sissy had work to do. Then she went about her duties—refilling coffee, bussing tables, and bringing out orders—all the while so very aware that his gaze traveled wherever she did, just moments behind.

Finally, he threw a couple of bills down on the bar, stood up, and adjusted his gun belt, then grabbed a toothpick and headed for the door. Bethel never made him pay for his breakfast, out of the goodness of her heart, Sissy supposed. But at least he always left a tip. For that, she could be thankful.

A lull usually occurred between ten thirty and eleven, when the breakfast crowd all shuffled out and just before the lunch rush started. That was when Sissy took a break. Today, she sat down in one of the booths with her own plate of a grilled ham and cheese and an order of fries.

The toasted sandwich reminded her of the "fresh" milk cheese she'd bought at Brubacher's the day before. After eating a salad and then chicken and potatoes from the Quiki-Mart, she did not let herself have a grilled cheese when she got home last night, as good as that notion sounded. That might just be her supper tonight. But for now . . . she took out a small notebook and pen and placed them to the right of her plate. Then she took a bite of the sandwich and chewed thoughtfully.

"What are you doing?" Lottie asked.

Sissy swallowed the bite and dabbed the napkin to the corners of her mouth. "I'm making a list of who could have killed Kevin."

"Land sakes, girl," Lottie exclaimed. "I meant what are you really doing?"

"That is what I'm really doing." Sissy held up her note-book, as if that provided definitive proof.

"Why, I never," Lottie said with a shake of her head. "Why would you want to go and do something like that for?"

"If I don't, I'm afraid Earl Berry is going to arrest me." It was the first time she had ever admitted it out loud, and it was a little disconcerting to hear her voice say those words to another. But all in all, it was the truth. She was worried that Earl Berry was going to do everything in his power—that he was *already* doing everything in his power—to send her up the river.

"Earl Berry is a toothless tiger," Lottie said.

"I'm not sure that makes me feel any better." A tooth-less tiger might not be able to bite, but it could sure enough scratch and claw. And if a man with no power was the one in charge of the good citizens of Yoder, what did that mean for her?

"All I'm trying to say is," Lottie started, "he's just a lot of hot air most of the time."

Most of the time.

"He probably thinks you have a clue, or that you saw something and you're not forthcoming with it. For what-ever reason. Like, say, because you're new in town, and he's trying to shake you up. He might want you to give up whatever it is he thinks you saw. Or kept."

That sounded reasonable enough, but it sent a pang of guilt slicing through Sissy's midsection. Funny how she hadn't thought about it again until right that moment. But she *had* found something that day. Stuck to the bottom of her shoe. A piece of fabric with tiny little checks. She had picked it up and shoved it into her pocket, and then she walked around the corner and found Kevin. Who could think about little scraps of fabric when a dead man was lying on the ground right in front of you?

"What is it, sugar?" Lottie asked.

Sissy coughed, then reached for her glass of tea. She swallowed a big gulp, but it didn't help. She coughed again and finally got herself under control. "Nothing." The one word was something between a choke and a croak, and it very quickly identified itself as the biggest lie she'd told in a long time.

Lottie eyed her for a moment, part concern, part suspicion. "Are you sure?"

Sissy's eyes began to water, but somehow, she managed to keep further coughs at bay. "I'm fine," she wheezed.

"You need the Heimlich maneuver or anything, you just say so. I saw how to do it on TV," Lottie said.

"Nope. All good."

Lottie looked from Sissy's red face and swimming eyes down to the notebook that sat in front of her, sharing the space with her partially eaten lunch. "If you're sure . . ."

"Positive."

Lottie gave one last nod. "Just quit worrying about all this murder business. It's enough to make a body collapse with the vapors."

"Does anyone actually collapse with the vapors these days?"

"You know what I mean," Lottie continued. "So stop worrying and let Earl Berry do his job. I'm sure it will all come out in the wash." And on that note, Lottie moved away, over to the cash register to ring out one last late-breakfast customer.

Sissy managed to get herself back under control. She even managed to work on the list and finish her lunch before her break was over. Not that making the list was such a good feat. It was short. Really short. In fact, it only contained Mike, the new milkman; Evan Yoder, mainly because Duke didn't like him; Josie because well . . . she sort of scared Sissy; and Darcy, because the widow was always a suspect. In truth, Sissy couldn't imagine Darcy killing her husband and purposefully widowing herself with ten children. That just didn't make sense. But the widow was always a suspect, yada yada yada.

"So who's on this list?" Lottie asked, as they began to get the lunch prep out of the cooler.

Sissy wasn't sure how to answer that. She wasn't ready to start blaming anyone, not even to Lottie. She gave a casual shrug. "You know, people." She chuckled albeit a bit nervously. "Mike, since he benefited by getting half Kevin's milk route. Though I can't imagine killing someone over something like that."

"That's true," Lottie said. She grabbed a huge tub of lettuce and carted it over to the worktable. "Anyone else?"

"No," she lied. "Not really. But can I ask you about Evan Yoder?"

"You don't think he's guilty?" Lottie stopped and propped her hands on her hips. "I've known that boy his whole life."

Who in this town had she not known since birth? But Sissy kept that question to herself. "No, of course not. I've seen him around town a couple of times, and every time Duke gets near him, he growls like crazy. I mean, Duke growls, not Evan." She let out another small, uncomfortable laugh. "Evan works with horses, so you would think animals like him. But I'm almost afraid Duke is going to try to bite him."

"That bad, huh?" Lottie said.

"I don't know. It just seems like something is off about the whole thing."

She leaned one ample hip against the worktable, and Sissy knew the gesture well. She was settling in for a bit of gossip. "Evan never wanted to work at the horse farm. At least, that's what everyone says. He and Darcy were going to run away. You knew they were a thing, right?" She didn't wait for Sissy to respond before continuing. "After Darcy threw Evan over for Kevin, Evan was so brokenhearted, he just kind of gave up, I think."

Sissy thought about the handsome man she had met out at the horse farm, and then again at the Quiki-Mart. He didn't look like the sort who would give up. But maybe that was what was behind those hooded green eyes. "You think he's resentful of animals?" It really didn't make any sense. Yet when it came to the human heart . . .

"Could be," Lottie mused. "See, his dad died, and he was left helping his mother run the farm. Darcy had gone off and married Kevin and already had a baby. What was he to do but soldier on?"

"And they were going to run away together? Darcy and Evan?"

Lottie nodded. "But that was a long time ago."

Yeah, it was, Sissy thought. Exactly ten kids ago.

All through the lunch rush, Sissy managed to push thoughts of Evan, Darcy, and Kevin from her mind. She almost forgot about Earl Berry, too, but something about being up for murder one tended to stick with a person.

Of course, it didn't help that the deputy came in for

pie. And during their busiest time. Who ate pie for lunch? Only someone on a stakeout.

But when things started to slow down once again, Darcy, Kevin, and Evan came crashing back into her thoughts. Truthfully, after her chat with Lottie, Sissy thought it best to move Darcy to the top of the list. Maybe Darcy killed Kevin so she could carry on with Evan.

"If she wanted to, she could just have had an affair with him."

Sissy spun around to find Josie standing right behind her. She really had to stop thinking out loud. But for today, it was too late. "Not if she wanted to marry Evan," she countered.

"Then she could have just divorced him."

That killed that theory, and Sissy was pretty much right back where she had started. And that was under the microscope, about to be arrested by Earl Berry, Deputy Sheriff, Yoder, Kansas.

"So," Sissy started, gaining courage as she did. "Did you have a thing for Kevin?" She turned and pinned Josie with a vicious stare. Well, she tried to pin her. Unfortunately, she had seen that look in the mirror, even practiced it to use on her brother. She knew for a fact that her vicious glare merely looked as if she might have a stomach virus.

Josie shrugged one shoulder, the one with the enormous Pegasus-looking tattoo. "He was all right, I guess." Every time Josie spoke, it surprised Sissy that she didn't have some exotic Russian accent that turned all of her *w*s into *v*s. "I really didn't know him except from here."

Sissy tried to nod thoughtfully, as if the words they were exchanging were of no consequence. If only she could find a reason to pin it on Josie. That would be perfect.

Not for Josie, though. And not for Bethel, seeing as how she would have to find another short-order cook. And maybe not for Sissy herself, in that making Josie out to be the murderer might possibly look like Sissy was trying to gain that job for her own.

In truth, there was no easy solution to all of this. If Darcy were guilty, then ten children would be without their mother *and* their father. Sissy supposed that April and some of the older children would be able to survive without their parents. But what about Dani and baby Dakota? What would happen to them? If Josie were guilty, Bethel would be without a cook. If Evan were guilty, his mom would be without his help at the horse farm. Whoever the guilty party was, they lived and breathed in this community. They walked and talked and worked and interacted with other people. They had moms, fathers, brothers, and sisters. No matter what the solution or the truth, someone—maybe even many "someones"—was going to be hurt. There was no way around it. The problem was, Sissy had to make sure that it wasn't *her* mother, father, brother—family—who was doing the weeping.

"Don't you have work to do?"

Sissy startled out of her thoughts, only then realizing that she was staring through Josie as she scraped the grill and prepared to turn it off for the afternoon. "Of course," she said.

She turned and pushed her way out of the kitchen and back into the front of the café. She had plenty to do. Restock the silverware rolls at the waitress station to get ready for tomorrow and wipe down all the salt and pepper shakers and ketchup bottles and other miscellaneous things that were left on the table each day. She had dishes to stack, chairs to move, a floor to sweep, a floor to mop. And a murderer to find.

"Excuse me."

Sissy nearly jumped out of her skin.

She turned to face the man who had spoken behind her. "Hey," she said stupidly. Clearly, she needed to add *not get so involved in your own thoughts that you don't pay attention to the world around you* to her list of things to do, right along with *stop thinking out loud.*

The man was tall, balding, with a sandy fringe of hair cut short and neat. He wore jeans and loafers and a pale pink button-down shirt that had been starched within an inch of its life.

"How can I help you?" she asked.

He shook his head and held up his phone. "Do you know the way to Darcy Saunders's house?"

Coincidence? Sissy thought, and thankfully kept the word to herself. But she must've paused too long, for the man continued.

"I have the address in my phone GPS, but it's not working right or something, because I keep coming back here."

"Let me see?" Sissy held out a hand, and the man offered her his cell phone. She peered at the screen. Funny how she had never noticed before, but the address to the Sunflower Café and the address to Darcy Saunders's house were almost the same. "Look here," she said, pointing to the screen. "You have the seven and the five in the wrong places. Switch those. And it's not Candles Street, it's McCandless."

He shook his head and smiled a little at his mistake. "So close. That's the thing about these GPSes. They work great until one little thing. Thanks."

"Anytime," Sissy said. "Why are you headed to Darcy's?" Perhaps she shouldn't have told the man where Darcy lived. But it wasn't like he didn't have the address almost completely correct. And yet . . .

The man tucked his cell phone into his pocket. Something about his demeanor was slightly aloof. "Just business."

Bethel picked that moment to stomp out from the back, where she had apparently been listening in. "You the insurance man?"

"That's right," he drawled. "Thanks again." Then he turned on one heel and left the café.

Sissy felt a wave of trepidation from the tips of her toes to the top of her head. Insurance man? He was awfully casual for an insurance agent, but she supposed it wasn't impossible for him to be in insurance.

She shook off the ill feelings. He had Darcy's address, she told herself. Mostly . . . But there was something in his smile that made her a tad uncomfortable. In all honesty, she couldn't figure out what it was. Only that maybe she'd been watching too many murder mysteries on cable.

CHAPTER TEN

The trouble with doing nothing is it's too hard to tell when you're finished.
—Aunt Bess

Sissy was just about to pull out of the parking lot behind the Sunflower Café when a familiar figure came along beside her.

"Gavin! What are you doing?"

He grinned at her. He had a nice smile, she decided. "I thought I would come by and see if you were ready to take a break. But I forgot that the café closes at two."

"Every day." She grinned back at him. "Are you walking?"

He jerked a thumb over his shoulder in no general direction. "It's not far from the newspaper office to here."

In Yoder, nothing was very far from anything.

"So . . ." he said, looking off in the distance. "Would you like to go to the Carriage House and maybe get a cup of coffee and a piece of pie?"

"Pie is definitely out, but I could have a coffee with you. Why? What's going on?"

"Nothing. Just thought you might take a break, but since you're not working . . ." He shrugged as he trailed off.

"Sure," she said. "Wanna ride over there?"

He seemed to think about it a moment. Like there was anything to think about; it was only two blocks away. She was already in her car. And he was already standing there. "I guess that'd be great."

She patted the passenger seat and waited for him to come around and get into the car. Then together, they rode the couple of blocks down to the Carriage House and pulled around the back to park. Gavin got out and waited while she put the top up, rolled up the windows, and locked the doors.

"You know your car would probably be fine out here with the top down or the very least unlocked," he said.

She grinned at him as she adjusted the shoulder strap of her handbag. "Just a habit, I guess."

"And you came here from Oklahoma City?" he asked.

"Tulsa," she corrected.

He pulled the door open for the both of them and waited as she stepped inside. Then he followed her in and opened the next set of doors. The first thing on her right was a display case filled with the most scrumptious-looking pies she had ever seen.

"Goodness," she said, looking at the pies and then glancing back up to Gavin almost in disbelief.

"They say they have the best pies in town."

"Don't let my aunt hear you say that."

He mimed turning a key in front of his lips and tossed the imaginary object over his shoulder.

Sissy chuckled as the waitress grabbed a couple of menus and took them into the restaurant. It was a series of cozy booths with a little piece of history placed on each table, telling about the Carriage House and Yoder and how it all began. It was fascinating as far as Sissy was concerned, but she had always liked history.

"You sure you don't want a piece of pie?" Gavin asked as the hostess moved away.

Sissy patted her stomach. "I feel like I've done nothing but eat since I got here," she said. At least tonight, she wouldn't be going out to her aunt's house and having a huge, greasy, buttery, creamy Amish meal.

"Maybe you should exercise a little more." He jerked his head into something that might've been considered a shrug had his shoulders been involved. "I mean, not that you need to exercise more, but I ride my bike a lot, and I suppose that lets me eat just about anything I want."

Sissy gave a smile and shook her head. "Lucky you. But just coffee for today."

The waitress came by to take their orders. Sissy had made her plan. She was sticking with coffee, and coffee only, while Gavin ordered a piece of peanut butter chocolate pie.

Heavens, was she going to be able to sit by while he ate that? It sounded dreamily delicious. But she could. She was strong. She had willpower. Why just the other night she had a salad.

"Tell me what's been going on at the café," Gavin said.

Sissy grabbed a packet of sweetener out of the condiment caddy on the table and shook all the powder down to one end. "Not much. Though I still think the deputy is coming in more often than he usually does in order to try to trip me up."

"He still thinks you're guilty?"

Sissy shrugged. "Lottie says she thinks he's trying to pressure me into turning over some piece of evidence that I might've found, or that I might have overheard something and I'm keeping it from him. Not that he really wants me to be guilty."

"And how do you feel about that?" He sat back as the waitress delivered their coffees to their table. She slipped the cup in front of Sissy, who immediately dumped in a package of Sweet'N Low. Healthy eating. No sugar. It was a start.

Then the waitress set the most beautiful piece of pie Sissy had ever seen in front of Gavin.

No, it was just an ordinary piece of pie, she decided. Yet she had allowed it to rise to the level of forbidden, and that made it look all the more delicious. But she didn't want it. Not at all.

"I think he wants to arrest me for the murder. He's just waiting to find more evidence that he can construe to look like I did it, and then I'm going to prison because I'm the new girl in town."

Gavin shook his head and took a tentative sip of his coffee. "You really think he's after you because he doesn't know who you are?"

"I don't know what he's thinking. But I know from Bethel that nobody wants to believe that Josie could've done it, even though she was in the kitchen right before it happened. And of course, Bethel and Lottie can't be guilty, because everybody in town knows them. That leaves only one person," she said. "Me."

"Or somebody who came up to the truck from the outside." Gavin forked off a piece of pie and lifted it to his mouth. Sissy tried not to stare. But the pie just looked so good.

"Like Evan Yoder? Nope. See, nobody can believe that Evan is guilty, because they've known him since he was born."

"Why would Evan want to kill Kevin?" He shook his head a bit. "I mean, sure I've heard that he and Darcy had a thing way back when. But that was high school. Folks move on. Right?"

"I still don't like him," Sissy snapped. It was a very poor reason to put someone on a murder list, but coupled with what motive he might possibly have, plus wanting his girlfriend back . . . well, that was enough for her.

"Who else?" Gavin asked. "Who else could have done it?"

Sissy opened her large bag and pulled out the stenographer's notebook she'd been using at lunch.

Gavin's eyes widened in surprise. "You've got a list?"

"Of course. With their possible motives." How else was she supposed to keep it all straight? She took out a pen and tapped it against Josie's name. It was the only one without grounds for murder listed next to it. But Sissy paused before adding the reason. Why, exactly, was Josie on the list? Because her brother was in prison? Because she looked like she could have killed someone? Because her tattoo made Sissy a little nervous? All of this—but were these really reasons? Not hardly. There wasn't one solid justification why she should put Josie on the list and so many reasons why she should take her off—like Lottie and Bethel swore that she would never hurt a fly.

"You know Josie and her brother had a really hard time growing up," Gavin said.

Sissy sighed. It was not what she wanted to hear. She needed someone to be guilty. And she didn't need for her soft heart to get in the way of creating a list of those persons most likely to be culpable. "Like what?"

Gavin paused for a moment, as if thinking back. "Like their house burned down, and when they were little, their mom died and their dad was an alcoholic. Their grandmother raised them, but she didn't have any money. She was a lot older. She didn't have much to offer them, and then Daryl—that's Josie's brother—he started running around with the rough crowd. For a while, even, I think he was hanging out with Kevin and his gang. But they weren't much trouble. Hardly more than a bowling league. And then the accident." He made a face, as if that was adjective enough to describe whatever this event was.

"Is that how he ended up in jail, in prison?"

Gavin savored the last bite of pie before answering. "I guess it's all in who you talk to about it. Kevin and Daryl were out drinking, and they got into some kind of argument with these other guys. It was late, and tempers were hot. Then a fight broke out, a physical fight. According to most, Kevin and Daryl were about to leave, and Daryl grabbed a baseball bat that Kevin kept in his truck. And he decided to go back and end the fight."

"But it seems that the fight had already stopped if they were at his truck."

"That's exactly what the judge said. Evidently, Daryl hit one of the guys. Now, whether he hit him too hard, or it was the fall to the ground . . . I don't know. But he died, and the DA managed to get the jury to convict Daryl on a premeditated charge, since all the witnesses said the fight had stopped. That they were at the truck. If he hadn't gone back with the bat. That showed intent."

Sissy *tsk*ed.

Gavin nodded and pushed his plate to the middle of the table. Sissy tried not to stare at the crispy-looking crumbs and the smear of chocolate. This was her new leaf; she would do well to remember it.

"Why did you tell me that?" she asked Gavin.

"I don't know." He picked up a corner of his napkin. "Maybe to say a lot of people do a lot of things for a lot of different reasons."

Sissy thought about that a moment. "Fair enough." She propped her hand on her chin and stared across the table at him. "But I really believe I'm gonna have to find out who killed this guy, or I'm going to end up in jail. I'm not joking. All the people here in town, and nobody wants to believe the worst of anyone they've known since diapers. But someone in this town is a murderer."

"It's always that way in a small town. People tend to take care of their own. When you have a town the size of Yoder, everyone belongs, even those who don't."

Sissy had never lived anyplace smaller than Tulsa, but she had read enough and seen enough movies that she thought she had a pretty good grasp on small-town life. She just wasn't quite used to it yet. "So how do you go about finding a murderer in a town full of good-old-boy innocents?"

"Let me think about it."

Sissy nodded.

The waitress came by and asked if they wanted refills on their coffee.

Gavin looked to Sissy, who shook her head. She was really going to have to get out of this wonderful-smelling restaurant in order to stick to her diet plan. And after what she had for lunch . . . She needed to do better at supper.

And pie was definitely off the list. And basil and sun-dried tomato cheese from Brubacher's was calling her name.

"Just the check, please," Gavin told the waitress.

She tore off the slip of paper from her order pad and laid it on the table in front of him.

Sissy reached for her wallet. "Let me get you some money for—"

"I got it." He shook his head and took his own wallet from his back pocket. "We pay up front."

He stood and stretched, allowing Sissy time to walk past him. And then he ambled behind her, through the small gift shop and over to the cash register. Sissy couldn't help but look around at all the wonderfully kitschy items displayed there. Most had something to do with Yoder or Kansas or sunflowers, seeing as how Kansas was the Sunflower State. But looking at all the beautiful sun-flower displays made her want to update the display they had at the café. Maybe that was something she could get into. After she caught the murderer, of course. Otherwise, she didn't think she would have time to do much more than learn the menu items before she had to don an or-ange jumpsuit.

"Hey, Gavin."

A familiar man was standing at the cash register. Sissy knew that she had seen him somewhere, but since coming to Yoder, she had met so many new people, sometimes it was hard to remember exactly who she was seeing, even if she recognized the face.

"English Ben," Gavin said with a grin.

The florist. That's right. English Ben was the florist who owned the shop next to the Quiki-Mart.

"Are you coming to eat?" Gavin peered behind Ben to see if he was alone.

"No," English Ben said with a small smile. "Abby and her cravings," he said. "Every day this week, I've had to come get fried green tomatoes. She can't get enough of them."

Sissy could understand that. And she could get behind it, too. Fried green tomatoes were the bomb.

"The little woman has a craving, and you have to run out and satisfy it," Gavin said. "Am I getting this right? Should I be taking notes for myself one day?"

English Ben just laughed. But Sissy could tell the real truth. He was worried about his wife and the pregnancy. "It's just been a long haul," English Ben said. He didn't need to say more for Sissy to understand. She had heard the talk in the town, all they had been through, the countless fertility treatments and this one last chance—such a far-fetched chance, considering their ages—and bam! A baby.

All she could think of was the fact that they would be in their seventies by the time the child graduated college. But like Lottie had said: When a couple wanted a child that badly and for that long, they would do anything to make it happen, at any age that they could. It just so happened this was their time.

"Roger's been coming in to help, though," English Ben said.

"That's good," Gavin replied.

Ben nodded. "He's a good boy. A good nephew."

"I'm glad you have him to help," Gavin added.

"We are, too," Ben said. "Though Roger has had to work a lot more lately since Abby . . ." He trailed off, in that way of men who were not comfortable talking about women's matters.

Their conversation was interrupted, as the hostess came back carrying a large paper sack, its heavenly aroma mixing with the already scrumptious scent of the restaurant. "Here you go, Ben," the woman said. Like so many other employees of the Carriage House, she was Amish, a little on the young side. She wore the strings of her prayer covering loose, dangling about her shoulders. "Double order of fried green tomatoes with extra-extra dipping sauce."

English Ben grinned in relief. "I should probably go ahead and order some more for tomorrow night, too," he said with a chuckle.

The hostess laughed. "Nah. We'll be here, waiting for your call tomorrow. About four o'clock?"

Ben paid his bill. Gavin paid theirs, and then they all left the restaurant.

Ben hurried in front of them, no doubt to get the fried green tomatoes home before they cooled too much. It was incredibly sweet, she thought, that he loved his wife so much. And it was romantic that he came out each night to get her fried green tomatoes, a double order with a double-double order of dipping sauce, since she had such a craving. Who said men couldn't be romantic?

Well, whoever it was, they were wrong. Because romance and the male species were alive and well in Yoder tonight.

CHAPTER ELEVEN

Every family tree produces some lemons, a few
nuts, and a couple of bad apples.
——Aunt Bess

Thankfully, Earl Berry didn't come into the Sunflower
Café on Saturday morning. Since it was the first
Saturday that Sissy had actually worked since coming to
Yoder to help her aunt, she wasn't sure if Deputy Berry
was working the weekend. Or if he would come in to see
if she was working the weekend, and if he did come in, if
she would be able to tell if he was there for her or not.
The thought was almost giving her a headache, so she
pushed it aside and thanked her lucky stars that he had
left her alone for one day.

But as she turned from the long row of dryers at the
Yoder Clean 'n Suds, she thought she caught a glimpse of
a patrol car rolling down the street. She wasn't sure, because she hadn't been looking directly out the window.

She had been more concerned with the little scrap of fabric she held in her hands.

It was the same scrap of fabric she had slipped on, that day Kevin was killed. She had only thought about it once, when Lottie had said something to her about Earl Berry thinking Sissy had evidence to help his case. After she had found it, she had shoved it into her pocket, and for the most part, she had forgotten about it.

She turned the little scrap over in her hands and studied it, front and back. It was only a couple of inches long, frayed on both sides, as if it had weathered a great storm. Or maybe that was just from being run through the washer and dryer.

She couldn't remember exactly how it looked when she found it stuck to the bottom of her shoe, just before she had stuffed it into her pocket, just before she had found Kevin. How was a person supposed to remember something so mundane as a little scrap of fabric just before finding a dead body? One thing was certain: After running through both machines at the Clean 'n Suds, the little scrap was completely useless as evidence. Any DNA has been washed away, and—since she had handled it and washed it with her own clothes—replaced with her own.

"What you got there?" She looked up as Gavin came striding between the rows of washers.

Once again, he was dressed in cyclist spandex, and strangely enough, she was beginning to get used to the look. That was something she never thought she would say. Yet somehow, on Gavin, the super-tight, black, brightly colored garments seem to suit him. And if he ate whatever he wanted and cycled to get rid of the calories, well . . . he must cycle a lot.

"Hey, Gavin," she greeted him. Somehow, she managed to drag her attention away from his washboard abs to the scrap of fabric she held in one hand. "It's a clue, I guess."

Gavin frowned. "A clue?"

She shook her head. "No. Probably not. I mean, not really."

He cocked his head to one side. "Would you like to explain that a little better?"

Sissy sucked in a deep breath. "I found it on the bottom of my shoe."

"O . . . kay." Gavin's expression turned from Joyful Greeting to Confused Man. "Just now?"

She shook her head. "On the day of the murder." She lowered her voice and cast her eyes from side to side to see if anyone near was paying attention. There weren't many people in the Clean 'n Suds at this time on Saturday afternoon. Just two young girls, who seemed to be washing their clothes from the night before, and one little old lady, who had a penchant for pastel-colored, polyester leisure suits. "Just before I found Kevin's—Kevin."

"Inside the restaurant, or inside the milk truck?"

"In the restaurant," she said, then quickly corrected, "the café."

"So it could have come from someone inside. Maybe Lottie tore her blouse or something?"

"You don't think it's a clue at all." She tried not to sound hurt, but a note of it soured her tone.

Plus most of the employees at the café wore cotton knit T-shirts with the Sunflower Café logo on them—a sunflower sun rising in the east.

Gavin shifted. "It's not that I don't believe it's a clue, but you washed it, right? I mean, that looks clean for something that was stuck to the bottom of someone's shoe."

"Not on purpose," Sissy said.

"Would you like to start at the beginning?"

Sissy checked the location of the two girls and the older woman. The young girls were sitting on a bench on the opposite side of the laundromat from Gavin and Sissy. Both were engrossed individually in their own phones and seemed not to realize that the world was going on around them. The older lady had sat down with an iPad and started tapping the screen. She seemed well into her eighties, with snow-white hair as fluffy as a cloud and more wrinkles than a shar-pei puppy. But she was plugged into technology, wireless headphones in her ears. As long as no one else came in, it seemed that Sissy would be safe telling her story to Gavin.

She led him over to the bench in the farthest corner of the laundromat. They sat down, side by side, and Sissy gathered her thoughts.

"On the day Kevin was killed," she started, "Bethel told me to go find out what was taking Josie so long with the milkman."

Gavin whistled low under his breath.

"I know, right?" Sissy couldn't believe it, either; it almost sounded like a foreshadowing to Josie's guilt. But other than her brother running around with Kevin eons ago, Sissy could find no connection to tie Josie to Kevin. At least none so large that murder could be involved. "Anyway, I went to the back, and before I came around the corner and saw him, I slipped. At first, I thought it was my shoes."

"What about your shoes?"

"I didn't buy high-quality shoes. Nonskid bottoms. I

bought them at Walmart, so . . . you know. And I was thinking to myself that my nonskid shoes were not as slip-resistant as I had expected them to be. Then I looked at the bottom of one and found this piece of fabric."

Gavin nodded, as if to let her know that he was listening. "Then what happened?"

"All I remember after that is finding Kevin."

And that had been traumatic enough without trying to remember clues that might not be clues at all.

"And the scrap of fabric?" He inclined his head toward the item in her hand.

"I guess I shoved it into my pocket."

"And then you washed and dried it along with your laundry."

She slapped his leg. "Stop saying that. It's not like I did it on purpose."

"I don't think you did it on purpose." He didn't have to say the rest. The emphasis was enough that she could figure it out on her own. Gavin might not think that she had purposefully washed what could perhaps be the only clue to who killed Kevin, but Earl Berry certainly would. Because he would think she was trying to wash away any of the evidence that led back to her.

"So what do I do?"

"Keep it to yourself, I guess." He thoughtfully rubbed his chin, and she noticed he had a small dimple there. Not a large one, like Kirk Douglas or Tom Selleck. Just a small one that could only be seen if the light was just right. "I mean, you could give it to the deputy if you wanted to."

Sissy shook her head. "No, no, no. He'll just think that makes me that much guiltier." And if what Lottie said was right, and he was thinking she was withholding evidence, that would just give him all the more reason to lock her up. "I suppose the only thing I can do, would be figure out how it got into the café."

Easier said than done.

Gavin's suggestion stayed with her all through the afternoon, even while she folded the clothes from the dryer, loaded them into the car, and then drove them home. Those words knocked around inside her head while Duke enjoyed his afternoon belly rub, and even as she got together a small, almost healthy dinner. Well, she had some green beans with her fried chicken. That counted for something, right?

She was just putting away the last of her dinner dishes when Duke trotted over to the door and braced his paws on the white-painted wood. He yipped, then turned back to look at her as if making sure she was watching him.

"You want to go for a walk, little guy?"

He barked again, which always made Sissy think he understood what she was saying.

"You got it."

He didn't get out to play nearly as much since they had moved to Yoder. Or at least it seemed like he didn't. And the walk would do her some good, as well.

"Give me just a minute," she said. She dried her hands on a dish towel and laid it out to dry before sitting down on the bed and putting on her running shoes. Then she snapped Duke's leash to his collar, and off they went.

It was a beautiful evening for a walk. The sun had just started to go down, and everything held the pink tint of sunset. Even though she lived practically in the center of town, she could still smell the scent of country in the air.

She didn't get a whiff of exhaust like she always did in Tulsa, but more the scent of flowers and possibly manure. It was farmland, after all. But somehow the smells combined just right to seem earthy, natural. Almost sweet.

Duke trotted down the road, almost running by each house they passed. His little legs worked overtime as he hustled ahead of her.

"What's your hurry?" She tugged on his leash to let him know he was going too fast. At the rate he was walking, he would be worn out by the end of the block.

She wanted their walk to last a little longer than that. It was a beautiful evening. And her neighborhood was nothing if not interesting. Aside from the fact that she herself lived in a converted chicken coop, there was a quaint Victorian house that had been flipped to form a B&B, the Little House which was bigger than the Chicken Coop though not by much, and a handful of white clapboards reminiscent of the Amish houses she had seen—the big exception being that these had electrical lines running to them.

One of these, she had been told, belonged to English Ben and Abby. It was too large a house for merely two people, but the rumor mill had it that they had bought the house anticipating the time when they would fill it with children. They just hadn't known it would take over twenty-five years for that dream to become a reality.

And right smack dab in the middle of the block was the most unusual house of all in her neighborhood—even more so than the one belonging to her landlady, Vera Yoder. Vera had a great love of concrete statues and yard windmills. But this lady was immensely more creative.

Sissy had never seen the woman who lived there. She supposed that whoever did preferred to do her gardening when Sissy herself was at work. And garden she did. If that was what one chose to call the redecoration of her flower beds on a daily basis. Sissy didn't know what else to call it but gardening. Though not many plants were involved. At least not live ones.

There were two flower beds in the front yard—"bed" being a convenient term for a patch of dirt with things planted in it, both real and silk. Each bed was enclosed with various pieces of stone and hard materials, bricks, broken patio pavers, and just about any size rock available. The mounds of dirt inside were filled with the treasure trove of miscellaneous items. Sissy did her best to take inventory of each one of them as she drove by every day, but sometimes it was just too hard to take it all in during the time it took for her to drive past. She didn't want to gawk. And she really didn't want to make fun, though that's exactly what it felt like. In the back of both beds were tropical plants made of silk that stood almost as tall as Sissy. One in each bed, and both seemed to be the focal point. From there, the contents went in and out of rotation every couple of days, while others appeared and then disappeared, never to be seen again. And she had been watching.

Sissy'd only been there a little over a week, and she was curious as to when things would pop back up. Like the large ceramic rooster that had reigned over Flower Bed One, or Tekno Robotic Puppy that had been such a hit back in the early 90s that had guarded Flower Bed Two from atop the engine of the push mower parked there.

Today's exhibit was much of the same, though there was no rooster and no robot dog. There was, however, the bottom half of a conventional charcoal grill, which held a collection of large, white pillar candles and a portrait of Jesus that looked like it had been done by a child.

Sissy did her best not to stare as she and Duke walked past. The sight of these very original flower beds and their decorations both warmed her heart and made her laugh. But she did not want to hurt the woman's feelings by laughing. Evidently, her neighbor had quite a passion for rearranging the items, seeing as how she did it every day. Or perhaps she was just a little eccentric. Whatever the case, she definitely had an interesting yard.

Sissy and Duke walked to the edge of the neighborhood and turned around at the main road. Sissy contemplated the handful of houses scattered about that made up this neighborhood. It wasn't like the neighborhoods back home, where the houses were in neat rows and the streets all straight. No—here, the road was diagonal, cutting across and giving Eccentric Garden Lady a triangular-shaped yard. Coming back from the other side, Sissy noticed yet another flower bed tucked in the back part of that triangle. But she couldn't see this one as well without walking behind the woman's house. And that just seemed a little too deliberate.

"Come on, Dukes, let's go home." She still had a ton of laundry to put away. But walking the neighborhood made her feel a part of the community. It made her want to be a part of the community. Maybe for even longer than six months. But the six months were a jump start to a new life. And she was grabbing it with both hands.

The Sunflower Café was closed on Sunday. So many of the businesses in town were wrapped up in the Amish community and shut down for the Lord's day. It seemed the others just followed suit. The Carriage House was open and the Bull in Your Eye Diner. But not much else.

And if Sissy was remembering correctly, this was a church Sunday for her aunt. That would mean that Bethel and the rest of the family had gone to worship and left Lizzie behind at the house by herself. It would've been the perfect time to drive out and visit with her cousin, but it was also optimal time to head over to Hutchinson to Walmart. Still, she couldn't very well go all that way without asking her cousin if she needed anything. When the Amish wanted to shop in Hutchinson, they had to hire a driver. So Sissy drove over to see if Lizzie wanted something from Walmart.

It felt like a different world, as she drove out to her cousin's. There were no buggies outside, no evidence of an Amish community right there among them. But that was Sunday for you. Sissy couldn't remember how many Amish church districts they said they had. Two, maybe three. Not many, so most all the buggies in the whole community would be parked at one house, maybe two, as they held their long church service today.

Armed with a small list her cousin had made for her, Sissy strode into Walmart. Lizzie had pouted when she'd told her that she was headed to Hutchinson, because Lizzie herself couldn't go. But Sissy had promised to pick up what items she needed, then come back for a nice long visit.

This Walmart seemed the exact opposite of the Walmart she had at home. At least, nothing was where she had thought it would be. She'd been once before but somehow managed to forget the differences. She walked up one aisle and down the next, looking for protein powder, a salt and pepper shaker set for the Chicken Coop, and some sort of mixing bowl that Lizzie had asked for. Her cousin had said that she thought it would be with the camping gear, though Sissy had no idea why. But Lizzie had insisted she check that section as she handed Sissy her list.

That's how Sissy found herself wandering through piles of Coleman lanterns, sleeping bags, and coolers big enough to put a body in. She left the aisle with the tents, turning the corner to the sporting goods. And there, standing right in the center of the aisle, was Darcy Saunders. Alone. Well, without any of her children. And standing next to her was the insurance adjuster who had stopped by the Sunflower Café asking for directions to Darcy's house.

Sissy took one look at the pair and turned back around before either noticed her. At least, she hoped they hadn't noticed her. The question was: What were they doing in Walmart together?

CHAPTER TWELVE

Women are made to be loved, not understood.
—Aunt Bess

Surely it was just a chance meeting.

Sissy wanted so badly to round the corner again, act like she was shopping on that aisle, get closer, and find out why the two of them were together. In Walmart. Together. She couldn't help but feel this was somehow significant. Yes, two people could go to Walmart. But who met their insurance adjuster there?

No one. That's who. Which meant it had to be a chance meeting.

But still, her reporter's gut wouldn't allow her to let it go. If she couldn't be in the aisle with them, she could do the next best thing. She walked quietly up the aisle next to where Darcy and her insurance adjuster stood and did her best to hear the conversation going on just a few feet away. It was tragic how much tents could mute a conversation. She thought she heard the word *Thursday*, but she couldn't be entirely certain.

She started moving the tents out of the way, hoping to get a direct line between herself and the couple in the next aisle. If she could only hear their conversation. She didn't know why it was so important; it just was. But as soon as she cleared the shelf to hear a little better, they started to move. They were walking as if to leave their aisle. Sissy tiptoed to the edge of the section, thankful she had worn her running shoes instead of a cuter pair of sandals that would click against the tile floor. The end cap of the aisle was filled with hydro flasks, water bottles that were supposed to keep liquids at the same temperature for twelve hours. But she didn't care about that. She only cared about the couple strolling away from her.

At least she could see them now through the tall cylinders of the flasks. *Stroll* wasn't the best word—they were walking slowly, as if Darcy didn't want to get to the front any faster than necessary. Or perhaps the insurance adjuster was the one who had set the pace. Either way, Darcy stopped. Just where Sissy couldn't see her.

Dang it. She gently scooted a couple of the flasks to one side, so she could once again view Darcy Saunders and her too-casual insurance agent. The outfit he wore today was almost identical to the one from the day Sissy had met him. Except today's shirt was light blue; the other day, it had been a pale baby pink. She supposed the man had a thing for pastel colors. A bold choice, but not that important to the whole of what was happening before her.

As she watched, Darcy pulled her handbag from her shoulder. She unzipped it and started digging around inside. Then she pulled out an envelope and flipped through whatever was inside.

Sissy couldn't tell for certain, but it looked like money. Possibly even the money that Sissy herself had taken to Darcy's house? The help fund they had collected at the café for the poor widow?

Surely not. Just as surely as this had to be a chance meeting. But who met by chance and offered their insurance agent money? It just didn't make sense.

The agent placed one hand over Darcy's and pushed the money back toward her.

Thursday, she thought she heard him say again. Then he turned on his heel and walked away, leaving Darcy standing in the middle of Walmart with a lot of bills in her hand.

"Can I help you?"

A voice sounded behind her, scaring the bejesus out of Sissy. She jumped, her arms flinging wildly and hitting several of the hydro flasks. The empty metal containers clunked and bounced against the floor in a metallic sound like huge coins falling from heaven. She placed one hand over her heart as the noise continued behind her.

The one time she didn't need any help, and someone at Walmart wants to assist her. The one time she needed to be unseen and unheard, and she knocks down half a display.

She turned back toward the widow, but Darcy was gone.

After she helped the poor girl pick up all the water flasks that she'd knocked down, Sissy gathered the rest of her things from Walmart and took them to the cash register. She paid as quickly as she could and carted every-thing out to her car.

She didn't see Darcy or her insurance agent again. Nor did she tell the young clerk which of the water flasks had dented when they hit the floor. She was afraid that if she caused too much damage, they would make her pay for it all. That might've been the best and honest thing to do, but she really didn't have the money to spare. Not now, anyway.

She drove back to Yoder with the top down and the radio off, her mind filled with what she had seen. But she was fairly certain the man who claimed to be Darcy's in-surance agent was not her insurance agent. Sissy had thought six ways to Sunday and still couldn't think of any reason to give an insurance adjuster money. You paid your insurance *agent*. Or the company. This man was sup-posed to be the adjuster. So why was Darcy handing this man money? That just didn't make sense. And what was going on Thursday?

She had no answers, even as she pulled into the drive-way at her aunt's house. It was before three, and she sup-posed everyone was still at the church service. So she went around to the side of the house and entered the same way as she had before.

"Lizzie," she called. "I'm here. Just didn't want to scare you."

"Come on in," Lizzie called in return.

Sissy toted her Walmart sack down the hallway to Lizzie's bedroom.

"I couldn't find that bowl," Sissy said. "I looked in the sporting goods section and . . ." She trailed off with a shake of her head.

Lizzie nodded. "They must be out. It's all the rage

right now, and I think they're selling out faster than they can get them in. Just next time you go, will you check again?"

Sissy smiled at her cousin. "Of course." She set the bag of Walmart purchases on the end of Lizzie's bed. Then she hesitated for a moment before pulling up the chair next to her cousin.

"Where's Duke?" Lizzie asked.

Sissy waved a hand. "Home. I didn't want him to have to wait in the car while I went into Walmart."

Lizzie nodded, though her face still showed her disappointment. Sissy supposed that it was miserable to be trapped in one room, not even able to move around, for months on end. Of course, her cousin was going to have two beautiful babies soon, and surely that would make it all worth the sacrifice.

"I'll bring him out on Friday. Promise."

Lizzie's eyes widened in something akin to horror. "Tell me you're not going to wait till Friday to come out here again."

That's exactly what she been thinking, but only because Sissy didn't want to overstay her welcome. Plus, she was starting to put on a few pounds, between the delicious greasy food at the café and the delicious high-calorie food she was getting at her aunt's house, and her lack of willpower the rest of the time. "Of course not," she heard herself say.

Lizzie settled back into her pillows, a satisfied look on her face. "Good. I like having you come visit," Lizzie said. "I like that you're here."

Sissy laughed. "I like that I'm here, too." And strangely enough, it was true. She took a breath and forged ahead to change the subject. "Lizzie . . . is anything happening on Thursday that you know about?" For a woman on bed rest, she seemed to keep her thumb on Yoder's pulse.

Her cousin frowned as she thought about it. "This Thursday?" she asked.

Sissy nodded.

Lizzie looked thoughtful again. "Not that I know of. The only thing I've heard about coming up recently, other than the regular Amish events—you know, singings and meetings and that sort of thing—is that Danielle Mallory has been getting a baby shower together for Abby Yoder. Have you met Abby yet?"

"I saw her at the funeral," Sissy replied. "But I haven't really met her."

"Poor Kevin," Lizzie said with a small frown.

Sissy kept forgetting that her cousin knew Kevin. Pretty well, it seemed. But of course, Lizzie's job was pretty much the one Sissy was doing now.

It was the perfect time to change the subject over to Darcy, but before Sissy could formulate her segue, Lizzie continued.

"You'll most likely be invited to the baby shower, too."

Sissy sat back, almost in surprise. "Well, I should hope so. I'm your favorite cousin, aren't I?"

Lizzie laughed and shook her head. "Not my baby shower. The baby shower Danielle is throwing for Abby."

Sissy chuckled in return. "I was about to say."

"Of course, Danielle is having it really early. But . . ." She shook her head. "That's the *Englisch* for you."

"What do you mean?" Sissy asked.

Lizzie ran a hand over her bulging belly. "It's fragile,

you know. And a little self-centered, I suppose, to automatically assume that the baby's going to be fine and
born and everything." She broke off with a shake of her
head. "It's just fragile," she said again. "But I believe
Yoder needs this. With Kevin dying and everything feeling shook up. I'm stuck all the way out here, and I can
still feel it. A baby shower is about the best thing that we
can do to come together again as a community. Even if it
is a little early."

"When is it?"

"Two weeks from yesterday, I think." Lizzie rested
one hand on top of the mound of her belly. It was one of
those unconscious gestures that pregnant women the
world over executed with sweet elegance.

Sissy thought about the woman dressed in black at the
funeral. The woman standing next to English Ben Yoder.
She had looked slim and trim in head-to-toe black. But
that, in itself, was slimming. Everyone knew that. And
Sissy hadn't really been looking at her belly. And yet . . .
"I don't think she's even showing. I mean—" Sissy
waved a hand toward her cousin's belly.

Lizzie laughed. "You can't go off my size. There's two
in here, remember?"

Sissy smiled with the warmth of excitement. "I remember." Twins. One boy, one girl, and she could hardly
wait to get her hands on those new little cousins of hers.
They had a little longer before making their appearance.
"Wait. If the baby shower's in two weeks, then you won't
be able to attend."

"The good Lord willing," Lizzie said, running her
hand over her belly once again. "We need these two to
stay right where they are for as long as possible. Promise

me something," Lizzie started, "if you go to the baby shower, please save me some cake."

"Of course," Sissy promised. "It's the least I can do."

Sissy was still smiling as she pulled her car into the drive at the Brubacher Dairy. She really had enjoyed that cheese she bought, and she was wanting to try a new flavor. Or maybe even some of the yogurt she had seen there. That would be a great breakfast, seeing as how she got up at the crack of dawn. And it would be a nice alternative to bacon and eggs, biscuits, and other wonderful-tasting, fattening items that the café served each day. She pulled her car into the drive and got out before she saw the CLOSED sign on the door of the little shack that served as the farm store.

Nuts! She had forgotten that it was Sunday. And though Jonathan Brubacher seemed to have left his religion behind, it was possible that the rest of the Brubacher clan were still practicing Amish. Sissy would have to come back sometime during the week. No worries, though. Maybe it was just a sign that she needed to get back home and let Duke out of his kennel.

"Tell me, Miss Yoder," a familiar male voice drawled. "Are you spying on me?"

CHAPTER THIRTEEN

If your face is ugly, you can't blame the mirror.
—Aunt Bess

Sissy scoffed, but the sound seemed less than genuine, even to her own ears. "Course not. Why would I be spying on you?"

"Why indeed?" Evan Yoder was standing on one side of her car, and she on the other. He crossed his arms in a manner that clearly stated he didn't believe her at all. Of course, that gesture was backed up with a suspicious light shining in his eyes.

Sissy pulled on the bottom of her T-shirt. "I came out here to buy some cheese."

"They're closed."

"I can see that now."

He cocked his head to one side, furthering his disbelieving pose. "And you didn't know it before." It was not a question.

She raised one shoulder and let it drop. "I didn't think about it. You know, about it being Sunday and them being Amish."

"Uh-huh." He didn't believe her.

"Fine," she said. "I'm spying on you. Why?"

He shifted in place. "You tell me."

"All right then." She crossed her arms in a gesture to mimic his. "I am secretly a horse breeder. And I came here all the way from Kentucky just to spy on you and your horse farm and find out what you're doing, because you're so successful in the equine industry, and I want to mimic your setup."

"Cute," he said. "How about this? You're spying on me because you think I have something to do with Kevin's death."

That hit a little too close to home. "Why would I think something like that?" She asked the question with all the pluck she could muster, but she still had to lift her chin a bit in an effort to keep him from realizing that he had landed on the truth. Well, it would have been the truth, had she really been thinking about it. But when she'd been driving out here, she'd only thought about cheese. It was only after she realized the dairy was closed that she also took into account that this farm was right across the road from the Yoder Horse Farm. And Evan Yoder.

"Yoder is a small, small town," Evan said. "You ask something about somebody, you can be sure it'll get back to them eventually."

Sissy tried to remember who all she had asked about Evan and Darcy. It seemed as if most of the information had been volunteered, and most of that by Lottie, but somewhere, she had slipped up if Evan knew she was asking questions about him. Best change the subject. "Why would an insurance adjuster be offering Darcy money?"

The question took Evan off guard, just what she had hoped. A frown wrinkled his brow. "How would I know? I haven't talked to Darcy since she threw me over for Kevin the summer after we graduated."

"That's a long time not to talk to somebody in a town as small as Yoder."

He shrugged, as if it were no consequence at all. "I have no reason to talk to her. She married Kevin, got pregnant, and the rest is history."

Maybe it was, maybe it wasn't.

"If you want to know why Darcy is offering someone money, I suggest you ask Darcy."

So simple and yet so impossible.

But Sissy was saved from having to answer, as the clomp of horse hooves grew near.

The sound seemed to stop right next to them, and Sissy peeled her gaze from Evan's to look toward the road. A beautiful horse of a reddish color, with a black mane and a white blaze across his face, was standing at the driveway entrance to the Brubacher Dairy. A petite woman, with ash-blond hair mostly hidden by a nut-colored cowboy hat, sat atop the beautiful stallion. Though she was tiny, especially in comparison to the big beast, it was obvious she was completely in control. "There you are."

Evan dropped his arms and turned to face the woman. "It's all right, Mother. I just had a bit of business to take care of."

The woman's eyes flickered to Sissy, then back to Evan. "I see. Don't be long." She snapped the reins and headed back in the direction she had come from.

Evan looked back to Sissy but didn't meet her gaze. "I gotta go. Stop spying on me." And before she could answer, he stalked away.

Monday morning brought with it business as usual, she thought, as Earl Berry swaggered into the Sunflower Café and planted himself on barstool number three. He propped his elbows on the counter and waited for his breakfast.

Naturally, he refused Lottie's help, instead insisting that Sissy come wait on him, like neither one of them knew his standard order. And like he would order anything different.

"So, I hear you been out to Brubacher's," Berry said in lieu of a customary greeting.

It hadn't even been a day, and Evan was already running to the police. "They've got really good cheese," Sissy said. She wasn't going to allow herself to be dragged into this.

"Seems to me that you were after a little more than cheese," he said.

Sissy ripped off his order from the top of her pad and slid it through the tiny window into the kitchen, where Josie and Bethel were working side by side. "And how did you come to that?" She was not about to be intimidated by him. She was strong, inventive, imaginative, worthy, and powerful.

And she hadn't done anything to Evan. She wasn't going to let Earl Berry intimidate her into a confession or worse. She was going to stand her ground.

"Won't do you no good to go running around town try-

ing to pin this on somebody that would never hurt a fly."
Berry shifted on his stool, and Sissy secretly hoped that
some part of his gun belt was poking him.

"I went out there for cheese," she said again. She plas-
tered a pleasant smile on her face and somehow managed
to keep it there as she filled his coffee mug.

"You've been here long enough to know they're
closed on Sunday. Ninety percent of the town is closed on
Sundays."

"It must've slipped my mind." With that, she turned
and made her way back to the waitress station. She
dropped off the coffeepot to keep it warm.

She was not going to let Earl Berry get the best of her.
The problem was, he seemed hell-bent to pin this on her,
and her list of suspects wasn't going anywhere. She had
the same suspects as before. No more, no less. She hadn't
been able to weed anyone out, either. So unless she did
something quickly, it was only a matter of time before
she was arrested.

And she had a feeling that little scrap of fabric she
found on the bottom of her shoe and inadvertently washed
and dried somehow could've cleared her. But she surely
couldn't hand it over to Earl Berry now. He would think
that not only was she hiding evidence, but she was also
altering evidence in order to make herself appear innocent. Convoluted as it was, she knew that was exactly
what he would think.

She managed to serve him, answer whatever questions
he had about nothing and everything and nothing again,
and get him out the door. She barely had time to catch her
breath before the Mafia-looking man walked into the
café.

She hadn't seen him since that day at Darcy's, when

he'd been staring at the house, standing right in front of her car as he watched Sissy leave.

He slid onto Earl Berry's stool and watched solemnly as Sissy approached him.

Did he recognize her? It wasn't like she didn't stand out from the crowd. Her mother used to say her hair would glow in the dark. Through the years, it had calmed down a little. But as Evan pointed out a few days ago, it was still as bright as a copper penny.

"What can I get you?" Sissy asked.

"I'll have a coffee and . . ." He stared up at the menu above him. "Number six."

Sissy turned over the coffee mug that sat in front of him and filled it with fresh brew. "How do you want those eggs?"

"Over easy."

"Tomato or cantaloupe?"

"Tomato," he said. "Does that always come with it?"

Those words alone told her he hadn't been to Yoder very often. "Always," she said. "Anything else?"

"Ketchup for my hash browns."

"You got it."

Unable to just hang around and hope she could discover something about the man and what the mob wanted with Darcy, Sissy moved to the waitress station and placed the coffee urn back onto the burner.

Lottie came up behind her.

"See that man over there at the counter?" Sissy asked in a quiet whisper.

Lottie turned toward the man.

"Don't stare," Sissy admonished as quietly as she could. "He's M-a-f-i-a." She wasn't sure why she had spelled it.

Lottie drew back, an incredulous look on her face. "I thought the Mafia was gone."

Sissy nodded in the man's direction. "Tell him that."

She tore the ticket from the top of her pad and slid it through the small window into the kitchen. Then she made her way back to the waitress station, where Lottie still remained. "I'm going to find out why he's here." Sissy started back to the counter.

Lottie snagged her elbow and held her in place. "Don't go sticking your nose where it doesn't belong. You might end up hurt."

"It's better than arrested."

"What about d-e-a-d, like Kevin?"

Sissy faltered. She straightened and grabbed a bottle of ketchup for the man. It was the perfect excuse to go over there again, but Lottie's words still had tingles running up and down her arms.

Was that a bulge under his arm? A gun of some sort? What kind of weapons did modern Mafia men carry?

She forced a smile to her lips and did her best not to look nervous as she slid the bottle of ketchup to him. Truth was, she hadn't been nervous until Lottie brought up Kevin. She needed to engage the man in a little conversation. She didn't have many customers, but she had no idea how to linger without looking suspicious. Or how to initiate the conversation without it appearing like she was prying. She couldn't just say, *So, been staring at Darcy's house lately?*

Finding no other reason to hang around, she moved back a step, until she was standing right next to the cash register. Surely she could find some busy work to do there.

"This is a pretty small town, yeah?" he asked.

Sissy stopped straightening the rack of potato chips that sat on the counter next to the register and gave the man her full attention. "It's a very small town."

"And pretty much everybody knows everybody else."

And everybody else's business, too, she thought. "I think that's safe to say."

"So you know Darcy Saunders."

Jackpot! "I've met Darcy a time or two," Sissy said. "I haven't been in town long. I just came to help my aunt. She owns this café."

She was trying to tread lightly here. She wanted to ask her own questions, but she didn't want to offend him. The last thing she wanted to do was anger the mob.

"Why do you ask?" Sissy asked innocently.

Mafia Man shrugged. "I went by her house earlier, but there was no answer."

"Maybe she wasn't home."

"She was home." His words were emphatic.

"Well, then, I suppose . . . she must've had a good reason for not answering."

All of her needy kids came to mind. Dani was sweet, and Dakota, and maybe some of the other younger children. But Darcy's older children were something of a handful. They were practically the same age as Sissy and still lived at home. They should be out on their own, working and providing for themselves. Even through trials and tribulations. Which was exactly what she was doing.

"Darcy has her hands full right now," she said. She gathered up her courage and asked, "Why do you want to talk to Darcy?"

"I'm Brian Carter. Her insurance adjuster. And, well, it's a sensitive matter. But I do need to talk to her."

"Number six!" Josie called from the back. She slid the order back through the window, but Sissy could only stare at the man.

Did she believe him? He seemed honest enough. But the way he was dressed, and that bulge under his right arm.

Truth was, she didn't know what to believe.

"Order up!" Josie called again.

Sissy looked at the man. She should be getting his order, but all she could think about was whether or not he was telling her the truth.

"Oh, for pity's sake," Lottie huffed, and moved behind Sissy in order to grab the number six from the window. She slid it in front of the man, as if it had been her responsibility all along. "Here you go, hun," she said.

"Thanks." Then, before he picked up his fork, he reached into his pocket. Sissy didn't know if she should hit the ground or run for cover. But he didn't flash a weapon. He pulled out a business card. Two, even. He gave one to her and one to Lottie. "It really is imperative that I speak to Darcy. If either of you see her, will you give her my card?"

"Of course," Lottie said, then elbowed Sissy in the side.

Sissy jumped, then nodded. She couldn't take her gaze from the card. It looked real enough. It was printed with the name he had claimed was his. Now, what kind of Mafia man was named Brian Carter? But still . . . "Right," Sissy said. "If I see Darcy, I'll let her know. I'm sure I'll run into her sooner or later."

Most likely sooner. Because the minute she got off work, she was headed to Darcy's house herself.

* * *

Sissy didn't have to worry about whether or not Darcy would ignore her knock. Dani let her in once again and directed her back toward the family room.

And just like the time before, the house was in complete chaos. In fact, it was in more chaos than it had been before. If that was even possible. The dog that Darcy had been carting around was running in circles and barking at a young man eating a corn dog. Kevin Junior or Joe, she supposed. Whichever son it was, he held the corndog in the air and laughed as the dog jumped for it. April slouched on the couch with a large glass of chocolate milk as she aggressively flipped through channels. Dakota was in the playpen once again, this time dressed in mustard-yellow overalls and a green shirt. Still had no sign of gender identity. And amidst all this, one little girl whom Sissy hadn't met before was sitting in the corner, her nose buried in what looked to be an ancient encyclopedia. At least, Sissy thought it was ancient. Did they even have those anymore?

She turned to Dani. "Is your mom home?"

Dani gave her that slightly vacant smile, though it was still charming all the same. "She's in the tub. You want me to go get her?"

A mental image of poor, stressed-out, worn-out Darcy Saunders, lounging in a tub full of bubbles with candles all around and a glass of red wine at her fingertips, passed through Sissy's mind's eye. She couldn't disturb that image. Not for anything in the world. But since she was here, and she had promised—albeit at Lottie's elbowing insistence—she should tell Darcy to contact Brian Carter. If he was Mafia, and not truly an insurance agent from

Alco Unlimited, Darcy should know the man was looking for her, right? And the most traditionally logical person to tell this information to would be April. She was the oldest. Kevin Junior and Joe might be next. Right.

She turned back to Dani. She might have her mental limitations, but Sissy had a feeling she would be the most responsible of them all.

"No," she said. "Don't bother her. Can you take a message?"

Dani's eyes lit at the thought of the responsibility. "Let me get a piece of paper. I'll write it down."

Sissy waited for her to rummage through the desk to find a pen and a notepad.

"A man named Brian Carter came by today, asking about your mom. He said he needs her to call him. Did you get all that?"

Dani stuck her tongue in the corner of her mouth and continued to neatly print on the piece of paper. After what seemed like an eternity of lit candles and dog jumps, Dani was finished. She dotted the final *i* with a flourish and looked up at Sissy with a smile. "Got it. Should I put a phone number?"

See? She knew Dani would be the most responsible.

Sissy shook her head. "I think she has it. But if she needs to, she can come by the café, and I'll give it to her."

"Bull in Your Eye, or the sunflower one?" Dani asked.

Sissy plucked at her Sunflower Café T-shirt and gave Dani a smile. "The sunflower one."

Dani grinned. "That one's my favorite. I like the name best of all."

Sissy nodded. "Me, too."

"Do you want me to walk you to the door?" Dani

asked in that formal way she had, that way that suggested someone had taught her these lessons and made her practice them daily.

"That's okay. I can find it," Sissy said. "It was good to see you again."

Dani grinned, as if Sissy had been her visitor and hers alone. "It's good to see you again, too."

Sissy was about to let herself out of the house when a picture just down the hall from the front door made her stop. She walked over to look at it. It was a blown-up snapshot, almost professional-looking. And there stood a young Darcy in a Barbie-pink bathing suit and nude-colored heels, her blond hair poofed up and sprayed within an inch of its life. In the crook of one arm, she held a huge bouquet of red roses, and the sash around her shoulder and midsection declared her to be Miss Kansas.

So it was true what Lottie had told her. Darcy had been a beauty queen and here was the proof. She was young and beautiful and not so tired-looking. But winning a competition like the Miss Kansas Pageant took a lot of dedication, a lot of practice, and a lot of discipline. A person had to throw their whole being into it if they wanted to succeed.

In that moment, it occurred to Sissy that Darcy couldn't be guilty of killing Kevin. Not to be with Evan; not so she could be without Kevin. And certainly not to be alone with ten ungrateful children. No, a person who could put everything into themselves and win a beauty pageant of that magnitude would give themselves to every part of their life. Including their marriage.

And just like that, Darcy Saunders fell off Sissy's suspect list.

CHAPTER FOURTEEN

Winning is a habit. Unfortunately, losing is,
as well.
—Aunt Bess

The office of the *Sunflower Express* sat on the corner just around from the hardware store and right before the railroad tracks. It was tucked back there so neatly, she would have missed it if she hadn't been looking for it. And of course, it was just like she had pictured it. She supposed there was a standard for small-town newspapers all across the country. Must have large plate glass windows in the front. The name of the paper should be painted on the inside, where it could be read from the opposite. Must have large, subtropical plants banking the doorway, and must be filled with cluttered desks and harried writers. And must, *must* have a ceiling fan twirling lazily overhead, while those reporters below frantically typed out their messages to the world. Sissy was certain somewhere in the office was a hard-bitten editor with his sleeves rolled up, his tie askew, waiting for the next big story to come in. *Dairy Cow Gives Birth to Twins*; *Bridge Out on the Old Highway*; *Sale on Rutabagas*.

"Sissy." Gavin stood as she came in the front doors. There were a couple of other reporters hanging around, but when they saw that Gavin had gone to greet her, they turned back to their computer screens.

"Are you busy?" Sissy asked. She was reluctant to take him away from a story if he was working, but she really didn't want to do this by herself. Who else but Gavin would be game to follow Kevin's route to see if perhaps they could figure out who killed him? And of course, that would be a scoop to get in on firsthand, right?

"No, no, I'm not busy at all." Gavin gestured toward his desk. "Won't you come sit down? Do you need a water? Something to drink?"

Sissy bit back a laugh. "No, thanks. I just came to see if you wanted to go on a little adventure with me."

She saw the light of interest in his eyes; then, Gavin casually leaned his hip against his desk and crossed his arms. "What kind of adventure?"

"The kind where the two of us follow Kevin's route and see if we can figure out if there's a pattern, or maybe something there that will let us know who killed him."

He seemed to think about it. "Okay." He closed his laptop and looked to the woman whose desk was opposite his. She looked to be in her late sixties, her hair dyed up with an orangey shade of copper mixed with fuchsia, which just so happened to clash horribly with her bright red lipstick. Sissy wasn't certain, but she thought the woman was wearing false eyelashes, but it was hard to tell through the lenses of her cat-eye glasses. "Shirley," he started, "I'll be out for the rest of the afternoon."

Shirley waved a hand at him but didn't take her eyes from her computer screen. She wasn't typing, per se, but every now and then, she would hit a key or two. Sissy figured she was either researching on the web or playing a very intense game of FreeCell.

"Let's go." Gavin grabbed her elbow and steered her toward the front. Then, as if he had just realized that he had touched her, he dropped his hand and opened the door. He stopped just outside, as if in his excitement over something new to do in tiny Yoder, Kansas, he had forgotten he didn't know what they were doing.

"Now what?" he asked.

They stood in the dusty sunshine for a moment as Sissy surveyed the scene. Two streets over from the railroad tracks was the café. She supposed that was the best place to start.

"I talked to Mike this morning. He's the milkman who took over after Kevin . . . died."

Gavin nodded while she spoke. "Yeah. I know him. Mike Harper. He's an okay guy."

"If you say so. He's just sort of . . ."

"Oily," Gavin supplied.

Sissy smiled at him. "Good enough. Anyway, I asked Mike what the route was. And he told me the two stops before the café and the two stops after. Now," she said, pointing in the direction of the Sunflower, "the café is that way. See, I figure that whoever killed Kevin walked to the café; so it couldn't have been too far, right? Or they would not have walked to begin with."

Gavin nodded. In this light, he really did look a little like Brad Pitt. Or perhaps he would if he cut his hair like Brad Pitt in *Moneyball*. Not that Sissy cared or anything. But Gavin's overly long blond hair tended to flop into his eyes. And he had nice eyes, she supposed. Clear and green, sort of blue. Somewhere in between. It was a shame that he kept them covered at all with his thick-rimmed geek glasses, but it was even more a shame that half the time, that thatch of hair was covering them as well. Sometimes it just made her want to reach up and—

"Why do you think they walked?" Gavin asked. He pushed his glasses up a little farther on his nose. And Brad Pitt turned instantly into a nerd.

"Because there were no screeching tires or burnout marks in the parking lot. Whoever killed Kevin did so, then quietly slipped away." Or maybe ran like mad; either way, they did it quietly.

"So they walked." Gavin shoved his fingers into the front pockets of his jeans and surveyed the area. "And you think someone from one of the stops around the café did it?"

Sissy shrugged. "I don't know. But it's a starting place. Come on." She hooked one arm over her shoulder and started in the direction of the Sunflower.

Behind her, she heard the shuffle of Gavin's feet as he set himself into motion. "We're walking?"

"Of course. If the killer can walk it, we can, too."

They walked the two diagonal blocks over to the Sunflower Café. Once again, she was reminded that Yoder seemed to be built on a slant. Or maybe she was just spoiled by the gridded streets of Tulsa.

The walk was a little longer than she had anticipated. Partially because they stayed on the streets and didn't cross like when she had walked Duke.

The café was closed this time of day. They stood in the parking lot—the empty parking lot, without any tire marks to speak of.

Sissy pointed to the back door of the small white building. "Kevin's truck was parked there."

"So someone could have come from either direction." He looked behind them. "From any direction, actually."

He was right. Drat him. But she was staying focused on her theories. "If you want to look at it that way, then anyone in Yoder could've killed him."

Gavin nodded. "Okay."

"For now, let's concentrate on the first two stops before the café."

"Which were?"

"The Carriage House and the meat market."

Gavin once again looked in one direction and then the other. "When's the diner?"

"After," she said.

He propped his hands on his hips, the sunlight glinting off the face of his watch. Not a smartwatch, just a regular old Timex. "But the diner's closer."

"I know," she said patiently. "But stabbing someone—" She closed her eyes and tried not to think about the image of Kevin's body lying on the cold floor while the lifeblood slowly drained from him. "That's personal, wouldn't you say? A crime of passion. And the knife they used was one of ours. So it's not like they brought the murder weapon with them." The killer would've had to have been in the back room of the café in order to get the knife. She shuddered as she imagined being in the same building with a killer.

"So you're thinking that he pissed someone off at one of his previous stops, and they followed him here to talk to him, but instead, ended up killing him."

It sounded even more logical when Gavin said it out loud. Proof that her theory was solid.

Sissy nodded.

Gavin pushed on the nose bridge of his glasses once again and struck a thoughtful pose. Hands on hips, staring off into the distance, in the direction of the Carriage House and the meat market. "So who works at either of those two places that Kevin might've had some sort of beef with?"

Sissy made a clicking noise with her tongue. "Now there's the question."

"I suppose the best thing to do is go eat at both places and maybe see if we can find out anything."

Sissy sighed. "That sounds easy enough," she said. "But you and I both know the Carriage House has so many employees. And the meat market does, too."

Aside from the charter school, those two establishments employed more citizens of Yoder than anywhere else in town. Just more and more people for Kevin to make angry.

Gavin shifted in place, but before he could speak, a small red car pulled up next to them.

Sissy turned as Lottie rolled down the window of her shiny sedan. "What are you two doing out here?" she asked.

Sissy jumped in before Gavin could answer. "Just out for a walk," she said.

Lottie nodded and gave a small frown. "Where's Duke?"

Sissy smiled apologetically. "He's at home." Stupid! She should've brought her dog along if she wanted to look like she was just out for a Sunday stroll. On a Thursday. In the middle of the afternoon. And with Gavin, nerd reporter extraordinaire. "It was sort of spur of the moment," she said.

Gavin nodded, albeit a little too enthusiastically. That flop of hair that couldn't seem to stay out of his eyes moved back and forth with the motion. "That's right. Totally off the cuff."

Sissy wanted to elbow him in the ribs to keep him from saying any more. Some ace reporter he was turning out to be. But she supposed there wasn't much call for subterfuge in Yoder. Not much sneaking around to get the scoop in such a tiny town that seemed to be an open book. Except for the murder of Kevin Saunders, of course.

"Poor baby," Lottie said. "Left at home all by himself and on such a beautiful day."

"Next time," Sissy promised no one in particular.

Lottie smiled and waved, then rolled the window back up.

Sissy and Gavin waved in return as she drove away.

"You want to go home and get your dog?" Gavin asked when Lottie's car had disappeared.

"No," she said. It was almost a lie. She would love to go home and get the dog, but . . . "If we decide to go into one of the restaurants, what would we do with him then?"

Gavin looked around as if just realizing something. "Where's your car?"

"It's at the house," she told him.

"So you walked from the Chicken Coop to the paper office?"

"I figured it would be easier," Sissy said.

"But a lot of steps," Gavin replied with a small whistle under his breath. "I bet your tracker is going crazy."

Sissy looked to the fitness tracker she wore on her left arm. Truth be known, she never managed to get all ten thousand steps in for the day. Not even when waiting tables at the café. As far as she was concerned, the darn thing might be broken. The only time it had gone off to let her know something important had happened was when the battery had run out of juice and she'd forgotten to recharge it. Then it had buzzed like crazy, and she thought she had hit her steps, but it was only the poor thing dying. "Not hardly," she said. "I cut over through my neighbor's yard."

"Which neighbor?" Gavin asked, a small frown puckering between his brows.

"The crazy lady who lives in the middle of the block. Big white house, extremely interesting flower beds." She chuckled at the memory of some of the displays she had seen.

"That's my aunt's house." Gavin said.

Sissy didn't know how to respond. "Your aunt?"

"Edith."

"Edith Yoder?" she asked, trying to bring a small bit of levity to the conversation.

"Jones," he said. "Her name is Edith Jones."

"I'm sorry," she said. "I meant no offense. It's just her yard—"

He nodded. "Aunt Edith is . . . well, she's sort of a Boo Radley kind of person." He didn't have to explain further for Sissy to get his meaning. A little slow, a little sheltered, a little bit feared, though harmless in her differences.

"I suppose I shouldn't be cutting through her yard." She grinned sheepishly and shrugged. "Easier, but . . ." She trailed off, not sure how to finish anyway. She'd never seen anyone out in the yard, and even though the flower beds changed daily, she supposed she'd thought it was okay to trespass, since she hadn't seen the owner out and about.

"Half the town cuts across there," Gavin said. "She was probably watching through the window as you walked by."

Now that thought was a little unsettling, as well.

"I'm really sorry," Sissy said.

Gavin shrugged. "If you ever catch her outside, you can tell her that."

Sissy nodded. Yet somehow, a bit of the camaraderie had leached from the day.

"So Kevin, or rather Mike, goes to the diner next?" Gavin said, pulling them back on the task. And for that, Sissy was grateful. Otherwise, she might continue on apologizing to Gavin for cutting across his aunt's yard. But that wasn't the true apology; the apology was for calling her crazy.

Note to self: Yoder is a small, small town.

"That's right," Sissy said. "Then he goes to the hardware store."

"The hardware store?" Gavin asked. "Why would he stop at the hardware store?"

"There's a drink box there. A cooler. It carries milk."

"I've been in there a hundred times, and I never noticed that."

"It's amazing what you miss when it's right underneath your nose," Sissy said. It was a simple fact she had learned early on in her journalism days.

"What's after that?" Gavin said.

Sissy shrugged. "I only asked for two before and the two after. I figured that whoever was walking, they wouldn't have been too far away."

"What about the Quiki-Mart?"

"What about it?" Sissy countered.

"When does Mike go to the Quiki-Mart?"

"Right after, I suppose." Now who had told her that? She couldn't remember, but she knew it all the same.

"Right." Gavin turned, put his back to the café, and surveyed the area. "Okay. If Kevin is coming from that direction. Or Mike. Whoever—" He pointed off to the right. "Then chances are one of his first stops is the discount market."

"Okay," Sissy agreed.

"Then the charter school. The Carriage House, the meat market, and then the café."

"We already established this," Sissy said.

Gavin nodded. "Just hang with me here." He pointed out to the left. "So from here, he goes across to the diner, then down to the hardware store."

Sissy followed the point of his finger as he outlined the suspected route in the air. "Seems to me the next logical place he would go would be the Quiki-Mart."

"And?" Sissy asked.

Gavin punched a couple of the side buttons on his watch. "Let's time this." He watched the second hand on his watch for a moment, then said, "Okay. Let's go."

"Go where?" Sissy asked as she followed behind him. He stopped at the road and waited for a car to pass, then crossed at a leisurely pace. "Kevin's route. Or Mike's, whatever." He continued to walk on to the diner. He stopped there, waited for a moment, then resumed his march to the hardware store. He walked on the street, not cutting across any space, until he reached the corner of the hardware store right around from the newspaper office. "Now. I suppose that Kevin would've parked his truck there." He pointed to the other side of the newspaper office and hardware store building. "Then when he left, he would go around this way."

Sissy followed behind him as he strode down the side road, up to the main road, across and down and over again, to get to the Quiki-Mart. It would've been nothing to cut across through the makeshift park, but only if one were walking.

"We have to take the roads," Gavin said. "Because that's how Mike would've driven. Kevin. Whichever."

He stopped in front of the Quiki-Mart, raised his wrist. Punched a button on his watch. And said, "Time." He shot her a satisfied look. "That took less than twenty-five minutes."

Sissy shook her head. "I'm not sure I'm following all this."

But Gavin was in form. "Add fifteen minutes for each stop. That gives us a total of fifty-five minutes. So let's just say an hour. Make it even. What time did you say Kevin"—he shook his head—"Mike, comes by the diner?"

"Eight o'clock always." She stopped for a moment. "Well, always since I've been here."

"Was it the same time that morning? When Kevin died?"

She nodded. "What does this mean?"

"Then he goes to the Quiki-Mart?"

"I suppose," she said.

"If Kevin is eating lunch at the Quiki-Mart, but it only takes him an hour to get from the café to the convenience store, then he's got to be padding his time. Or somebody somewhere is not telling the truth."

CHAPTER FIFTEEN

Plow with the horse you have.
—Aunt Bess

"Or he's eating lunch at nine a.m.," Gavin continued.

Sissy stared in the side window of the convenience store, not really seeing anything at all. There was something about this whole issue that was nagging at her. But she couldn't figure out just what it was.

"Who said that he had lunch at the Quiki-Mart?" Sissy asked.

"You did," Gavin said. He frowned at her as if she'd lost her mind.

"No," she said. "Who told me?"

"Oh." Gavin raised his chin, as if that served as an agreement. "I don't know. Who told you?"

Sissy snapped her fingers. "Freddie."

"Freddie?" Gavin frowned at her.

"Howard," she replied.

"Both of them?" Gavin asked. "Howard Yoder?"

Sissy shook her head. "Freddie Howard. He's the young kid who works on the weekends. Well, Saturdays. He helps us get everything ready to be closed on Sunday."

Gavin nodded. "Got it. I don't think I've ever met him."

It stood to reason. Freddie was only seventeen. And unless Gavin had a penchant for Hutchinson High School basketball games, there was really no reason for their paths to cross.

"He works here, too." Sissy pointed to the building next to her. "At the Quiki-Mart. At the funeral, he told me a story about a man. A Yoder."

"Those are hard to come by around here," Gavin joked.

Sissy held up one hand. "Hush. I'm trying to think." She searched her memory for more details. But she hadn't been paying enough attention to Freddie at the time. They were at the funeral, and she had been looking for suspects. "Seems like maybe he has a scooter."

Gavin frowned again. "Like an Amish scooter? A couple of families have them, but not like you see from Lancaster and stuff."

Sissy wanted to ask him how he knew about Lancaster but decided against it. She needed to keep her focus. "No, not a scooter like one of those. I mean the motorized chair thingies that some handicapped people use."

"A Jazzy?"

Sissy snapped her fingers again. "That's it."

"That would be Winston Yoder. He's the only one around here with one of those. Or at least the only person who takes theirs out on the street." And suddenly, Sissy was so very glad she had dragged Gavin along on this little venture.

"Yes! Winston. Where do we find him?"

Gavin consulted his watch once more. "About this time of day, he's over at the VFW."

"Yoder has a VFW?" Sissy asked.

"Doesn't every small town?" Gavin returned. "Though this one is supposed to serve the greater Yoder/Reno County area."

"Why did you look at your watch before you answered?" Sissy asked.

"Winston is something of a character," Gavin started.

And it seemed Yoder was full of those, as well.

"And he has a pretty tight schedule. For a man who's retired."

"Yeah?" she asked. "Like what?"

"Like, if we wait here fifteen minutes, he will probably be coming through. As long as the weather's nice."

"And what does he do?"

Gavin thought about it a moment. "I don't know what he does for breakfast. But he likes to come through here around lunchtime to go over to the Bull in Your Eye."

"Does he eat at the diner?"

Gavin shook his head. "Sometimes he does, sometimes he doesn't."

"When he leaves the diner, does he come through here?" Sissy asked. She knew the space was generously called a park. Though there were no swing sets, no jungle gym, no slides. Just a covered concrete slab with a few picnic tables bolted in and a basketball hoop on the other side.

"Yeah."

Sissy nodded. "So that's what Freddie was talking about . . ."

"What?" Gavin asked.

"Freddie said that Winston got mad when he couldn't get through the alleyway. I suppose he was trying to come through here. And I'd bet anything he was on his way to the Bull in Your Eye Diner to get some lunch."

"Right. The timing's right. Except—" Gavin broke off.

"Except there's no reason for Kevin to be here at noon if he can . . . could make it here from his stop before by nine o'clock."

Gavin turned on his heel and walked to the edge of the parking lot.

"Where are you going?" Sissy asked.

Gavin looked down the main road once and then twice, back and forth, before coming back to her side. "See that road? The one on the other side of that is the highway."

"I can see that," Sissy said.

There was a small patch of grass between the road and the highway, which ran parallel to each other. "If Kevin's route went down the highway, he might have a stop or two."

Sissy saw where he was going with this. "But enough to take up three hours of work time?"

Gavin shrugged. "I don't really know. Who knows how his route was?"

Sissy grinned. "Mike."

"Maybe," Gavin said. "But who's to say that Kevin followed what he was supposed to be doing?"

He had a point. Unfortunately, he had a very good point. If there was one thing she had learned about Kevin during all of this, it was that he seemed to march to the beat of a different drummer. Gavin pointed to the grassy area behind the Quiki-Mart. "Right on time."

Amazing, was all Sissy could think. Amazing that a man could be so predictable that a town member, who had maybe never even talked to him before, knew his schedule. And amazing was the sight he made coming across the grassy area.

The Jazzy itself was painted bright purple, and she figured Winston had to be a Kansas State man. Why else have a purple Jazzy? There was an American flag flying from the back off a pole that bent and curved in the wind. It wouldn't have looked quite as interesting had it been a small flag, say five by seven or eight by ten inches. No, this one was something more to the tune of three by four feet and barely missed scraping the ground as he went over a bump. And then there was Winston himself. A black leather motorcycle vest covered the paunch of his middle. Said vest was covered in a multitude of patches, including an upside-down Jayhawk and a Confederate flag. Under the vest, the man wore a faded black T-shirt, its short sleeves showing off arms covered in white hair and tattoos that had faded and slightly warped with age.

But it was his leg that really took her aback. Well, one of them, anyway. And not just because it was missing. His hat declared him to be a Vietnam Veteran, and she had seen plenty of men who had come back from that war missing limbs of any different number. It was the replacement he had that made her look twice. The prosthetic had been painted to look even more elaborately tattooed than his arms. The drawings were vibrant and held their color on the smooth material that made up that leg. A hula girl; a Hawaiian flower; something that looked like an Asian man in a rice paddy with the moon overhead. She wanted to stare, to take it all in. Ask him to hold up the leg so she could see every inch of it. But she didn't think he would take kindly to that. Something in the slant of his mouth, the fact that he looked at her and Gavin, one eye squinted even though the sun was not in his face. "What are you two young'uns doing out here in the middle of nothing, just staring?"

"Hello, Mr. Winston," Gavin said. "You remember me? I did an article on you in the *Sunflower Express* newspaper."

The man grunted. "I remember," he said. When he talked, Sissy could see the stain of tobacco juice at the corners of his mouth.

"This is my friend, Sissy." He gestured toward her, and Sissy gave a small nod.

"You got yourself some red hair there, girl."

Like she didn't already know that.

"Sissy's aunt, Bethel, owns the Sunflower Café."

"Don't eat there no more," Winston Yoder said. Every time he spoke, his mouth returned to its previous frown, and Sissy was beginning to suspect that frowning was his normal expression. She supposed with all the man had been through, even from just what she could see, he deserved to wear that frown if he wanted to.

"I'm sorry to hear that," Sissy said. Not really knowing what else to say.

"Bethel quit serving chili dogs," he said. "Got on some health-food kick or something or another. I like chili dogs."

"Chili dogs are very yummy." Seriously. How was she supposed to answer that, anyhow?

"Mr. Winston," Gavin started in that gentle yet persuasive way he had. "You like to go through the alley when you come eat lunch, is that right?"

"Is this for something for that paper of yourn?"

Gavin shook his head. "I was just telling Sissy here about Yoder. She's new in town. And I told her you like to come through here every day on your way to eat lunch."

"It's a heck of a lot easier since Kevin's not here anymore. I hate to see a man go like that, but at least I don't have put up with his truck always being in the way."

It had to be an exaggeration. Kevin's truck could not *always* be in the way. It wouldn't have been there on a Saturday or Sunday. Just the days in the week, but she wasn't about to correct the man.

"Wouldn't it be easier to just go around if Kevin's parked there?" Sissy asked.

"Last time I checked, this was America, and if I want to go through the alley when I go to lunch, then I want to go through the alley."

Okay, then.

"What about Mike?" Gavin asked. "He's the new milkman. Doesn't he park there during lunch?"

"Nope. Never seen him at lunch. I guess he just doesn't come and stay half the day."

Sissy murmured something that she hoped he took as agreement. She had no idea whether Mike stayed there half the afternoon or not.

"Now if y'all are done interrogating me, I'd like to be on my way."

"Of course," Gavin said. "It's nice to talk to you again, Mr. Winston."

The man grunted once again, then put his Jazzy into drive and buzzed away.

"And what do you make of that?" Gavin asked once Winston Yoder was out of hearing range.

"Are there any normal people in Yoder? Besides the Amish?"

"Hey!" Gavin pretended to look hurt. "I'm about as normal as they come."

Sissy nodded. "Tell that to your spandex pants."

His pretend-frown turned into a real one. "They're aerodynamic."

"Yeah," Sissy said. "Well, I suppose I can only say that he's exaggerating. Kevin couldn't stay here all day."

"Of course not," Gavin said. "But if he was here, say between eleven and one, then he would've definitely been here on Winston's way to lunch, or perhaps on his way back."

"Why would he stay here from eleven to one? They do call it a lunch hour for a reason."

"So maybe he was skimming a little off the top from the dairy," Gavin said. "Padding his hours. Then again, we don't even know if he gets paid by the hour."

"Good point," Sissy said. She made a mental note to call the milk distributor and see how their drivers got paid. Perhaps she would pretend she was hiring a former employee.

"What's that?" Gavin said.

Sissy looked around. "What?"

"That look on your face. What's that look on your face about?"

Sissy shook her head. "Nothing."

"And now you're lying."

Sissy sighed. She knew better than to try and pull something over on a fellow reporter. "I was just thinking about calling the dairy, pretending I was hiring someone, and seeing maybe how they pay their employees. Maybe then we can find out what Kevin's true schedule was, or what he was turning in to the company. Perhaps he was here between eleven and one."

"We can go in and ask." Gavin jerked one thumb over his shoulder.

"I say we do both." Sissy shot him a cheeky grin.

Together, they walked into the Quiki-Mart. The man behind the counter was large. One of the largest men, perhaps, she had ever seen. Tall and broad, with dark skin and a thick black beard, thick and slightly curly. The hair on his head was the same, black as pitch, very thick, and with a slight bit of curl to soften the look.

"Hey, Eddie," Gavin greeted the man.

Of course he knew him. Gavin knew everyone in town. It was Sissy who needed to get out a little more.

It all had to be an exaggeration. There was no way Kevin would stay half the afternoon in the alleyway between the Quiki-Mart and the flower shop. It was just dumb to even think that was a possibility, but they had to find out for certain.

"This is my friend, Sissy." Gavin gestured toward her.

Sissy nodded to the man behind the counter, who inclined his head in turn.

"It's nice to meet you, Sissy." Eddie's accent was so slight, it could barely be heard. And she wondered if he worked at keeping it in check. Yoder was not the best place to stand out.

"It's nice to meet you, too," Sissy said. "I came by the other night and got gas. I met your daughter Lina."

Eddie gave her a warm smile. "My Lina is a good girl."

"I totally agree," Sissy said.

"Eddie," Gavin started, "we've been looking into Kevin's death."

Eddie shook his head. "It is a sad, sad thing."

"Yes, it is," Gavin returned. "And we're hearing that he kept his truck parked here between the two shops for long periods of time during the day. Is that true?"

"Kevin took his lunch here," Eddie said. "He might have stayed longer some days than others." His big, big shoulders rose and fell in the tiniest of shrugs. "It never bothered me any."

"So he came at the same time every day?" Gavin asked.

Eddie shrugged again. "I have deliveries coming and going all day long. I never noticed who came when."

"Only that Kevin was here during his lunch."

"Sometimes. I'm not here every day at lunch, so I couldn't tell you on those days."

"If you're not here, then Lina is here?" Sissy asked.

Eddie shook his head. "My wife, Nan. She works the day shift when I'm not here or Freddie Howard."

Sissy nodded. "I know Freddie."

"Lina and Freddie share the evenings, when he's not playing ball. And I have other employees, but they work evenings and weekends, too. Not during the day for deliveries."

Gavin rapped his knuckles on the counter. "Good enough. Thanks, Eddie."

"Are you helping the police?" Eddie asked.

"Something like that," Sissy said and ducked out of the store.

"Now what?" Gavin asked.

"I should probably be getting home to Duke," she said. "He's got a tiny bladder."

"Uh-huh," Gavin said. "No, seriously."

Sissy glanced quickly over at the florist shop. "I really should be getting home," she said. "But maybe I can take

some flowers out to Lizzie tonight." It was Monday, and
she wasn't expected out at her aunt's for supper but buying flowers for her cousin gave her a reason to go into the
florist shop and a reason to drive out and see Lizzie. And
she could find out a little more about some of the characters she had experienced now that she'd been in Yoder for
another weekend.

"But . . ." Gavin prodded.

"I think I'll just pop inside the florist for a moment."

Gavin nodded. "I'm right behind you."

Sissy's heart thudded in her chest as she pulled open
the glass door that led into the brightly lit florist shop.
She wasn't sure why her heart was beating so rapidly.
Perhaps she was just expecting more from the visit at the
Quiki-Mart, and since she didn't get it, she transferred
that longing to the flower shop. Or perhaps she was
merely letting her imagination get away from her.

She stepped inside the cool, fresh-smelling shop and
felt almost as if she had stepped into a jungle. There were
plants everywhere. Peace lilies and azaleas in pots; tulips
in pots, even though they were out of season. There were
tall plants, short plants, miniature succulents, large tropi-
cals, and even prickly cacti. One whole wall was taken up
with a cooler filled with buckets of fresh flowers, some
already made into bouquets with cards just waiting for
someone to deliver them. Or maybe pick them up. The
opposite wall was covered with bows done up in every
color that she could think of and then some. They were
beautiful and unique. Two colors were twisted together,
and some with two sizes and two different colors of ribbon meshed to make a perfect bow. It was an overload to
the senses. Straight in front of her, the cluttered, dull-brown
counter sat unapologetically amid the lovely chaos. A small

bell was perched on top to summon a worker from the back room. That, she supposed, was where all the magic happened.

English Ben came out from the back. There was no chime on the door, and neither Sissy nor Gavin had rung the tiny bell on the front counter. It was as if he had some type of sixth sense to know someone was in his shop. "May I help you?" he asked, his gaze quickly flowing from Sissy to Gavin. "Hi, Gavin."

Gavin nodded toward the man. "Ben."

"I'd like a bouquet of daisies," Sissy said. "Nothing too elaborate. Just a friendship sort of thing."

Ben looked from Sissy to Gavin, a small frown puckering his brow as he wrote out the ticket.

"I'm taking them out to my cousin, Lizzie Schrock."

"Lizzie, yes," English Ben said. "How's she doing?"

"Physically, I think she's fine. Mentally, I think she's going a bit stir crazy, shut up in her room twenty-four-seven."

"I do hope she's being careful." Another woman's voice joined the conversation. Sissy looked up as Abby Yoder slid in next to her husband. Abby had a pallid look, as if pregnancy was not quite agreeing with her. Or perhaps her skin always had such a sallow color. It wasn't like Sissy could ask outright. But she did notice the bags under Abby's eyes and the lankness of her hair. Whereas Lizzie was glowing, the picture of health, though a little frustrated with her extended bed rest, Abby Yoder, despite her smile and her uplifted chin, looked as if this baby were already getting the best of her. The curve of her lips had a feeble slant, and her eyes held no sparkle. How sad that the one thing that she had wanted most hadn't added a joyous spring to her step.

"As careful as she can be," Sissy replied.

"Good." Then Abby patted her husband on the arm and moved toward the bank of coolers on the left-hand side of the shop. "I'll get it. I know just the thing."

Sissy caught the concerned frown on English Ben's face as he watched his wife move away. For a moment, she thought he might protest. But when Abby turned back with a pre-made bouquet in her arms, the starch left his shoulders.

"That's lovely," Sissy said. And more than what she had anticipated. Not only were there the requested daisies; the bundle also held pink roses, a few sunflowers, and a couple of orange day lilies for good measure. All in all, the bouquet was gorgeous. "But—"

"I know what you're going to say," Abby interjected. "But I made this one this morning, and the fellow who ordered it changed his mind. Rather than see it go to waste, I'll let you have it for half price."

"Deal," Sissy said with a smile. Lizzie was going to love the flowers.

She paid and thanked the Yoders, then she and Gavin made their way out into the waning sunlight.

Sissy wanted to ask him what he thought about Abby Yoder and her despondent air. But even though Gavin was a reporter, he probably hadn't noticed Abby's sadness. It wasn't like she was curled up in a corner and sobbing her eyes out. She seemed to be going about her day like a florist normally would. But Sissy could tell that something was off. She knew just the person to offer an opinion, and she was headed out to see her now with a bundle of flowers in her arms.

CHAPTER SIXTEEN

*Worrying is like paying on a debt that may
never come due.*
—Aunt Bess

Sissy loved the look on her cousin's face when she
walked into her room with the bundle of flowers later
that afternoon. She had forgotten what such a small surprise could do to lift someone's spirits.

"Will you get some water for these?" Lizzie asked
with a small clap of her hands. "There should be a vase
under the sink in the kitchen."

"Of course." Sissy set down her handbag and unhooked Duke's leash. She lifted the pup onto the bed,
where he cuddled into Lizzie as if he never got the attention he felt he deserved. "Rotten dog," she muttered af-
fectionately, then made her way down the hall and into
the kitchen. She found the vase just where Lizzie had said
it would be. She filled it with water, then returned to the
bedroom.

"Where's your *mamm*?" Sissy asked. She pulled the chair closer to the bed and set the vase in its seat.

"At the doctor." Lizzie made a face. "I hope she gets a new cast soon. One of those really made to walk on."

Sissy chuckled as she unwrapped the daisies from their green floral paper. The bundle of stems that made up the bouquet were tied together with a slim piece of ribbon. Sissy pulled it free from its bow and placed the bouquet into the vase. "If she's not careful, she'll crack the one she has."

Lizzie nodded. "That's just what she's done."

Classic Bethel. Her mother had tried to warn Sissy when she made the decision to come up to Yoder to help the family. Mary Yoder had explained what Bethel Yoder was like. Sissy tried not to laugh as she scooped together the mess and trash left after she had placed the flowers into the vase. But the ribbon—the little piece of ribbon that had been used to tie flowers together—gave her pause.

There was something about it. Something she couldn't pinpoint, a familiarity and yet not. It was like she'd seen it before, but she knew she hadn't. The ribbon was thin, only about half an inch wide, and of a pattern of checks in black and white so tiny that from a distance, it appeared to be solid gray.

She ran one finger over the long piece of ribbon, just to touch it.

"Set the flowers on the dresser, please." Lizzie pointed to the large piece of furniture that sat against the wall directly in front of her. "That way, I can see them all the time. They so brighten up this room."

Her cousin's enthusiasm was enough to make Sissy wish she had thought to bring Lizzie flowers days ago.

"You got it." She abandoned the cleanup and carried the vase full of flowers to the dresser as instructed. Then Lizzie directed her. Up, back, left, right, just a little more. Until they were exactly as her cousin wanted them.

Sissy went back over to gather up the trash. She wadded the paper and any of the little stems together but held out the piece of ribbon. "Do you want to keep this?"

Lizzie glanced at it. "What for?"

What for, indeed! It was a piece of ribbon. Sissy shook her head at herself. "I'm *so* turning into my mother." Mary Yoder saved everything, in case she needed it. Or in case she wanted to make something out of it. Or in case there was a (insert natural disaster here), and she needed it. But something about the piece of ribbon . . .

Sissy wadded it up with the rest of the floral paper and showed the ball to Lizzie. "I'm going to throw this away. Be right back."

Lizzie idly stroked Duke's head where it lay next to her large belly. He let out a shuddering doggie sigh, unconcerned with anything at the moment. Not that he gave much thought to anything other than riding in the car, eating, and sleeping. Not necessarily in that order.

Sissy made her way to the kitchen to throw away the trash and somehow managed to resist the urge to pull that piece of ribbon from the ball she had made and shove it into her pocket. It was ridiculous. Almost a compulsion. And once again, she reminded herself that there were worse things than turning into one's mother. Especially when you had a mother like Mary Yoder—kind and understanding. A woman who had been through so much that she had a wide world of relevance from which to dole out advice.

Which reminded her: Sissy needed to call her mom

when she got home this evening. She hadn't talked to her mother much since arriving in Yoder. But in all fairness, three days after her arrival, Kevin was killed. And she didn't want to share such news with her mother, seeing as how Mary Yoder would worry about her only daughter. That was to be expected. Yet Sissy was afraid that if she started telling the story, more and more of it would slip out, and her mother might do something absolutely horrible like send her brother after her, to check on her, to move her back to Tulsa to the wreckage of her life, or even just to come up and meet everybody.

She was just now starting to make friends. She still had a few casual friends back in Tulsa, but if she were planning on staying in Yoder for any amount of time, she needed more friends on her side than merely her cousin Lizzie. So the last thing she needed was Owen, the shining star, coming up here and ruining everything for her. Owen didn't set out to blow her life out of the water; he was just so spectacular, everyone else fell short of whatever mark they were after in his presence.

Sissy reentered Lizzie's bedroom and pushed the thoughts of the ribbon and Owen and even her mom to the side.

Duke, so content to lie snuggled up in the curve of Lizzie's side, barely acknowledged that his mistress had come back into the room.

"So how are things going at the café?" Lizzie asked. "I asked Mamm, but she never says."

"Fine," Sissy replied, settling down into the chair next to the bed.

"That's exactly what she says, too," Lizzie said. "Not the answer I want to hear. I want to know what's really going on."

"Well," Sissy drawled. "Earl Berry came in last week and actually ate cantaloupe instead of the piece of tomato with his number eight breakfast. And then little Carly Yoder accidentally spilled her drink, and it took a whole roll of paper towels to clean it up. Then—"

"Not what I meant, either." Lizzie shot her a plant-withering look. Good thing the flowers were nowhere close.

"No one wants to worry you," Sissy explained. "You're supposed to be on bed rest. Not worrying about what's going on at the tiny café in little bitty Yoder, Kansas. You've got babies to grow."

"Bed rest can be a joke," Lizzie said. "I worry more just laying here not knowing what's going on than if some-body would actually tell me a few things for a change."

"All right, then," Sissy said. "When is an insurance ad-juster not really an insurance adjuster?"

Lizzie stopped. "Is this some kind of joke?"

"No, I really want to know. When is an insurance ad-juster not an insurance adjuster?"

Lizzie face pulled into a most thoughtful pose. "When he's not really an insurance adjuster."

Sissy nodded. "That's what I was afraid you were going to say."

Lizzie continued to watch her as Sissy pulled a small notebook from her handbag and started jotting something down.

"What have you got there?" Lizzie asked.

Sissy gave a small, one-armed shrug. "Just a list of people and things."

"For?" Lizzie pressed.

No sense in trying to keep it all from Lizzie. Protecting

Lizzie was one thing; protecting herself was another. And frankly, she could use Lizzie's help on the matter.

"This insurance adjuster came in. I mean, I think he was an insurance adjuster. He was dressed sort of casually, and when I asked him, he said that yeah, he was something like that."

"What did he look like?"

Sissy described the man, including as many details as she could remember. Like his fringe of dark blond hair, shiny top of his bald head, and his overly starched shirts. "Oh," she said, almost forgetting. "And he had a pinky ring."

"A what?"

Sissy held up the aforementioned digit. "A pinky ring. A ring he wears on his pinky finger."

"*Jah*," Lizzie said. "I've seen guys like that. It's a strange look, I think."

Sissy wondered if any jewelry didn't look a little off to Lizzie, considering the Amish wore none. "It's usually reserved for gigolos and mob bosses," she joked. But once the words left her mouth, she immediately sobered.

At her change in attitude, Lizzie pushed herself up a little farther on the bed. "What?" she asked excitedly. "What is it?"

"It's probably nothing," Sissy said.

Lizzie gestured around her with one sweep of her arm. "I have less than that going on right now."

"I just heard a couple stories that maybe Kevin owed money to some very not-nice people in Kansas City."

"Who said that?" Lizzie asked.

"Mike," Sissy replied.

Lizzie shook her head. "Mike Harper? You can't believe half of what he tells you or the other half of what he says."

"I sort of thought the same thing," Sissy said. "This is a little different. It feels different, anyway."

"How so?"

Sissy told Lizzie about the man in the suit, the Mafia-looking man who gave her a card that said he was the insurance adjuster. "But then there's this man, who *claims* to be the insurance adjuster."

"And that's the guy with the pinky ring?" Lizzie asked.

Sissy nodded grimly.

"Could there be two insurance adjusters?"

"I suppose. If there are two insurance policies. But . . . Kevin didn't look the type to be that thorough." She sighed. "So what does it all mean?"

Lizzie thought about it for only a moment before replying. "It means that the man in the suit who gave you the card is most likely the true insurance adjuster. And the other man . . ." She trailed off. It was Lizzie's turn to shift uncomfortably in her seat.

"What?" Sissy asked.

"Maybe you just got them backwards, and this man with the pinky ring, he's your Mafia."

"There is no Mafia. There is no Mafia. There is no Mafia," Sissy repeated to herself as she drove home. But it began to take on the rhythm of *there's no place like home*. And when she looked around, she was still in Kansas, Toto, *thankyouverymuch*.

And Kevin was still very dead. Two men were asking about his widow, and Earl Berry still wanted to pin the whole thing on her.

No place like home. Check.

She put the top up on her car, got Duke from his seat, and let herself into the Chicken Coop. She had headed for home as soon as her aunt and Daniel got back from the doctor. She hadn't wanted them to feel obligated to invite her to supper, though she knew Lizzie would enjoy her being there all the same. It was just that she was on her own now. She didn't have a boyfriend, she didn't have a roommate, and frankly, she wasn't used to eating her supper alone. But she needed to get used to it. Because in the future, she might not have a roommate, she might not have a boyfriend, and she needed to learn to live with her own company. It was something she had never managed to do. And now that she was turning over a new leaf . . .

She opened the refrigerator door, looking for something to cook, telling herself she shouldn't call Gavin and invite him to the Carriage House to eat. Of course, their chicken fried steak sounded heavenly right about now. But a minute on the lips . . .

She shut the refrigerator and opened the cabinet door next to it. Canned soup, canned pasta, canned tuna. Everything packaged and ready to eat in a few minutes' time, yet it held no appeal. Or maybe it was just the thought of dining alone that held no appeal.

Duke barked, as if to remind her she really truly wasn't alone. Or maybe he just wanted to be fed, as well.

Sissy shook her head at the little dog. "Come on, then," she said. She hooked one arm toward the kitchen and got out a can of food for him. She plopped it into his bowl and stood back as he begin to devour the big mound of food. Honestly, she didn't know where he put it all.

He was more than halfway finished before she pulled a can of ravioli from the cabinet and popped open the can.

She should heat it up. Put it on a plate. Maybe even make some bread to go with it.

Yeah, and use her best china and light a candle. She shrugged and took a fork from the drawer began to eat the stuff right from the can. Pathetic, she knew. And just when she thought she'd been doing so good, she turned pitiful once more.

Plate empty, Duke sat back on his haunches and whined. Sissy shook her head, still scooping out the ravioli bite by bite. "You don't want any of this," she told him. "Honestly. You really don't." Duke whined a little more, then barked and braced his feet up on her leg. She rubbed his head and took another bite straight from the can. Tomorrow, she promised herself. Tomorrow she would work on this evening-alone stuff. She would work on getting her life back together. She would work on being not quite so pathetic.

"There he is again," Sissy said, nudging Lottie as they passed.

It was lunchtime, and though it was only a Tuesday—and people hadn't yet grown tired of packing their lunch for the week—the café was almost to capacity.

"There's who?" Lottie asked. She gestured wildly with one arm, as if to say the place was full of *he*s and that Sissy would have to be a tad more specific if she wanted a proper reaction. "The casual man. The one who said he was an insurance adjuster."

Lottie glanced over in the direction that Sissy had nodded. Actually, it was more of a sideways tilt of her head, just to let Lottie know where to look.

"That's not the insurance adjuster. The insurance adjuster was that little guy. With the dark hair and the thick mustache."

"And the black suit." Sissy nodded. "But this guy told me he was an insurance adjuster."

"He's awfully casual for an insurance adjuster," Lottie said.

"That's what I thought," Sissy exclaimed.

"You want to take that table?" Lottie asked.

"If you don't mind," Sissy said. "You can have the tip; I just want to be able to talk to him for a bit. You know, without seeming suspicious."

"Whatever cranks your tractor," Lottie said. She grabbed an order from the kitchen window and started toward the booths on the far side of the restaurant.

Sissy took up the coffeepot and headed toward the other side, where the insurance adjuster wannabe had settled down into the booth on the end. She noticed he sat with his back to the wall. From his angle, he could see the entire restaurant. Only the kitchen was not visible to him.

Sissy stopped in front of the booth. "You want coffee?" she asked.

He looked at the pot she held at the ready. "Everyone drink coffee at lunchtime around here?"

Sissy shrugged. "I guess so. It seems to be the most popular drink."

He nodded and pointed toward the upside-down mug sitting in front of him. "Go ahead."

Sissy flipped over the mug, then filled it with the hot fresh brew. "You want a minute, or do you know what you want to eat?"

"How's today's special?" he asked.

"Very special," she returned with a grin. "You want that?"

He gave a quick nod.

"One special," she said. "Coming up." She made as if to leave, then stopped, turned back around to face him. "So the other day, Darcy Saunders's insurance adjuster came by. Gave me his card and everything."

The man sat back in his seat and picked up his coffee mug with such deliberation that it darn near mesmerized Sissy. "Is that a fact?" He took a sip of his coffee and eyed her over the rim of the steaming mug.

"That's a fact." Sissy did everything in her power to make her voice sound flippant and carefree, but inside, she was quaking, heart pounding.

"So I guess I didn't tell you the entire truth," the man said.

"Yeah?" Again with the flippant tone, again with the pounding heart.

"Yeah," the man said. "See, Kevin and I are . . . friends."

CHAPTER SEVENTEEN

*You've got to go out on a limb if you want
to get the fruit.*
—Aunt Bess

*F*riends?

There were a hundred ways to interpret that word. But the man's tone suggested they weren't friendly at all. In fact, an almost lethal thread ran through it.

Was she just hearing things? Because if this man wasn't an insurance adjuster, and Kevin did owe money to the KC mob . . .

That left Pinky Ring here as the mobster. And though she'd had almost twenty-four hours to think about the possibility, it didn't seem any more feasible than it had last night. Pinky ring aside, the man did not look like a mobster.

Add that to the fact that she didn't know if the KC mob was even a thing anymore; he could just be a . . . friend of Kevin's.

While the man ate, she did everything in her power to hover near, hoping maybe he would get a phone call or he would say something or do something, pull something out of his pocket like a mob ID card, anything to let her know who he was. But alas, he finished his meatloaf special, left a generous tip, and walked out the front doors, leaving Sissy sorely disappointed that she hadn't found out more about him.

Perhaps he was CIA, deep undercover, pretending to be a mobster in order to bring down a hotbed of illegal gambling.

Or perhaps she had watched way too much crime television before she made her way to Yoder. She had hoped her lack of cable at the Chicken Coop would serve her well. But all it had seemed to accomplish was fueling her already overactive imagination, firing it back to life with cockamamie ideas and theories and larger-than-life scenarios starring the most unlikely characters.

Maybe it was time to get TV after all. She was still mulling it over when Gavin walked in a little while later. "I've got him," she told Lottie.

The woman looked from her to Gavin and back again, a matchmaking light twinkling in her eyes.

Sissy shook her head. "Don't even think about it. He's my friend. And he's helping me with"—she almost said *finding this murderer,* but she somehow managed to keep that part to herself—"a special project."

"So that's what they're calling it these days," Lottie murmured. Jokingly, albeit, but still, Sissy managed to turn beet red. Not that she could see her own face, mind you, but she could feel the heat coming off her freckled skin in what surely amounted to the waves coming off the asphalt in July.

"Calling what?" Bethel came out of the kitchen and stomped behind the counter, over to where the two of them stood.

"It's not like that at all," Sissy said.

Lottie glanced back over to Gavin. "He's cute, though, right?"

"I guess so. I hadn't really noticed." Which was a lie. She had thought that Gavin was cute in a certain light in a certain way, with stipulations. But she had noticed. Not that it made a difference. Not that it made any difference at all.

She grabbed a glass off the waitress station and automatically filled it with water. She knew before even going over to the table to ask that Gavin would want water.

Lottie nodded toward the tray. "You know what he's going to get before he even orders?"

Sissy rolled her eyes. It would do no good to argue. Lottie and Bethel would think what they wanted to, despite any argument of hers. "Whatever," she said, then headed off to give Gavin his drink and see what he wanted to eat this afternoon.

"I took the liberty of pouring you a drink," Sissy said, as she slid the glass in front of him.

He smiled. "A girl after my own heart."

She felt the heat rise into her cheeks once again. Why was everything about romance these days? She didn't want a romance. She didn't have time for romance. She had more important things to do, like, *I don't know . . . keep myself out of jail!*

Okay, so she was being a tad dramatic. But only just a tad. Yes, she was doing her best to keep herself out of jail, but she wasn't there yet. And that was saying something. Right?

"What will it be?" she asked him, pulling the ticket pad from her apron pocket and getting her pencil ready to write.

"Just a hamburger, no bun, and a side salad," he answered quickly. Then he unwrapped a straw and took a long draught of the cold water.

"Back in a second," she told him, more accustomed than she realized to his unique tastes. She took the hastily written ticket to the back kitchen window and called out the order. Bethel was still standing next to Lottie, watching her as if she were part of a real-life reality show.

"Who are you hollering at, girl?" Bethel demanded.

Sissy turned to face her aunt. "I'm guessing Josie, since you're up here."

"Nope. She's not here, either. But I'll get it." Bethel's new cast thumped against the floor in a strange *tick-tock*, in rhythm with her cane.

Sissy shook her head and walked back out to where Gavin sat. She knew Josie's situation, because she had been told enough times, but it just seemed strange to her that the woman never seemed to be at work. What did she do for money?

Perhaps she had made some kind of deal with Darcy over the insurance money. Or maybe now Sissy was really grasping at straws.

They weren't very busy, so when she got to Gavin's table, she slid into the booth opposite him. "Order's in," she told him. "Tell me something. Is there still a mob in Kansas City?"

"Guess so. I mean, I don't know. When everything went down in New York . . ."

"So you don't think it survived," she supplied.

"I'm not saying that." Gavin sat back in his seat and waited for her to continue. "Are you going to tell me what this is about?"

"The other guy who was looking for Darcy came in today to eat."

"The insurance adjuster?" he asked.

She shook her head. "The man we *thought* was the insurance adjuster. It turns out that the insurance adjuster was the man that I thought was in the Mafia."

"But he's not," Gavin asked.

"Well, he said he was the insurance adjuster. I can't imagine any insurance adjuster also being part of the Kansas City mob, can you?"

Gavin shrugged. "I guess it's possible."

"I hate when people say that," Sissy said. "Anything is possible. Is it happening? That's the question."

"Just because the man you thought was the insurance adjuster is actually in the Mafia, it doesn't mean that the man that you thought was in the Mafia is actually the insurance adjuster." He frowned. "Or the other way around."

"I understand what you're saying. But you didn't hear what he said."

"What *who* said?" Gavin asked. "I've lost the thread of the conversation here."

"Pinky Ring."

"Huh?" He shook his head. "Insurance adjuster? Or Mafia?"

"The one I thought was the insurance adjuster, but now believe might be Mafia."

"Got it," Gavin said. "What did he say?"

"Well, I told him that the insurance adjuster had come in, sort of insinuating that if the insurance adjuster came in and it wasn't him, then he couldn't be the insurance ad juster, like he had claimed to be the time before."

Gavin thought about it for a moment. She could almost hear the pieces locking in place. "Okay, got it. Continue."

"And then he said"—she paused a moment for extra emphasis—"that he and Kevin were friends."

Gavin simply looked at her. "And that's why you think he's Mafia?"

"Yes!" Sissy exclaimed. "No, I mean . . . he said *friends*. Doesn't that seem odd to you?"

"Not if they're friends," Gavin said. Patience colored his expression.

"You didn't hear how he said it," Sissy complained. "That was the real clincher. He said it like *friends*. Like they really weren't friends at all."

"And that's why you think he's Mafia?"

"I don't know." She sat back in her seat and shook her head. "Mike said that Kevin might owe somebody a lot of money, and he insinuated—actually, he came right out and said it—Kevin most likely owed money to the mob. Gambling debts and stuff like that."

"You can't believe half of what Mike Harper says, and the rest of it is a lie." Sissy couldn't help but take note that two people—Lizzie and now Gavin—had said the same thing about Mike Harper. "He loves to exaggerate and stir up the pot."

"Maybe, but somebody killed Kevin," Sissy pointed out unnecessarily, as far she was concerned. That was the whole reason for all of this.

"Yes," Gavin agreed. "Kevin is dead. And the murder's taking a toll on the whole community."

True. The murder had taken its toll on the community. People were a bit more cautious now, friendly but their eyes not so openly expressive. It was like everybody had something to hide now, and everyone was wary of their neighbor. But only one of those neighbors was a murderer. And if they found out the murderer truly was a stranger, from another town, and was Mafia . . . "Don't you think it would be better if whoever killed Kevin doesn't live in Yoder?"

"Of course I do," Gavin said. "But that doesn't change the facts. Whoever killed Kevin killed Kevin. And wherever they live is where they live."

"I guess you're right," Sissy grumbled with an exasperated sigh. "It's just this town," she said. "Nobody wants to believe that the people they know are guilty. The local deputy wants to blame me, because I'm new in town."

"To be fair, you did find the body," Gavin said.

"To be even fairer, I didn't kill him. Plus, I wasn't the one in the kitchen that day. I was manning the counter. Taking orders and such."

Gavin's smile was meant to be reassuring. "I know Earl Berry can sometimes be a little hard to handle. But if you didn't do anything wrong, he's not going to be able to manufacture evidence to arrest you."

She blew an errant strand of hair from her face. "I guess you're right," she said. "But it's a little unnerving to have him breathing down my neck all the time. Plus, like you said, the community is suffering from it. That's why I think it's so important that I find out who did this."

"I see where you're coming from," Gavin said. "And just because Earl Berry isn't doing his job doesn't mean that you're supposed to step in and do it for him."

Sissy shook her head. "I don't see I have any choice in the matter." Before she could say anything else, Lottie called her from the waitress station. "I guess I better get back to work."

"I'll see you tomorrow?" Gavin asked.

Sissy nodded. "Tomorrow."

"You want me to what?" Gavin asked the following day.

Sissy had a feeling, when he promised they would see each other today, that he didn't have any clue that she would ask him to follow Josie.

"There's no harm in following her. No law against it."

Gavin grimaced. "There might be a law against it. You know, stalking and all that."

"I'm not stalking." Sissy lifted her chin in the air at a haughty angle. "I'm just trying to find out all I can about one of my coworkers."

"So you can trap her in a murder charge," Gavin finished for her.

"No," Sissy said with a shake of her head. "I'm trying to prove her innocence. See, I have this list, and I can just knock her off the list as one of my suspects, say, by following her around town today to see if she does anything suspicious, or perhaps not. Then I'll know whether or not she should remain on the list."

Gavin shifted his weight to one leg and crossed his arms. Again, today he was wearing jeans, tennis shoes, a button-down shirt with short sleeves, and a tie that didn't quite go with the whole thing. Of course, he was wearing those nerdy thick glasses, and his hair needed a trim in front. Once again, it was falling over his eyes, but Sissy didn't care about that. "I know you mean well, but that does not sound like you're trying to prove her innocence. If you follow her around all day, and she doesn't do anything suspicious, how are you able to cross her off your list? It's just one day."

She didn't want to have to do this, but desperate times and all. Sissy laced her fingers together like she was praying and leaned toward Gavin. "Please," she begged. "Please, please, please, go with me today and see what Josie does. Just one day. Surely you can do that for me."

"This is ridiculous, you know," Gavin said. "But if that's what you want to do . . ."

She clapped her hands and jumped up and down in place. "That's exactly what I want to do!"

He looked at her car, then back at her. "And you don't want her to know that you're following her, am I correct?"

"Right," she replied.

"You won't be able to follow her around in Yoder in that."

Sissy turned and gazed at her car. Her sweet little Italian convertible. As far as she knew, she had the only convertible in town. Most people around these parts drove a truck or a tractor.

She shrugged indifferently. "So we'll take your car," she said. "I'll buy the gas."

Gavin shifted, suddenly appearing uncomfortable. "I don't have a car."

"What?" Sissy asked. For a moment there, she thought he had said—

"I don't have a car," Gavin repeated.

"How can you not have a car?"

He shrugged. "I just don't. They're terrible for the environment, and I don't have any place I need to go that's so far away I can't ride my bike."

"How about Walmart? You want to go to Walmart, don't you? That's miles from here, not even in the same town."

"When I need to go there, I do what the Amish do: I hire a driver."

And she supposed that would work, as well. The Amish had been driving around in other people's cars for as long as there had been cars. The original Uber.

"Then I guess we have to take my car," she said. But he was right: Her car would be so conspicuous in little Yoder. Josie would know they were following her by the second or third stop they made. And surely, she would recognize her car if Sissy parked it anywhere near her front door. How was she supposed to keep a potential killer under surveillance if she didn't have the proper equipment?

"Nah," Gavin said. "I got a better idea."

Ten minutes later, Sissy was staring at what had to be a nightmare. A pair of black spandex shorts with a padded rear end. Who came up with that? No woman she knew wanted her butt to look bigger. A rash guard–type shirt in the same black with splashes of neon green. And though the sizes were designed to fit Gavin, they fit him like a second skin, which meant they would fit her pretty tightly, as well. Gavin wasn't bulky. He was slim and trim. That's just what she needed to do—show off every roll of flab she had. Spandex, her old nemesis.

"I am not riding a bike all over town."

"It'll be fun."

She shook her head, unable to take her gaze from those black and brightly colored spandex garments. They lay on the bed and taunted her. They mocked her over every slice of pizza and every cookie she'd ever eaten when she knew she needed to stop and some of the ones that maybe she actually needed.

"What have you got against biking?" he asked. "Everybody loves riding a bike."

"Yeah," Sissy said. "When I was ten."

"Despite the number of years in your age now, you're still the same girl you were when you were ten."

"I . . . I don't have a helmet," she said. That should do it. Helmets were a necessity these days. There had been a couple of times when she was growing up where she had managed to run off without her bike helmet, but no one today did that. Most little kids she saw riding bikes had elbow pads, kneepads, wrist braces, helmets, shin guards, and a plethora of other protective gear. It might as well have been chain mail and a coat of armor to protect them in case they had a wreck. She surely couldn't go without a helmet.

"I've got an extra."

Oh, joy.

"And I don't have the shoes. And I'm sure your shoes won't fit me," she protested.

"We'll stuff paper in the toes. Or you can wear your own shoes. Either way, it works. You don't have to have that much special equipment to go biking. Pretty much just a bike and a helmet."

"If I say yes, then I wear my own clothes."

Gavin shrugged one shoulder. "Fine," he said. "But it seems to me that these clothes might be a good disguise.

Going around in your own clothes, Josie will surely figure out who you are. But cover your hair with a bike helmet and disguise your frame in black spandex, and *voilà*,
no one's going to know the difference."

And that's exactly how Sissy got talked into riding a
bike around Yoder to follow Josie and find out if she was,
once and for all, Kevin's killer.

CHAPTER EIGHTEEN

Martyrdom covers a multitude of sins.
—Aunt Bess

Sissy wasn't certain what she expected Josie to do to show herself as a murderer. It wasn't like there was a club she could go into, like the VFW, or some special handshake. Not even a T-shirt she could wear around: I KILLED KEVIN SAUNDERS. And for someone who appeared as exotic as Josie, her day off proved more boring than Sissy's own.

Josie mailed a letter, picked up some dry-cleaning, and bought cigarettes at the Quiki-Mart. As far as Sissy was concerned, the most suspicious thing she did was the dry-cleaning. She'd only ever seen the woman in a wifebeater and a pair of jeans. Who dry-cleaned things like that? But Gavin had reminded her then that Josie visited her brother in prison regularly and most likely wore something nicer than jeans and a tank top on visitation days. Josie lingered for a while in the Quiki-Mart, while Gavin and Sissy pretended to be doing something in the park.

"So," Gavin started, "what you think?" He nodded toward her bike.

For a moment, she thought about pretending she didn't understand what he was talking about, and she tossed back her head and straightened her shoulders. Of course, then she had to straighten her helmet, as well, the motion knocking it a little sideways. Perhaps she needed to adjust the chin strap a little more. "It's fun. I guess."

Okay, the truth was, it was more than a little fun, seeing charming Yoder from the seat of a bike. It was strange how the world appeared so different just from a slight change of angle. Or perhaps it was the speed. One couldn't go nearly as fast on a bike as they could in a car. Slowing down allowed a person to see things that perhaps they had missed on the first trip through. Or the second, or the third, or even the ninety-eighth.

Of course, they stayed in town. And once again, Sissy questioned her own methods. Silently, of course, and definitely not where Gavin could hear. Just what had she expected Josie to do?

"Do you need anything while we're here?" Gavin asked as they stood outside the discount store.

Josie had been inside for fifteen minutes or so, while Gavin and Sissy waited outside near the ice machine. He had produced money from some magical pocket in his skintight shorts and bought her pop with it. The fizzy drink was cold and delicious, and the day was hot. She rubbed the can across her forehead.

"I don't believe so, no," she said. She could always pick up a couple of things, but she wanted to be ready to hop back on her bike once Josie came out. Surely she had something sinister planned today. Something that would link her to Kevin's murder.

Gavin nodded and took a drink of his own soda.

"You know, I don't think I've ever seen you drink anything but water."

He shrugged. "I usually don't. I figured today I deserved a treat."

She was about to ask him why when Josie came out of the store, carrying two large shopping bags. Instead of replying, Sissy nudged Gavin in the side with her elbow and nodded toward the cook.

She could've turned around and spotted them so easily, but she kept walking around the side of the building.

Gavin held one arm out as if to hold Sissy back as they waited, listening for the sound of the door opening, closing, maybe opening again, and then her car starting.

He crunched his can in one fist and tossed it into the trash nearby. "Come on," he said. "Let's go."

Following someone driving a car while riding a bike was not nearly as easy as it looked on paper, even through a town as small as Yoder.

Gavin had reminded her that cyclists were expected to follow the same rules as any other wheeled vehicle—car, truck, motorcycle, or horse-drawn buggy—but they didn't want to draw too much attention to themselves by pulling up behind her at a stop sign or staying too close as she drove through town. So they stayed back as far as they dared, hoping that since Yoder was such a small town, they could keep track of her from a distance. But when she turned down McCandless Street . . .

Sissy stopped, then called for Gavin to do the same.

"What is it?" he asked, circling back to her.

By then, she had dismounted and walked her bike onto the sidewalk. "Darcy's house."

"And you think Josie is going there?"

"See for yourself." She nodded in the direction of the little colonial that Darcy Saunders, her ten kids, and once upon a time, her husband Kevin, called home.

As they watched, Josie knocked on the door. They couldn't see who opened it, but Sissy supposed it was most likely Dani, since the image of Darcy—dog in one hand, cigarette in the other, while straddling the tract for the sliding-glass door in back—was burned into her brain.

"She's taking them the groceries." Gavin bobbed his head toward the door, where Darcy was handing off sacks of goods, the very same sacks of the very same goods that she had bought at the discount market, to the person on the other side of the threshold.

They must've said something, for Josie shook her head, her long ponytail swishing out behind her. Then, whoever was standing at the open door of Darcy's house grabbed hold of Josie's elbow and pulled her inside.

"What do you make of that?" Gavin asked.

"Maybe she feels guilty?"

"I thought you were trying to prove she was innocent." Gavin frowned at her.

Sissy nodded. "I am. I am. It's just that Josie seems . . ." How could she say it without sounding critical? How to say that Josie seemed only to be concerned about Josie and not whether Darcy, whose husband Josie might have had a hand in murdering, had something to eat? ". . . more like the kind of person who worries mostly about herself. And figures each man is on his own." It was the nicest way she could say it.

"And someone who wants to take care of their own personal life wouldn't bring groceries to someone else's house after they lost a spouse?" Gavin shook his head. "That's just Yoder," he said. "Everyone here takes care of everyone else. It's not like a big city."

Sissy scoffed a bit. "I would not call Tulsa a big city."

"It's a heck of a lot bigger than Yoder," Gavin pointed out.

That was true enough. But could she believe that Josie had no other motive for bringing Darcy groceries, other than she was a person in need in their shared community? That just didn't seem like Josie. Or maybe alien pod people had taken over her body. It was about as logical as anything else.

"Are we going to stand out here until she comes back out?" Gavin asked. "I mean, she could be in there for hours."

"Only for a few minutes," Sissy countered. "I don't think Josie and Darcy are the kind of people who would hang out together."

Gavin gave a casual shrug. "I suppose you're right about that. But you are in Yoder. Friendliest little town in Kansas."

Sissy shot him a look. "They should put that on the sign."

Gavin laughed, and then a wheeze escaped him as she elbowed him in the ribs. "That's him," she said, using everything in her power to keep her voice out of the range of shouting. "That's Casual Man. The one who said he was the insurance adjuster—but now we know he's *not* the insurance adjuster."

"You're right, he doesn't look like Mafia. But I think those days are gone, anyway," Gavin said.

"I thought you said the mob was no longer in Kansas City," Sissy demanded. "Make up your mind."

"They're still there," Gavin replied. "I Googled it. But I don't think they look like the Italian dons of the eighties any longer."

"But do they look like that? Like an aging frat boy?" It was the best description she could come up with for the man—starched button-down shirt, jeans, no socks, loafers. It seemed to be his standard uniform.

"In all honesty, I have no idea what they look like. I mean, it's not like I run in those circles."

"And Google didn't have pictures. But it is possible," Sissy said. "It is possible that this guy could be from the mob. And it is possible that Kevin could have borrowed money from them. Or maybe a marker in one of their casinos."

"And the mob killed Kevin?"

"That's what we're trying to figure out."

"I thought you thought Josie did it," Gavin countered.

"I don't know who did it; that's why we're investigating." She looked up and saw that Casual Man was staring at them. "Crap! We've been made."

Gavin's gaze jerked in the direction of hers, and he saw the man, as well. Then he turned back to Sissy.

"He's seen us," she said. "What do we do?" Before she could say one more word, Gavin wrapped his fingers around her upper arms, pulled her to him, and kissed her soundly on the mouth.

It had been her experience that unexpected kisses were generally a welcome treat. And this one had her heart pounding. Not because she was so attracted to Gavin, but a potential mobster had found them surveying Darcy's house in their quest to follow Josie. Hopefully, the man would not be able to identify her at this distance. Not with the clothes she was wearing and the fact that her hair was covered. Mostly, anyway.

And this kiss . . . this kiss was most unwelcome.

Just as she started to raise her arms to push Gavin away, his lips moved across her cheek and to her ear, his breath tickling the hairs that had escaped her helmet.

"Don't move," he whispered.

She shivered. "What's he doing?" she whispered in return.

"It looks like he's getting into his car and driving away. But just wait a moment." He raised his head, only to press his forehead against hers. Or rather, the front of his helmet against the front of her helmet. He reached a hand up and brushed his fingers across the slick plastic, as if he were brushing back her hair. All in all, it was a loving gesture. And it made her uncomfortable. They were standing entirely too close to each other. He had turned her so that her back was to Darcy's house. How was she supposed to know what was going on if he was kissing her and distorting her view? And the worst part of it all? Kissing Gavin was a little like kissing her brother. Not that she had ever actually kissed Owen. But it had the same vibe. Despite her pounding heart and suddenly dry mouth. That was definitely due to Casual Man/Casual Mobster.

"Is it safe now?" she asked. She needed to step away. She needed a good breath of air. She needed to see what was happening behind her.

"Just one second now . . ." he murmured. His eyes kept looking back and forth between the happenings behind her and straight into her own.

She was not good at all this acting stuff. It had never

been her style. Not even in high school, when everybody was talking about the theatrical production they did of *Oklahoma!* It had just never been on her radar to pretend to be something other than what she was.

She started to step back, but Gavin held her firmly in place. "Just one second now," he murmured. "Here comes Josie."

"Did she leave the groceries there?"

"It looks like it."

"Gav–viinn," she said, drawling out his name until it had three or four syllables extra.

Then, just as suddenly as he grabbed her, he turned her loose. "There," he said.

Sissy glanced backward, down the street, just barely catching the brake lights of Josie's car at the stop sign a block away before she turned out of sight. Josie was gone; the Casual Mafia Man was gone—now what?

"Now what?" Gavin asked.

Sissy shook her head, suddenly exhausted.

"You want to follow Josie some more?" he asked.

"No," she said. "I think it's time to call it a day."

"You have to step it up if you're going to get through the breakfast shift, girl," Lottie said the following morning.

"I'm stepping it up as best I can," Sissy replied. Every muscle in her body ached. Butt, hips, thighs, feet. Even her arms hurt. Why were her arms hurting if she'd been riding a bike? Her shoulders were stiff, her neck ached, as if she had slept crooked, but still . . .

Lottie stopped. "You're young. Why are you moving like an arthritic old man?"

"Gavin," she said, and Lottie shot her a very questioning look. "No, no, no," she started once again. "Nothing like that. He talked me into riding his extra bike yesterday."

"I see," Lottie said. "Seems like you've been spending a lot of time with Gavin lately."

Sissy shook her head. "It's nothing like that. We're just friends." And even as she said the words, the thought of his lips on hers came crashing back in. Brotherly. Definite *ew* factor. And her heart racing and her breath stopping had everything to do with being found out by the Mafia and nothing to do with Gavin's attention on her. Nothing at all.

"That's what they all say," Lottie said with an apologetic shrug. "You start off as friends, and then it goes on from there."

"I am not in the market for anything like that. I'm only here to help my aunt; then I'm going back to Tulsa." To the haggard remains of an almost-successful life. Yup. She would go back to Tulsa to no apartment, no boyfriend. A clean slate to start over. At least she still had Aunt Bess. As if that were any consolation.

Come to think of it, she might stay here for a while. But that still didn't mean that there would be anything between her and Gavin. It just wasn't possible. But thinking about her defunct life in Tulsa made her wish that she were writing again. Not the column, but articles, news events. She missed the deadlines and the rush of digging around and finding the right information to make the piece complete and doing it on such a quick turnaround. It was challenging; fun, even. Definitely more fun than carrying around the large bus tub full of dishes. She sat it on the back table next to the sink and sighed as her arms turned to wet noodles.

Maybe when this was all over, when she'd managed to clear her name and find out who really killed Kevin, she could write some sort of editorial about it. She could freelance. Maybe sell it to the *Sunflower Express*. Heck, maybe she could even sell it to *The Kansas City Star*. But the first thing she had to do was clear her own name. She could get herself back to herself.

She pushed back through the doors that led to the dining area of the café. As luck would have it, Earl Berry was coming through the door from the outside.

Oh, joy.

She was not going to let him get the better of her. Not today. Or maybe she should say especially not today, seeing as how she felt like hammered dog poop. Emphasis on *hammered*. It was Friday, and tonight was the weekly dinner at Bethel's house. Sissy would love nothing more than to go home and soak in the tub. But the Chicken Coop only provided a shower. What she wouldn't give right now for some lavender bath salts and her mom's pulsating garden tub. That would feel really great on her sore muscles.

Except for another bike ride, she would pretty much prefer anything other than having to face Earl Berry. But such was life.

The deputy sheriff slid onto the third barstool at the counter and rapped it lightly with his knuckles. "Thought any more about that morning?" he asked Sissy.

"Good morning to you, too, Deputy Berry." Sissy grabbed the coffeepot from the burner at the waitress station and moved to fill the ready mug sitting in front of the man.

"You leave the girl alone," Bethel grumbled.

Her reproach warmed Sissy's heart. Her aunt might not be the most affectionate person in the world, and she surely didn't act like she wanted Sissy there in Yoder at all, even if she was there to help, but she never let Earl Berry get the best of her. That was one thing she could say about Bethel.

Still, Sissy got the feeling she could stay there for years and years and still be considered an outsider, that she still would not belong to the town.

Sissy grabbed up the second bus tub filled with dishes from their breakfast rush and headed through the kitchen doors once again.

She moved toward the back counter, setting it on the sink edge, and tried not to look at the back door, or remember it being open, or Kevin's truck pulled up to the back, and Kevin himself lying on the cold, wet floor with a knife blade sticking up between his shoulders. She turned, intent on calling out to Josie. But when she spun around, the cook was right there next to her. Only inches away.

Sissy stifled a shriek of surprise. Then managed to pull herself back together. "Earl Berry's here." She didn't bother to put in a regular ticket order for the man. They all knew he ate the same thing every day. And Bethel never charged him. Not once.

Josie nodded, that dark ponytail of hers swishing with the motion. "So I heard." She turned to go back over to the grill but stopped, spatula in hand, held out menacingly toward Sissy.

"And if you want to start following people around town," she said, "I suggest you don't do it wearing black and neon green."

CHAPTER NINETEEN

Experience is a hard teacher. She gives the test
first, then the lesson afterward.
—Aunt Bess

"And then what happened?" Lizzie asked. Sissy's cousin pushed herself forward in the bed, as if somehow, that would make the story even more suspenseful.

Duke, who had immediately curled up and gone to sleep next to Lizzie when Sissy had brought him into the room, stirred. He frowned a small puppy frown, then rolled over and went back to sleep. Seconds later, the sounds of his soft snores filled the room.

"Well?" Lizzie prompted.

"Well, what?" Sissy asked.

"What happened then? What happened after you saw the casual man?"

That's when he kissed me. But she kept that comment to herself. Not because she minded her cousin knowing that Gavin had kissed her, but simply because it was not important. Sissy shrugged to show just how unimportant it was. Because it wasn't important at all. "We went home."

Lizzie flopped back against her pillows. "It's not Josie," she said, running a hand across her large belly. "Of that much I'm certain."

Sissy felt for her cousin. Her belly seemed to grow by the hour. And she still had another month to go. And poor Lizzie was confined to the bed, allowed only to get up and go to the bathroom when absolutely necessary.

Sissy had assumed this last part had been added when Lizzie, bored with four walls and nothing to do except read and crochet, had to go to the bathroom *a lot.*

It sounded great on the outside, lying in bed and reading all day. Sissy would love her chance to catch up on her books. Her to-be-read pile was stacked almost to the ceiling—theoretically, since it was truly a string of files on her e-reader. But she also knew that the reality of bed rest had to be excruciating. It was one thing to lounge about because one wanted to for an hour or so on a Sunday afternoon. And another altogether to be confined to one spot, unable to have the freedom to move around, because you had two precious lives depending on you. It was definitely a daunting prospect.

"You seem pretty sure of that," Sissy said. "That Josie isn't guilty."

Lizzie continued to rub the large mound of her stomach. "That's because I *am* sure. Josie's had a really tough life, and she's had a lot she's had to deal with. If she hasn't murdered someone before now, she isn't going to this year."

Sissy laughed. "If that's your official stand on it."

"That is my official stand." Lizzie bowed, well . . . as much as one who was propped up on pillows while sitting in bed can bow. "And I don't think it was Darcy either," Lizzie added.

Sissy had to agree with her on that. Ten ungrateful, needy children were too much for one person to handle. Actually, they were too much for five people to handle. There was no way Darcy was forcing single parenthood and widow-dom on herself by killing Kevin. Even in a crime of passion, it didn't quite make sense.

"How well did you know Kevin?" Sissy asked.

"I guess about as good as anyone else in town."

"Mike—" she started, and Lizzie rolled her eyes.

"May the good Lord save us from Mike Harper and his mouth," her cousin quipped.

"Is he really that bad?" Sissy managed to avoid him most days. It wasn't her job to let him in the back or to check the order. She only did so when both Bethel and Josie were too busy to drop whatever it was they were doing and check Mike in. So she had only seen him a couple of times since Kevin's death.

Lizzie shook her head. "What is he saying now?"

Sissy jerked her head to one side, somewhere between a nod and a shrug. "What he's been saying all along," Sissy replied. "That Kevin had a gambling problem. That he's probably into it for a great deal with the Kansas City mob. And when he says that, he winks, so I'm not sure what that means."

"I'm not sure what any of it means," Lizzie said.

"That the mob knocked Kevin off because he owed a lot of money."

Lizzie frowned. "But he's not to be able to pay them if he's dead."

"Insurance payout," Sissy said. Which was exactly why she thought Casual Man was hanging around Darcy's house. Was he just waiting on the real insurance adjuster to write Darcy a check? It was the most logical explanation for all that she had, and considering it contained a mob hit, it wasn't logical at all.

"What's a lot of money?" Lizzie asked.

Sissy shrugged for real this time. "Six figures, I guess. Maybe seven."

Lizzie's eyes grew as wide as saucers. "A million dollars?"

"Gambling is a slippery slope," Sissy said.

"But a million dollars?" Lizzie repeated once again. "That's more than a slippery slope. That's an avalanche."

Sissy chuckled. "I still don't know if that's the real case or not. But something's going on."

She shook her head at herself. She hated when she said things like that. Of course *something* was going on. A man had been murdered; two strangers were in town, only one of whom was an insurance adjuster; and Gavin had kissed her yesterday.

Time for a change in subject. "What are you working on?" She gave a cursory nod to the basket of crochet that waited on Lizzie's other side. Other than reading, yarn crafts were how Lizzie filled the rest of her days alone.

Her cousin smiled and pulled the half-finished project from the basket. It was made of soft white yarn, with tiny stripes of yellow and green. "It's a baby blanket. For Abby Yoder." Lizzie lowered her arms and let the tiny blanket rest on the mound of her belly. "It feels too soon to be making something for her, but since her sister is having her baby shower in a week, I wanted to send something."

Sissy's mouth twisted into an apologetic grimace. "You're not getting to go, are you?"

Lizzie's smiled to tell Sissy that everything was all right. "No, but it's okay. You're going, right?"

"I don't really know—"

"I don't want to hear it. You live in Yoder now, and when the Yoder community has an event, you should go."

"Without an invitation?"

"Because you're living in Yoder, you're automatically invited."

"If you say so."

"I say so," Lizzie said with an emphatic nod. "But if you want me to call Danielle and have her send you a formal invitation, I can do that, too."

Sissy chuckled. "That's not necessary."

"One favor, though," Lizzie said. "Will you take it to the baby shower for me? You can pick it up when you come by next Friday for supper."

"Your *mamm* isn't going?"

Lizzie shrugged. "I don't know, but if I make you take my present, I know you'll have to go."

Sissy shook her head but was still smiling. "I should have known," she said. "I should have known."

It was Saturday afternoon, and Sissy was tired. A six-day workweek—even if it was only half days—and trying to run down a killer could really take it out of a person. Once she was home from work and had taken Duke out for a small walk to potty and take care of other necessities, she was going back to the Chicken Coop and taking a nice long nap. But when she got back home and let the dog from his leash and climbed onto the large bed that took up most of the space in the tiny one-room flat, she found her mind to be restless.

That was the way it was. So tired she couldn't rest.

She pushed up from the bed and put her shoes back on. She had changed clothes when she got home, so at least she wasn't wearing her smelly work jeans and Sunflower Café T-shirt.

"Let's go for a drive."

Duke, chin on his front paws, shot her a dubious look without lifting his head.

"You want to go bye-bye?"

That did it. The pup was on his feet in seconds. He let out a sharp bark as Sissy retrieved his leash.

With no particular place in mind, she locked the front door, strapped Duke in his doggie car seat, and put the top down.

A drive. That should clear her head. She hoped, anyway. Solving murders was tiresome business. Especially when she felt like she was only chasing her tail. She had no new leads, no new suspects. Just the same old clues, which basically amounted to nothing. It was enough to make her want to give up the investigation and just start praying that Earl Berry would, too.

Fat. Chance.

"There's just something we're missing, Duke," she told the pup.

He barked in response and turned his face back to the wind. What was it her journalism professor had said? When all the obvious aspects run out, look for the *unob-vious*. And what was the unobvious here?

Josie's brother was serving a life sentence for a murder that witnesses say Kevin Saunders had egged him on to.

Josie was the last one in the kitchen when Kevin was found. And her family had been broken apart when her brother was shipped off to jail. That was obvious.

Kevin had reportedly gambled away a lot of money and owed the wrong people a large amount. That was obvious.

Darcy seemed smart enough. Smart enough not to kill her own husband and land herself widowed with ten children who bickered and fought and leeched off everything. It was sucking the life out of the poor woman. That was obvious.

And then, take her, for example. She had found the body. She had touched the knife, so therefore, her fingerprints were on it. She had gotten into an argument with Kevin just the day before. That was obvious.

So that meant neither she, nor Darcy, nor Josie, nor Casual Man Possibly of the Mafia, could have committed this crime. Then *who*?

The only other person tied to Kevin in a way that suggested a personal relationship that could possibly lead to murder was Evan Yoder.

Evan had everything to gain where he was. An heir to a beautiful horse farm in this quaint little town. A mother who was somewhat overbearing, but nothing that a grown man shouldn't be able to handle. And yes, his girlfriend had thrown him over for another, and he somehow had never managed to marry. But that wasn't obvious. Killing your high school nemesis decades after he stole your girlfriend from you was not obvious at all. Senior year, maybe; day after graduation, maybe. She would even give him a five-year leeway. But that had long since passed.

She looked over to her dog. Duke had his paws braced on the edge of his seat, ears flapping in the wind.

"You know what, pup?" she said. "I think I'm in the mood for some cheese."

Sissy had a feeling the minute she pulled up in front of the Brubacher Dairy that Evan Yoder would know she was in the area. She wasn't sure how he could tell she was around. Only that it seemed like whenever she came by, he came over to tell her that he knew she was following him or some such nonsense. So all she had to do was go into the shop, look around, pick out some cheese, maybe even another yogurt, and Evan would be there. Then all she had to do was engage him in some conversation, maybe trip him up, and find out if he was the real killer.

Or maybe she had seen too many episodes of *Scooby-Doo*.

"Sissy, right?" Jonathan Brubacher came from behind the table that served as the cash-register stand and nodded in her direction.

"That's right," she said. "And thank you for remembering, Jonathan."

He smiled, then went back to his work. He had a pen stuck behind one ear and a calculator out, adding numbers from a ledger.

Sissy browsed in front of the large coolers. She had only come by because she knew that if she did, Evan Yoder would buzz over from across the street and confront her like he had every other time she had been here. She really shouldn't buy any more cheese. Even though it was incredibly delicious. It seemed to hold its freshness longer than anything she had ever had, and the herbs and spices that the dairy added made it just perfect for a grilled cheese on sourdough bread. Yum. Yum. But she should be strong.

"We have a new cheese over there. Garlic herb with fresh scallions." Jonathan looked up from his figures.

Sissy pointed to the refrigerated section in front of her. "Here?"

He nodded. "Right there on the right."

She found the cheese. It sounded so good. Maybe just one brick. And yogurt wasn't so bad, health-wise. And before she knew it, she had all sorts of milk products sitting on the cabinet, waiting for Jonathan to ring up. Raw milk. Who knew?

Jonathan gave her his total and she reached into her purse to pay him.

"You know my aunt, Bethel Yoder?" Sissy asked.

Jonathan nodded and punched some numbers into the cash register; then, he pulled the handle on the side. The money drawer opened with a *ding*. He put her money in and counted back her change. "Yes. I do."

"And your mom's Amish, right?"

"If I'm remembering right, so is yours." He said the words, but his eyes twinkled, taking any sting from them.

"So the bishop doesn't mind you not being a part of the church and still working with your family?"

"I never joined the church," he said. "I don't know if it was being mixed with all the English kids at school or what, but it just never seemed to fit me. My wife joined."

"And she's shunned?" Sissy asked. "If you don't mind my asking."

"As much of anybody is shunned around here, I suppose. We make ways to get around it. And we attend the

Mennonite church, so the bishop doesn't frown too heavily upon us. I guess because we still live here, we still take care of the family dairy, we still do all the things that we would normally do as if we were Amish. Because of all of that, I suppose he doesn't mind so much." As he spoke, he loaded her purchases into a large brown paper sack.

Sissy dropped some coins into the tip jar by the register. "If you do all the things the same as you would when you were Amish, why did you leave?"

"Freedom of choice is a very powerful thing."

"Well, well, well," Evan said as she came out of the tiny store. He had one hip braced against the driver's side fender. His arms were crossed, and he looked completely casual, while behind him, Duke growled as if he were a ninety-pound guard dog.

Sissy shifted her purchases to one arm and pulled her sunglasses back into place. "Evan Yoder," she said. "Fancy running into you here."

He pushed himself to his feet, though his arms were still crossed. "Yeah, fancy that. And just what brings you out today, Ms. Yoder?" He made to look at what was in her sack, but she sidestepped him, opened her car door, and placed the dairy goods on the back seat of her convertible.

"Tell me, Evan," she said, crossing her arms to mimic his pose. "Why is it that you never married?"

He shook his head. "That's a very personal question. I don't think we know each other well enough for me to reveal all my secrets."

"Was it because you were so in love with Darcy that you didn't want to let go? Couldn't let go, even when she chose Kevin over you?"

Those green eyes turned stormy. "Nah," he said, his tone still casual and directly at odds with those fierce eyes. "I was going to break up with her anyway."

"I saw a picture of her. Miss Kansas, right? She looked amazing. So beautiful."

Evan's face shifted into a mask of indifference. But it appeared on the verge of cracking. "She was very beautiful." His lips hardly moved when he said the words, as if he were afraid of cracking it himself.

"It must've been hard for you to see your beautiful girlfriend reduced to—" She didn't have to finish for him to get the gist of it.

"She deserved so much better than him. So. Much. Better."

"It's always tragic to see such potential wasted." Though she wondered if her parents—despite their insistence otherwise—thought the same thing about her. Still, she wasn't the one with a horse in this race.

"What do you want, Sissy Yoder?"

"Did you talk to Deputy Berry?" she asked. "Did you give him your alibi? Do you *have* an alibi?"

She didn't know where her courage was coming from. It was just suddenly there. Maybe because she was tired of dealing with Earl Berry's insinuations every morning, or the fact that somebody out there had killed Kevin and was willing to let her take the fall for it while they walked away scot-free. Wherever it came from, she was glad to have it.

"I'll tell you what I told him," Evan said. "Darcy and I

were over a long time ago. Two guys went up for one girl, and he won. More power to him. But Kevin had some shady dealings all over. He bed-hopped, he gambled, he drank, and heaven only knows what else. You may have me at the top of your list, just as Earl Berry has you at the top of his. But I'll tell you this: You'd be hard-pressed to find five people in this county that wouldn't pay to see Kevin Saunders dead."

CHAPTER TWENTY

When you sweep the stairs, start from the top.
—Aunt Bess

"Where have you been?"

"Hi, Gavin, it's good to see you. Yes, I have had a good afternoon. Thanks for asking," she replied.

"I've been calling your phone for the last hour, and you haven't answered. Pardon me if I'm worried. There is a murderer on the loose."

Sissy got Duke from the car and handed his leash over to Gavin. Then she reached into the back seat and grabbed the bag of goodies she'd bought at the dairy. "I didn't mean to worry you."

"Then why didn't you answer your phone?" He shook his head. "Sissy, that man could be Mafia. And he could have recognized you."

"Maybe." She shrugged and dug out her keys to open the door of the Chicken Coop. "Josie did."

Gavin still held Duke's leash, so he threw the other arm up in the air and let it fall back quickly to his side, a sure sign of exasperation. "See? Now why didn't you answer your phone?"

"I didn't hear it." She unlocked the door and stepped into the tiny apartment. Gavin followed behind with Duke. "Oops, there's why." She pointed to the kitchen counter, where her cell phone sat.

Gavin shook his head and pressed his lips together. That lock of blond hair dropped over his eyes once more. He pushed it back with his free hand. "In this day and age, it is not safe to go around without a phone."

She gave him a strange look. "Even in Yoder?"

"Two weeks ago, I would've told you no. But in case you've forgotten . . ." He trailed off.

"There's a murderer on the loose. I haven't forgotten." And she wasn't about to tell Gavin that she confronted the last person on her list. The one person who was not obvious and yet could still be guilty.

She looked at Gavin, noticing for the first time since pulling up that he was still wearing his work clothes. "You're not biking today?"

He shook his head. "I was in Buhler today. There's a lady missionary who lives there. She goes to Africa, takes care of these children over there. It's a really great thing. I do a piece on her every so often, just to keep her organization fresh in everybody's mind."

Sissy stopped unloading her dairy products and gave Gavin a smile. "That's really sweet of you."

Gavin turned loose of Duke's leash and shoved his fingers in the front pockets of his jeans. "I do what I can." He shrugged.

Don't they all.

"Why are you here again?" Sissy asked. She put the last of the dairy goods she had bought at Brubacher into the Coop's tiny refrigerator and closed the door. Then she turned around to fully face him.

"About the other day," he started.

Sissy's heart jumped into her throat, and it took a second to swallow it back down. This was about the kiss. The kiss he gave her to keep Casual Mafia Man from noticing that she was there. Was Gavin going to say that it had affected him in ways that he had never dreamed? How was she going to answer if he did? Maybe she had felt a little something. Or maybe it was just shock. Or even the excitement of tailing someone, then finding out that the person you were tailing was being tailed by someone else. "Yes?"

He shifted in place. "It's just . . . well, I enjoyed riding bikes with you. I don't mean to be presumptuous, but if you wanted to have my old bike, and you wanted to ride with me, I would let you have it." He shifted again. "But only if you want it."

Sissy stared at him. She blinked. Then she tried to assimilate his words into something that she could understand. He was talking about the bike. *The bike*. Not the kiss. *Bike*. "You want me to ride bikes with you?"

"Well, yeah." He shifted once more. "I thought you had a good time. I normally ride alone, but I kind of enjoyed having company. You wouldn't have to go as much as I go, or you wouldn't have to give up your car or anything. But if you wanted to keep my old bike here and use it whenever you want, or perhaps ride it over to my house and we'll go somewhere together. I don't know; it just sounded like fun."

Fun. He thought riding bikes with her sounded like fun. But there was no mention of the kiss.

See? She'd blown it all out of proportion. The kiss was nothing to her. It was nothing to him. It was nothing to get excited about. They were talking bicycles.

"I suppose I might be persuaded to ride with you again," Sissy said. "Though we can't stay on them quite so long. I could barely walk the next day. Even my hair hurt."

She couldn't believe she was admitting this to someone, but it wasn't just anyone. It was Gavin. Gavin, her buddy, her old Building and Loan pal. Probably her best friend in Yoder. It would be like telling Stephanie back home, before Colt had flaked and cheated and the ruin of that relationship had ruined the other. And that ruination had caused Sissy to pack up everything and move to Yoder. Ahem . . . it was a just-between-us-girls kind of thing, like she had once had with her bestie and roommate, but it was between her and Gavin. Who wasn't a girl, but was more like a brother she could enjoy being around. A brother who didn't try and outdo her at every turn. Or something like that.

He nodded. "Okay, sure. We don't have to ride for hours, but maybe tomorrow afternoon?"

She shook her head. "Let's shoot for next Sunday. I think my thighs still need a break from running around after Josie."

"Yeah. Right. The first couple weeks are always the hardest." Gavin smiled that crooked, nerdy grin of his, and she was happy. Everything seemed to be back to normal.

* * *

Sunday. Was there ever a better word in the English language? As far as Sissy was concerned, there was not. Sunday morning sleep-late, Sunday morning brunch, Sunday newspaper, lazy Sunday afternoon, easy like Sunday morning. Sunday with nothing more to do than laundry.

Okay, so the laundry was kind of a letdown, but what was a girl supposed to do? Not everybody could be independently wealthy and throw their clothes away and just buy new ones when they needed something clean to wear. So laundry it was. The good news was, since she came to Yoder, it seemed as though she didn't wear as many clothes.

She didn't have a roommate, so she didn't have someone constantly passing judgment. Therefore, the same pair of pajamas could be worn two or three or six days in a row, and there was nobody there to call her out on it. In fact, there was no one to call her out on the three-in-the-afternoon pajama-mode that occurred when she got home from work, decided she wasn't going out again, and put on her pajamas. See how much laundry that saved?

But today, for the Amish—which meant for Bethel and the family—it was a nonchurch Sunday. That meant Lizzie would be at home surrounded by family and not alone. Though Sissy loved spending time with Lizzie, and Duke did, too, she figured today was as good a day as any to let her cousin relax and enjoy her family without the interruption of the English cousin from Oklahoma.

So once the two loads of laundry were done, she took her clothes back to the Coop and grabbed Duke's leash and a quilt. "You want to go on a picnic?"

Duke stood on the bed and barked three times in rapid succession.

"I'll take that as a yes."

She scooped the fearless puppy off the bed before he

could take a blind leap to the floor. She wrapped the leash around the doorknob as she started to gather up the rest of the supplies they would need for a picnic.

Duke paced back and forth in a small circle. He never got far enough to pull the leash taut, but it was as if he knew he was tethered. He whined and walked and whined and walked and whined and walked.

"Hush, silly," Sissy said. "I'm getting us a snack. Cheese and crackers for me, puppy kibble for you, light beer for me, water for you. Okay, maybe you can have a sip of beer." She had never met a dog that didn't like beer. Or peanut butter. Peanut butter and beer. Couldn't go wrong with either one of those, as far she was concerned. Just one of the many reasons she considered herself a "dog person."

She gathered up everything in a large beach tote that had never seen the sand, grabbed a quilt and a floppy hat large enough to shade her shoulders, and out the door they went.

They didn't have far to go. Less than fifteen feet from the house was a large oak tree. Sissy wasn't certain if it was planted on the lot where the Chicken Coop was built or if it belonged to the neighbor next door. That neighbor, like the one across the street with the eccentric flower beds, never seemed to be at home. So she didn't think that if it was his tree, he would mind her sitting underneath it to enjoy a beer, some "fresh" milk cheese from a local dairy, and the beautiful Kansas day.

It was a different angle, watching Yoder from the spot under the oak tree. At first, she just plopped down and enjoyed all the sights and sounds around her—the soft rumbling of a small town on a Sunday afternoon. An occasional car would go by and, from time to time, she could hear the squeal and laughter of children. Maybe a dog bark, a car door slam, the gentle sounds of life.

But then she began to notice things—nothing of earth-shattering importance, of course. After all, it was a Sunday, and Yoder seemed to have come to a screeching halt sometime after dark on Saturday night. No, she just began to notice—or maybe appreciate was a better word—the eccentricities of the town. And there were plenty of those in the small unincorporated space. It was not just the mix of Amish and English that brought about such a variety. But the way the whole town was set up. It was as if angry siblings had set up camp. Angry so they turned their backs on one another, instead of all facing front.

Take her road, for example. She couldn't really call the road a street. It was packed red dirt, packed hard enough that it wasn't nearly as dusty as it sounded, which in itself was a miracle. At least it was straight, even though it only lasted for a block before it ended in another hard dirt-packed road, this one more of a diagonal angle that bisected and met the other diagonal street just one house down. And how interesting it was that because her neighborhood was set on such an angle, she could see almost to the café from here. She thought about Winston Yoder and his purple Jazzy and "tattooed" prosthetic leg. How he liked to cut through places. This was definitely the town for him. She wondered if his propensity for cutting across had come naturally, or if it was a part of his environment. She could never imagine cutting through her neighbor's yard in Tulsa. Well, her parents' neighbors' yard. She always lived in an apartment, so the grass in her neck of the woods was common area. She would never think to cut across Jordan Lance's yard next door to Mary and James Yoder. The young investment banker most likely had more security than Fort Knox. And he would certainly come unglued if someone dared step on his precious Bermuda sod. But right now, if she wanted to, she could get up, cut straight across through either of the Yoders' yards, through the flower bed, and straight over to the Sunflower Café. From there, if she chose, in another five minutes she could be at the Quiki-Mart. The whole trip would probably take her less than fifteen minutes from side to side, almost the whole town of Yoder.

Duke whined as she stopped rubbing his belly and stood to get a better look. But if she could run straight across from here . . . She moved to the edge of the grass and looked back in the opposite direction. In her mind's eye, she drove the streets to get there and see where exactly it would be, that point on the diagonal line that could very well be Darcy Saunders's house.

"Well, that's no help," she said.

"Who are you talking to?" A male voice sounded close behind her. Sissy slapped a hand over her heart to keep it from beating out of her chest and whirled around to face . . . Gavin. "You scared me," she said. She'd been too wrapped up in her own thoughts to pay attention to what was going on around her. Or perhaps the whir and click of his bicycle had just become part of the white noise that was Yoder on a Sunday.

Gavin shot her an apologetic grin and removed his helmet. "Sorry. I didn't mean to. You were just so wrapped up in your thoughts."

"I suppose," she said, and sucked in a deep breath to calm her nerves.

"What is it you're looking at?" he asked. He took a step closer and peered in both directions, as if trying to see from her point of view.

Sissy shrugged, the magic of the moment lost. The ideas that she'd had, which seemed miraculous moments before, were now downgraded to nothing more than afternoon daydreams. "Yoder."

"That's interesting enough," Gavin replied with a chuckle. "Wanna go for a ride?"

She gave him a tight smile. "I'm good."

"You're not going to chicken out on me, are you?"

She shook her head. "Nope. But I can be honest and say that I'm too far out of shape to ride the way you do. Maybe once or twice a week—at the most. Maybe."

He shook his head sadly. "You'll never get in shape with that attitude."

Sissy shot him a cheeky grin. "I'm okay with that. Want some cheese? Some beer?"

He patted his trim midriff. "Better not."

"How about we split the difference, and I get you some water?" she asked.

He grinned, that thatch of hair flopping over into his face once again. "I'm not sure how that's splitting the difference, but it sounds like a plan."

Duke trotted along behind her as she went into the Coop to get a glass of water for Gavin. He really was good on the leash—Duke, not Gavin—and, though he talked a big game when he wanted, the little dog was a mama's boy.

Together they came back out of her flat and took the water over to Gavin.

He was now standing where Sissy had been moments before, gazing across Yoder in one direction, then turning and studying the other. "What were you looking for?"

She shrugged and handed the plastic tumbler of water to him. He drank it thirstily as she answered, "Nothing, really. I just have never looked at the town from this angle before."

He nodded as if understanding. "I guess I haven't, either. But there's a diagonal line right through the center."

"And so I was thinking—" She broke off, unable to decide if she should continue or not. It was pure speculation on her part. She had no proof to back any of it up, but . . . "We determined that the killer left the café on foot," Sissy verified.

"It seems more likely than not," Gavin agreed.

"And no one saw him leaving. No one saw which direction he went."

"No one saw anything, as far as we know," Gavin pointed out. "It might not even be a *he*."

"Right," she said. "But if Earl Berry has been going around talking to the citizens of Yoder who would've been walking down the street during that time . . ." She paused once more.

Gavin took another step forward, looking left and right, his body angled in the same diagonal as the crazy line that bisected the town. "He might not have seen them, because they could've been cutting through someone's yard." Gavin turned back around, excitement lighting his sea-colored eyes. "Get Duke his leash, and let's check this out."

Sissy looked down at her bare feet. "Give me a second to get some shoes."

She shoved her feet into running shoes without bothering with socks. She locked the Chicken Coop and hustled back to Gavin's side.

"You want to pick up this mess first?"

With an aggravated growl, Sissy gathered everything

up from their picnic and hustled it back into the house. Cheese in the refrigerator, remainder of beer down the drain, blanket wadded up inside the beach bag; she could deal with the rest later. Right now, she wanted to retrace those steps. Or trace them. They didn't actually know if somebody made them, but it seemed more likely than not that whoever killed Kevin had cut across to get to another part of town—easy, quick, and without suspicion.

CHAPTER TWENTY-ONE

It is easier to stay out than get out.
—Aunt Bess

"Gavin," Sissy said, hesitating as she drew near. The Chicken Coop was locked up, Duke was on his leash, and everything that she had dragged out of the house for the picnic was at least put inside.

"Ready?" he asked.

She nodded.

He turned to go, but she caught him, one hand on his arm. "Wait," she said. She pulled her other arm from behind her back and showed him what she held. A small plastic bag, with the scrap of fabric she had found at the café tucked neatly inside.

"What about it?" Gavin asked. They had already determined that it was useless as evidence, seeing as how any DNA that was on it had been washed away and replaced by her own.

"It's bothering me," she said. "I mean, I can't stop thinking about it. I can't shake the feeling that it's a clue."

"A completely immaculate clue," he said. "You washed and dried it, remember?"

She resisted the urge to stomp her foot at him. "I did not do it on purpose."

He held up his hands in a gesture of surrender. "All right, all right," he said. "You didn't do it on purpose, but you still did it."

She shot him a look. "This is why no one likes you," she groused.

Gavin chuckled. "Remind me not to send you any of my money."

"Hardy har har," she said. "But look at this. What if someone got it stuck on their shoe?"

He stopped, frowning a bit as he mulled over what she was saying. "So you're thinking that whoever came into the café and killed Kevin dragged that piece of fabric in on the bottom of their shoe."

Well, when he said it like that . . . it didn't seem feasible at all. But in her head, it had seemed perfectly logical. People just didn't go around murdering other people without leaving some shred of evidence. *CSI* had taught her that. There had to be a clue; there had to be something that linked the killer to the crime scene, and seeing as how this was all she had to work with . . .

"Think about it a second," she said. "There are a lot of yards between here and there." She pointed in both directions along that diagonal line. "A lot of garden flags, street memorials, wreaths." A lot of debris that someone could pick up and bring along for the ride.

He shifted in place and looked at the little scrap of fabric, still sealed in the plastic bag. "So in their haste to get to Kevin, they picked this up running through someone's flower beds or yards. And they just so happened to drop it in the café. What would have been their haste with coming into the café? Before killing Kevin?"

Heavens up above, she hated when he got all logical on her. "It could have happened either way. I don't believe that this was in the café originally. Someone brought it in from somewhere." And it still had a vaguely familiar look to it. Like she'd seen it somewhere before. Which was ridiculous. She wasn't into crafting like her mother or Owen's girlfriend, Sydney. But she had seen it somewhere.

"So can we walk it or not?" Gavin asked.

"Let's go," Sissy said. She shoved the plastic bag, containing the only clue she truly had in this whole murder mystery, into her pocket and started behind him.

Duke trotted casually between them. Several times, she had to remind Gavin not to walk quite so fast. Duke's legs were incredibly tiny. And that was exactly why she couldn't get a good brisk walking pace going when she had her dog with her. He just couldn't keep up.

"When we get there, we walk back really slow, agreed?"

She nodded but couldn't keep her eyes from straying to either side of the street as they walked. If the piece of fabric had been from a door—say, on a wreath—it would've been from someone's front yard. Unless it had been a backyard wreath and not one for the front door. She didn't see any street memorials between the Chicken Coop and Sunflower Café, but that didn't mean there wasn't one on the other side. She wanted to look, examine, get down on her hands and knees and crawl around the yard until she found it. This need she had to solve this mystery was strange, nearly overwhelming. But somehow, she managed to keep walking next to Gavin, Duke between them, until they got to the café. There he turned around and pointed back in the direction they had come from.

"We need to go slowly as possible."

"Until someone's dog chases us from their yard?"

"You are such a pessimist." Gavin adjusted his goggles/glasses, then motioned for her to begin.

That first step she took seemed momentous, but she chalked it up to her writer's imagination. There was nothing spectacular going on, just an investigation, trying to track down a clue that might not even be a clue. But its familiarity was what held it for her. They would probably investigate and find out that it came off one of those banners at the car lot.

Side by side, they walked, the line cutting across backyard after backyard. It was summertime, and the decorations were out in full force. Mostly, there were outdoor wreaths and the occasional flowerpot decorated with some sort of something or another. But nothing that had fabric like the piece she had found.

Even though they walked slowly, it seemed to take no time to get right back where they started.

"What's that?" she asked, pointing to the rose of Sharon bush in his Aunt Edith's yard.

"It's a rose of Sharon," Gavin replied helpfully.

She sighed. "I know that. Is that garden hose wrapped around it?" Of all the crazy things she had seen, she'd never seen anyone decorate a bush with a bundle of garden hose.

She had to remind herself that this was Gavin's aunt.

And he probably wouldn't appreciate her poking fun, but it truly was the strangest thing she had ever seen. Had it always been like that? She couldn't remember. And if it had, why hadn't she noticed it before now? There was just so much the human eye could take in in one glance. And with as much work as Edith Jones secretly put into her yard, there was no telling when or how many times it'd been changed since Sissy had moved in across the street.

"Why would she do that?" Sissy asked.

Gavin stopped. "She didn't do it. I did."

Sissy stopped as if her feet had been glued to the ground. "What do you mean *you* did it?"

"That bush has a tendency to flop over. The longer the branches get, the more they splay out over on top of the grass. I've tried to shape it up a bit for her."

"With a garden hose?" Surely he could have found something nicer or even prettier to tie the plant up with. Even just a simple piece of rope would look better than a bush covered in a garden hose.

"The hose kind of protects the plant from getting damaged. It's easier on the trunks."

Learn something new every day. Even then, the yard retained its eccentric vibe. There was still the small piece of plastic yard fencing that was braced up against the legs of the round-bottomed charcoal barbecue grill. The kids' toy car, the kind older toddlers could climb on to drive around the yard, and a bright green seed spreader. Of course, each was embellished with some sort of silk flowers all tied up in ribbon in a familiar pattern that—

"Wait!" Sissy pulled the little bag from her back pocket and held it up. The same check. The same checker-patterned ribbon that had been wrapped around Lizzie's flowers was also wrapped around one leg of the barbecue grill. And it was identical to the scrap in the bag. "It's not fabric," she said. "It's ribbon."

"If I turn it over to Earl Berry now, he'll think I've been withholding evidence," Sissy argued as they sat at the Carriage House Restaurant that evening.

Of all the places to eat in Yoder, the Carriage House was the only one open on a Sunday evening. And Sissy noticed the absence of any Amish waiters or waitresses in the place. She supposed they all had Sunday off, and the entire English crew worked. Such was life, she supposed.

After discovering that a representative of the scrap of ribbon she had found the day Kevin was murdered was also present in Edith Jones's yard, Sissy and Gavin had examined the bow in question. The only problem was it looked new. At least, too new to have been out in the weather for more than a couple of days. It showed no signs of fading, and no spots were raveling as one would expect something similar to do in the strong Kansas wind. Which had deflated both their hopes. Chances were, the ribbon hadn't been there when Kevin had been murdered. At the very least, the scrap hadn't come from that bow, regardless of the fact that it had to come from somewhere.

Sigh. Of course it came from somewhere, Aunt Bess would say. Everything came from somewhere.

"It just doesn't seem like a good idea," Sissy said.

"But if you can give him more than just 'here's this piece of ribbon, and oh, by the way, I washed all the DNA off of it,' then perhaps he won't feel that way," Gavin contended.

Sissy took a sip of her iced tea. "That's a great thought; too bad it's not going to happen." And it was too bad that they didn't have any more to give him.

"If you present it to him right, it might get him off your case." Gavin squeezed his lemon into his water and stirred it around with her teaspoon.

"I suppose," she said noncommittally. Okay, so the truth was, handing Berry the evidence might get him off her case. It might show him that there was another suspect out there somewhere, just waiting to be discovered. Or it might make him think she was presenting him with false evidence to do the same thing. Nope. That wasn't a chance she was willing to take.

Gavin sighed. "What did you order again?"

She supposed he thought a change of subject was due.

"Chicken fried and a piece of chocolate peanut butter pie." That's all she'd been hearing about since she had set foot in Yoder: the chocolate peanut butter pie at the Carriage House. And she had sat in a booth across the restaurant a week or so ago and watched Gavin devour a delicious-looking piece. She had been dreaming about it ever since.

The words no sooner left her mouth than the waitress stopped at the table. She held her notepad up and gave Sissy an apologetic smile. "We just ran out of chocolate peanut butter pie. Can I interest you in chocolate silk, or maybe apple?"

Sissy pouted her disappointment. There was always next time. "Chocolate silk."

The waitress noted the change on her ticket, then moved away to resubmit the order.

"The chocolate peanut butter pie must be popular," Sissy said.

"It's the best," Gavin agreed.

She waggled a finger at him playfully. "Best not let my aunt hear you say that."

He chuckled and took a sip of his water. "Never."

Seconds later, their food arrived, and thoughts of ribbons and chocolate peanut butter pie were pushed to the side.

"Let me see it again," Gavin said.

The food had been delicious, the coffee served hot, and the pie out of this world. Now the dirty dishes had been taken away by the waitress, and there was nothing more to do than pay the bill and go home. Still, she and Gavin lingered at the table.

"Let you see what again?" she asked.

He reached a hand across the table, palm upward, and wriggled his fingers. "Come on. Let me see that piece of ribbon."

She dug the plastic bag from her back pocket and slid it across the table to him.

He held it up to the light.

"What are you doing?"

He tilted his head back so he could study it better. "I wish the piece was bigger. It's familiar somehow."

"Well, yeah. Your aunt had it tied on the legs of her barbecue grill."

"No, it's something else." He shook his head. "But the piece is too small to tell."

He set the bag down on their freshly cleaned table and took a sip of his black coffee. His hair did that flippy thing again, and he was still wearing his goggles, a kind of hunky, dorky nerd. But in a cute way.

"If only it were a little bigger."

Sissy sat back in the bench seat of the booth with a sigh. "From your lips to God's ears."

"That's it!" He sat up fast.

"What's it?" What had she said?

"Aunt Edith." He grew even more excited. So much so, he picked up the baggie containing the scrap of ribbon and shook it at her enthusiastically. "She not only used the ribbon to adorn the legs of her grill—this is also what she used to tie up her rose of Sharon."

"And . . ." They were close to something. She could feel it.

"And I had to cut the ribbon off the bush. I tried to pick up most of it, but the wind was blowing so hard that I know I didn't get all of it."

"And whoever killed Kevin could have picked up a piece from your gardening efforts."

"Right."

That was great news. A terrific breakthrough, but she had no idea how he'd gotten from what she said to the answer.

"So does this prove it?" Sissy asked. "Does this prove that whoever killed Kevin cut through your aunt's yard to get to and from the café quicker?"

Gavin slumped back again. "Maybe. I don't know, really."

"When did you do all this rigging with the garden hose and the rope to protect the plant?"

He shrugged. "Before Kevin died."

"How long before?" she asked. "With the way the wind blows here, if it was too long ago, it might not matter at all."

He drummed his fingers on the tabletop in a thoughtful gesture. "Maybe that Monday night before."

"I spent that night at my aunt's house."

"But you had already been by the Chicken Coop. Right?"

She shook her head. "I didn't see the Chicken Coop until the next day."

He grimaced. "So why does it look so familiar to you?"

Sissy gave a small shrug. "My mother's a crafter; my brother's girlfriend is a crafter. I'm sure that ribbon has been used a thousand times in a million different crafts over the years. I mean it, it's ribbon."

"So you don't think it's a clue to this mystery?"

"It's definitely a clue. The only way it could've gotten into the Sunflower Café kitchen, at the time that it had gotten in there, would be on the soles of Kevin's killer. So if we can figure out who cut across your aunt's yard that day, we may have this solved."

What had seemed like a fantastic breakthrough the night before had dulled to merely ordinary information the next day. Anyone—*anyone*—could have come through his aunt's yard. Anyone could've picked up that piece of stray ribbon and tracked it into the Sunflower Café kitchen. Which left anyone to be responsible for Kevin's murder. But the thing she kept coming back to was, of all the people she knew, all of those whom she felt could possibly be involved in Kevin's murder—all those people on her suspect list, whether they had been crossed off or not—of all those people, only Darcy lived within that diagonal line.

And though Mystery Solving 101 always stated that the widow was a prime suspect, Sissy couldn't imagine Darcy having a hand at making herself sole caregiver to ten churlish children.

Of course, to hear Lottie talk, there were only five or so of the children who should be living at home. Even Dani was possibly able to move out and be successful in a single-person residence. Or maybe even with a room-mate. She was just a little slow, but meticulous and care-ful. And Sissy was sure she had been trained to be cautious her entire life.

Maybe that was the plan, Sissy thought, as she pulled the dirty dishes from the table and piled them into the bus tub. Perhaps the plan all along had been to get rid of her husband, pay off his gambling debts, and then, with the remainder of the insurance money, set herself up some-where nice and with only half of her children.

Five. Even on a good day, five children sounded like a nightmare. And despite the fact that Darcy seemed to be the most logical person to run kitty-corner across Yoder to get to the Sunflower Café, she continued to stubbornly stay at the bottom of Sissy's list.

It was two o'clock. The restaurant was closed. It was yet another workday over, and Sissy hadn't figured out who killed Kevin. She was about to take it as a personal affront.

She set the bus tub full of dishes on the counter next to the sink and grabbed the mop bucket and mop.

Some investigative reporter she was turning out to be. Although she had never investigated anything other than who had eaten her yogurt out of the breakroom icebox, it was still her chosen field.

Okay, so she wasn't reporting on anything. This was

actually more than just getting a story; this was poten-
tially keeping herself out of prison. Earl Berry could be
as inept as he wanted to be, but he had a badge and a gun
and a standing in this county, in this town, that she didn't
have. Her innocence would pale by comparison.

She filled the bucket with hot water and cleaner, then
rolled it back out of the kitchen and down into the dining
area. Lottie had already taken all the chairs up, setting them
butt down on the tabletops for easy floor-cleaning access.
Then she swept, and Sissy mopped.

Sissy started in the far corner, where an old candy machine sat. It wasn't the fancy kind with a digital readout.
You put your coins in a slot and pulled a lever, and out
came a candy bar. She wondered if, when tobacco became taboo, whoever owned the machine had converted
it to candy out of sheer self-preservation.

She mopped under the booths, working her way backward to the opposite wall. The same thing every day. But
at least it gave her time to think.

There was something to this ribbon business, she just
knew it. Somehow, she knew it. Whoever had killed
Kevin had dragged that piece of ribbon into the café. It
had still been early, and Lottie and Josie were meticulous
in their cleaning. Why, after Lottie was done with the
kitchen floor this afternoon, Sissy would bet a person
could eat off it, germ-free. Yeah, it was that clean. So to
have a wayward piece of ribbon just floating around at
eight o'clock on a weekday morning was ludicrous at
best. So who had tromped through Edith Jones's yard to
get to the Sunflower Café? And when they tromped
through Edith Jones's yard, did they already have murder
on their mind?

No, she decided. If they'd had murder on their mind,

they would've brought their own weapon. They had used a knife they had found on the counter in the back by the sink. A knife that everyone who worked at the Sunflower Café had touched at one time or another, since it had been washed again. That would make it a crime of passion. And where there was passion, there was usually a woman involved.

Darcy Saunders's face popped into Sissy's head once again. Her tired, weary, exhausted face that had once belonged to a beauty queen. Only this time, it refused to go away.

Perhaps Kevin was leaving her. Sissy had heard enough stories around town about Kevin and other women to know that the idea of him having an affair was not totally out of the question. If he was having an affair, and had fallen in love with the person he was having an affair with, perhaps he planned to leave Darcy and their children behind. Mix in a few gambling debts at the casinos, and the possible involvement with loansharking and the mob, and Darcy may have knocked Kevin off herself in order to pay Kevin's debts. Perhaps she thought if she were going to be left alone regardless, she might as well get something out of it.

Sissy stood up so straight and so quickly, she almost fell backward. But thankfully, the wall was there behind her. She had made it to one side of the café to the other without even pausing to rinse her mop. She would have to go back and do it again, she thought.

She started toward the mop bucket, but her hair was caught on something behind her. One of those faded sunflower decorations on the opposite side of the café.

"Ugh!" she said, trying to free her hair from whatever

had grabbed it. But it was behind her, and she couldn't see what it was or how to get loose.

"What are you doing?" Lottie came bustling out of the kitchen.

"I got too close to the wall and my hair is caught on whatever this is behind me and I can't get free," she said on one rush of air.

"Land sakes, girl." Lottie bustled over and started freeing her hair from whatever object had claimed it.

"We might have to cut you loose."

"No!" Sissy exclaimed. "Just get me untangled, but don't cut it."

"Give me a minute," Lottie said, her lips pursed. It took only a couple of seconds, but it seemed like a heart-wrenching hour that Lottie worked at pulling Sissy's hair free from the wall decoration behind her.

Once her hair was untangled, Sissy turned around and glared at the object. And there it was. That checkered ribbon again.

CHAPTER TWENTY-TWO

*A man who totes a cat by the tail learns something
he can't learn any other way.*
—Aunt Bess

"Where did this come from?" Sissy asked, pointing
to the grapevine wreath decorated with ivy, sunflowers, and black-checkered ribbon. More importantly,
why hadn't she noticed it before now?

Because she'd been thinking about the piece of material that she had found on her shoe in the kitchen the day
Kevin was murdered as a piece of fabric, not ribbon. And
it wasn't like she paid the fading decorations any mind.
They simply were a part of the café as a whole.

Lottie waved a negligent hand toward the decoration.
"That old thing?" She shook her head. "It's been here as
long as anyone can remember."

Sissy had made note of those decorations right when
she first arrived, but it wasn't until now that she made the
connection between the two.

"I doubt anyone even knows anymore," Lottie said.

"But it was bought locally?" Sissy asked.

Lottie shrugged. "Maybe. Maybe not."

Sissy smoothed down the hair on the back of her head, thankful that at least Lottie hadn't had to cut the mess out of her hair. It didn't matter where that particular ribbon came from. She was fairly certain that the ribbon she had found in the kitchen had been the same ribbon that Gavin's Aunt Edith had tied around her rose of Sharon to keep it from sagging to the ground. The coincidence was too much. Though with every nail of certainty she hammered in, it appeared more and more that the killer was Darcy Saunders herself. And perhaps, that was something Sissy wasn't ready to face.

The week went by uneventfully, if a person could call the same set of events as the rest of the week *uneventful*. Earl Berry coming into the café every day, sliding onto stool number three, ordering the same breakfast, and hassling Sissy with the same accusations of withholding evidence or not remembering the events correctly. She could only hope that he wasn't the only officer assigned to the case. She truly prayed that someone else was out there, tracking down clues. And she sincerely hoped that person was better than her. Because, checkered ribbon aside, she had come to a dead end.

"The wrapping paper is over there," Lizzie said Friday evening at supper. She had finished the baby blanket and had it ready for Sissy to take to the baby shower the following day.

Sissy was still a little uncertain about just showing up without an invitation, but once again, Lizzie assured her that everyone in town expected her to be there, whether she had been invited or not.

She supposed that since she was bringing Lizzie's present, and Lizzie herself had been invited, maybe that invitation would serve for her, as well. If nothing else, at least she came bearing gifts.

She wasn't sure what to wear to an all-town baby shower, but when she got off work Saturday, she took Duke for a quick walk, jumped in the shower, and then stared at the contents of her closet. She had only brought a couple of dresses with her. Though neither was as cute as the black peasant dress with the drop shoulders that she had worn to Kevin's funeral.

She pulled it from the small rack that served as a closet and turned toward the nearby mirror. It was the cutest dress she owned by far, but would it be beyond tacky to wear a dress to both the funeral and the baby shower?

Yes, she decided. And she hung it back on the rack. She pulled out the next dress, just a basic shirtwaist, something akin to one of the dresses Alice Kramden might've worn on *The Honeymooners*. It was pale yellow with white pinpoint polka dots that suited her redheaded complexion. At least it didn't make her freckles stand out quite so bad, and the soft yellow didn't compete so much with her hair, as other colors might. For now, it would have to do. She slipped into her dress, donned a pair of sandals, then grabbed her own baby present from the end of the kitchen counter. The little sleeper she had bought in soft yellow with a teddy bear stitched to the front was nothing compared to the handmade blanket that Lizzie was gifting. And though Sissy had never been much of a crafter before, seeing that exquisite gift made her wish she could produce one of her own. Maybe, just maybe, she would ask Lizzie to teach her to crochet. Then perhaps, when the next baby shower came up, she would have a handmade gift to offer the expectant mother. Plus, wouldn't that be an Aunt Bess sort of thing to do, crochet?

"I know. I'm sorry," she told Duke as she shut him back in his extra-large kennel. He braced his little paws up on the wire door and whined. "I won't be gone long," she promised. "And when I get home, we will snuggle on the bed and eat popcorn."

He barked in return. Sissy turned on the lamp that sat on the nightstand and made her way out the door.

The baby shower itself was to be held in the gymnasium at the charter school. Sissy felt more than a little uncomfortable as she pulled into the parking lot at the school and slid into a space between a truck and a tractor. Both Amish and English were out tonight. She shouldn't feel out of place, but she did. But if she decided to stay in Yoder, maybe soon she wouldn't feel like the new girl in town, or the odd man out. Perhaps it was only a matter of time before she felt like a Yoderian or . . . whatever.

She locked the doors of her little convertible and made her way to the entrance of the school. Just inside and off to the right, she could hear sounds of the party. A light shone under the set of double doors with small windows filled with safety glass. The muffled sounds of music and talking and shuffling around. That must be it.

"Hello, hello," a woman greeted her as she stepped into the gymnasium. "I'm Danielle Mallory. I don't believe we've had the pleasure of meeting. You're Sissy, right?"

Sissy resisted the urge to take a step back from the woman's enthusiasm. "That's right."

"I'm Abby's sister," she said. "Come in. Come in. Food's to the left; games to the right. And don't forget to sign the guest book."

Sissy held up the two presents. "Where do you want these?"

Danielle laughed. "Silly me. Far right corner, on the other side of Pin the Gender on the Baby."

Now there's something you didn't want to miss. Sissy surely hoped they were using gender glyphs and not body parts. But with the crazy characters that Yoder had to offer, she was almost afraid to look.

"Hey! Welcome." The young dark-haired girl motioned for Sissy to come closer. She looked no more than seventeen, maybe eighteen, with a wide smile that just matched that of Danielle. "I'm Hope," she said. "Abby's niece." She pointed to the HELLO MY NAME IS sticker that she had pressed to her shirt. "And you are?"

Uninvited.

"Sissy," she answered. "I'm Sissy Yoder."

Hope gave her that stunning smile once again. "I'm pleased to meet you, Sissy. Please take a name tag and print your name on it, or I can if you would rather. Then sign the guest book. Abby is asking for everyone to guess the date the baby will actually arrive, the time, its weight, and its length. You can put that right under your name in the guest book."

"What's this?" Sissy pointed to the large chalkboard set on an easel next to the table. Actually, there were two tables put together, both covered in disposable plastic tablecloths, one pink, one blue. The blue one had all the presents stacked up on top in a plethora of pastel shades and patterns depicting everything from ducks in raincoats to teddy bears asleep on the moon.

"I did that." Hope dimpled again. "This is a chart starting from when Abby and Ben got married to where they started their treatments and a little bit of what they went through. Then there's the date of the last treatment, and now they're pregnant. The last date is their official due date."

"Neat," Sissy said in response. She didn't really know what to say, but she felt like she should say something. Hope was obviously very proud of herself and her efforts. "Her last treatment was in October last year?" Sissy asked.

Hope leaned forward so she could see the front of the chalkboard sign. "Yep. It looks like it."

"And she's due in September of this year," Sissy confirmed.

"I know! It's exciting, right?"

Sissy wrote her name on one of the placards and stuck it to the front of her dress. "Sure is." She tossed the backing to the sticker in the trash and started to wander away.

"Uh-huh," Hope chided. "Don't forget to sign your name and write your predictions."

Sissy took the pen that Hope offered and stepped back toward the table once more. She penned her name in the book and looked at everyone else's forecasts about the baby. Just about every day in September was taken, and Sissy had to wonder: If the last treatment was in October, then wouldn't her baby be due sometime in August, maybe even the end of July, depending on when in October she'd actually had the procedure? Something was clearly off. She was chalking it up to bad math on the part of the effervescent Hope. Or maybe it was just some of that new "math" she'd been hearing about.

She chose a day in early September, wrote a couple of

random numbers that seemed like a good weight for a
baby, and put the same number of inches as the person
before her had. Yeah, that was cheating, but she really
didn't know what to write. Considering how the whole
chart seemed just a tad off anyway, did it really matter?

She smiled at Hope and handed her back the pen.
"Thanks," she said.

Hope flashed her award-winning smile once more.
"No. Thank you."

And Sissy wandered off in search of food.

"I didn't expect to see you here."

Sissy turned. "Gavin? I didn't expect to see *you* here."
He was wearing his customary button-down shirt, blue
jeans, and running shoes. He had a camera strapped around
his neck. "You're working." It wasn't quite a question.

He nodded. "The news never sleeps."

"I guess not," she said.

"Small-town paper, small-town news."

Sissy let her gaze wander around the gymnasium full
of people. "It's a pretty good turnout for a baby shower."

Gavin nodded. "I think with all the Kevin stuff . . ."
He shook his head. "I guess everybody's ready for some
good news now."

And what could be better news than a baby?

"I suppose you're right," she said.

He paused for a moment. "Do you want to go for a ride
tomorrow?"

A ride sounded like fun. Well, kind of. The ride itself
sounded like fun. It was the limping around all day Monday that didn't seem so great. "I thought it was supposed
to rain."

He squinted at her. "Not all day. And I believe that you
are now trying to avoid going out on another ride with me."

She scoffed. "Why would I do that?" Aside from the sore ankles, sore feet, sore back, sore arms, sore thigh muscles, sore knees, and sore everything?

"I don't know. You tell me."

She crossed her arms and eyed him, even though he had hidden his face behind the camera.

He turned the lens, adjusting the focus, and snapped a couple of shots.

"I'm not," she said emphatically.

He pulled the camera from his face and grinned. "Good," he said. "Then I'll see you at ten."

Gavin gave her a quick salute, then got back to work, snapping pictures while Sissy gazed around at the party-goers.

It took a moment, but she found Abby seated with a plate of food perched in her lap and an anxious English Ben hovering beside her. She was smiling at something someone was saying to her, and Sissy was surprised to see that it was an Amish man.

She started in that direction, thinking she would make her presence known, then skip out. What did it say about her sense of adventure that she would rather cuddle with her dog than attend a baby shower overrun with strangers?

And did it even matter?

"Hi, Abby, Ben," she said as she drew even with the couple.

"Hi, Sissy." Abby smiled at her, the happy curve of her lips backing up the warmth in her voice. "Do you know Amish Ben?" She nodded toward the man she had been talking to before Sissy had come up.

"I believe so," Sissy said, recognizing the man as one of the Friday regulars in the café. "I just didn't know you were the infamous Amish Ben."

"None other." His beard was long and streaked with gray. He had iron-colored hair with an indention that circled his head, most likely the spot where his hat usually rested. Blue eyes sparkled, and a map of wrinkles was sketched across his face. Other than the name, she couldn't see one thing he had in common with English Ben.

"I'll leave you to it," Amish Ben said.

"Don't go on my account," Sissy countered. "I didn't mean to run you off."

"No, no, it's time I be getting home," he replied.

"Say hello to Dorothy," Abby said. "And thank her for the gift. It's really special."

Amish Ben nodded once more, then moved away, leaving Sissy at the center of Abby and Ben's attention.

"Did your cousin like the flowers?" Abby asked.

Sissy had to admit, she looked a little better today. Not quite as weary as she had the day before, but there was still a sadness about her that Sissy couldn't fathom. She had gotten what she had wanted after years and years, according to the town grapevine. She should be over the moon with joy. But Sissy supposed that if Abby had been ill with morning sickness or even working too hard . . . perhaps that accounted for the fact that her mouth turned down at the corners when she thought no one was looking.

"She loved them," Sissy replied. "And she told me to tell you that she was sorry that she couldn't come tonight. She's still on bed rest."

Abby shook her head in commiseration. "I know that's got to be tough."

"She seems to be handling it well," Sissy said, but she knew her cousin was bored to tears, even on the best of days.

"It's these babies," Abby said, a wistful note creeping into her tone; then, just like that, it was gone, replaced with a thread of steel. "They are truly what's important. More important than anything else in the world."

All the hot water and all the Epsom salts in the world could not smooth out the kinks in all of her muscles. It was her stupid competitive nature. Or perhaps she should just blame it on Owen being so good at everything that when someone presented her with a challenge, she rose to it immediately, hoping that in some way, she would be better than her brother. It might be the truth, and it might not. But if she could blame it on Owen somehow, she was darn sure gonna do it. And this had Owen written all over it.

Monday morning, Sissy fell out of bed.

No, that's not exactly right. She tried to get out of the bed, and when she put her feet on the floor, her legs refused to hold her up. She crumpled like a marionette without a master.

Ever try getting off the floor while a three-and-a-half-pound dog licks your face? It's not easy, especially if your muscles are so sore you can barely stand it and you don't want to crush said dog. Somehow, she managed to haul herself to her feet, and miraculously, the second time they hit the floor, her legs held her up.

When she saw Gavin again, she was going to—

Scratch that. The next time she saw Gavin when she wasn't in excruciating pain, she was going to trip him. Yup. Right on the floor. Stick her foot out and make him fall. And then, she was going to laugh. But until such time, she was going to have to concentrate on just putting one foot in front of the other and walking, taking out orders, and ignoring the scream in every muscle fiber of her body.

"Sissy, can you check the milk order?" Lottie asked. "Mike should be here any minute, and Josie's got four orders waiting."

Sissy nodded. As much as she hated dealing with Mike and his insinuations and body jokes, it was better than trying to run around and get food to people's tables while it was still hot. Josie was behind the griddle, and Bethel had taken off to go to the doctor. Something totally unrelated to her broken ankle this time. "Yeah, sure." She made her way to the back and let Mike in.

"Hey-hey, sexy lady," Mike said. "Decided to go out with me yet?"

Sissy shot him a dubious look. "Aren't you married?"

He shrugged. "I don't care if you don't care."

"I bet I can name someone who would."

"Sissy!" Josie called from the direction of the grill. "I can't read what you wrote here."

Sissy looked back to Mike and the order he had.

"I can't wait all day," he said.

But she wondered how more much more accommodating he might be had she agreed to go out with him. The snake.

"Just put it in the cooler," she told Mike, then turned back to Josie.

The cook pointed to the marks on the ticket with the tip of the spatula. "What's this say here?"

Sissy squinted at her own handwriting. Even her hands ached today. She was certain from holding onto the bike and the brakes and the fact that she was a little terrified that she might fall. But she was new at this adult biking thing, and a bit of fear was natural, right? Or maybe not. "I believe that's a number four with sausage instead of bacon and an extra order of hash browns."

Josie turned the ticket upside down, then right side up again. "If you say so."

Sissy nodded. It might not be legible, but she was pretty certain that's what the man at the table had ordered.

She turned back to go check in the milk order, but Mike was already gone. The back door shut behind him. She heard the truck drive off and shook her head.

"Let me just go make sure." As gingerly as possible, she made her way to the front to the man's table.

"I beg your pardon," she said. "But could you repeat your order to me, please? There's been a small mix-up in the kitchen. I just want to make certain you get the correct food."

He frowned a bit, but repeated his order.

It was just what Sissy thought. She nodded and headed back to the kitchen.

"Miss?" someone called from the opposite side of the dining area.

Sissy made her way over as swiftly as possible, which was something akin to a snail on laudanum. "Yes?" she asked.

"We need some cream for the coffee."

"Powdered creamer or half-and-half?" Sissy asked.

"Half-and-half, please," the woman replied.

Sissy gave a quick nod, then regretted it as her neck muscles clenched and locked in place. Hopefully, her face wouldn't start hurting anytime soon. She shot the couple a smile and pretended that everything was hunky-dory. "I'll be back in one sec."

What a lie. She would be back as soon as she managed

to get her tired and beaten body into the cooler to find the
half-and-half and back out to the dining area. They would
be lucky to have it before the lunch rush hit.

She walked into the cooler, past the order that Mike
had just brought in. She never had an order with a problem before and didn't anticipate one today. Though she
would have to check it in ASAP. Right now she needed
half-and-half, but the space where the half-and-half was
usually kept was bare.

Sissy came out of the cooler and glanced over to Lottie. "Do we have any more half-and-half?"

"Did you check in the milk order? There should be
some in there."

Dang it! She really didn't have time to do this, but she
didn't have time not to, either.

Sissy started unstacking the milk crates that Mike had
just brought in, peering into each one, and checking the
purchase order against the actual product. There should
have been six quarts of half-and-half, and there were actually . . . none.

Sissy groaned and came out of the cooler. She held up
the purchase order, as if Lottie could see it at that distance. "There's not any half-and-half in the order, and
we're supposed to have six quarts according to this."

Lottie rolled her eyes and shot her an exasperated
look. "You didn't check the order before Mike left?"

"It's not like we're a little busy here or anything. What
do I do?"

"See if you can catch him. He can't have gotten far."

"Are you serious?" Her legs were killing her; she
wouldn't make it to the parking lot. At the rate she was
going, Mike would be halfway back to Hutchinson.

"Just cut across the park. It won't take you long to catch up with him at the Quiki-Mart. I'll try to hold things down here."

"If I have to," Sissy grumbled.

"You have to," Lottie said. "If you had checked in the order like you were supposed to, this wouldn't be happening. Take some money with you, and if you happen to miss Mike, buy some half-and-half from the Quiki-Mart."

"They have half-and-half at the Quiki-Mart?"

Josie turned from her spot at the grill. "If they don't got it at the Quiki-Mart, you don't need it."

Despite all her aching muscles and sore, tired everything, Sissy laughed. She grabbed a ten from the petty cash jar and headed out the door.

I can do this. I am woman. I am strong, she silently chanted. She was positive. She was powerful. She was hurting so bad, it was unreal. She could do this. She was powerful. She was woman. She only got through her chant three times before she actually made it to the Quiki-Mart. He must've been slower than she thought, for Mike was still there, parked between the two buildings in that way that drove Winston Yoder absolutely bananas.

Sissy opened the door to the Quiki-Mart. An electronic chime sounded as she stepped inside. Lina was standing behind the counter.

"You don't have school today?" Sissy asked.

Lina shrugged. "My parents had to go to the doctor in Hutchinson. They left me in charge."

And how old was the girl? Barely fifteen, if Sissy remembered correctly. "I'm looking for Mike."

"Milkman Mike?" Lina asked.

"That would be the one," Sissy replied.

"I just saw him in the back, but if he's not there now, I guess he went over to the flower shop."

"I was shorted on my milk order. Can I look in the back room? Or can you go get him for me?"

Lina jerked a thumb over her shoulder toward the storeroom. The door was propped open. From where Sissy stood, she could see crates of soft drinks and boxes of potato chips and all sorts of goods held up on pallets. She didn't even have to enter the room to see that he was nowhere to be found.

She came back to Lina. "You think he might be at the flower shop?"

"Yeah, he goes over there and stays a bit. You know, picks up flowers for his wife and stuff."

Picks up flowers for his wife? Sissy shook her head. Mike was just a blowhard. Evidently, he wanted the same ladies' man reputation that Kevin had borne so proudly.

"How did he get there without coming through the front?" Sissy asked.

"There's a side door that leads to the alley. And then one into the flower shop. Just buzz right across," Lina said with a small wave.

And if you do so, you won't have to actually walk in front of the two stores and risk someone seeing you.

It was slightly unnerving to walk into the back of the store, where no one knew you were there. But Lina assured her that they did it all the time. The spot where she entered the front of the flower shop was the exact spot Abby had come through the morning that Sissy had bought flowers for Lizzie.

Mike caught sight of her first. He straightened from

his place at the counter. "Hey," he said. "Look what the cat dragged in."

English Ben looked up from the flowers he was arranging. Those flowers that Mike would reportedly take to his wife that night.

The hair on Sissy's arms stood up. Something about wives. She wasn't sure what it was. But something . . . "I think you forgot to give us a crate."

"Give me just a minute," he said to Ben. Then to Sissy, he said, "Let me check the truck."

She followed behind him back down the hall and out to his milk truck. There was the crate of half-and-half. "Sorry about that," he said.

"No problem," she lied. It *was* a problem. A very big problem. It was a very big, sore muscle problem, and now she had to cart this back to the café? No way.

"I gotta get back to work," Sissy said. "But I'm not carrying this back to the Sunflower. I'll take one carton, and you bring the rest back when Ben finishes, deal?"

"Deal," he said. He started toward the side door to go back into the flower shop, but then he turned and eyed her once more. "How did you know to come through the side door?" he asked.

"Lina told me. She didn't tell you?"

Mike shook his head. "No, Kevin did."

He opened the side door of the flower shop.

"And don't forget to bring the other five quarts!" she called behind him. She started to turn and head back to the Sunflower, but something stopped her. Something niggling at the back of her mind. Like a wisp of smoke, the scent of a familiar fragrance from long ago. A ghostly memory that would not materialize.

Lina didn't tell Mike about the side door; Kevin did. Suddenly, it all clicked into place. Flowers and wives and incorrect dates.

Sissy's mouth went dry. She almost dropped the half-and-half on the asphalt in the alley but managed to catch it before it hit the ground. She sat the quart on the bumper of Mike's truck and started back into the side door of the flower shop.

The two men were chatting as she came in from behind. And there it was, right there on the wall. A beautiful wreath made of sunflowers, cotton bolls, and black and white checkered ribbon.

She knew now. She knew who killed Kevin the milk-man.

The men stopped as she came up behind them. Mike was facing her, and he stopped mid-laugh. Ben must've caught the strange look on Mike's face, and he, too, turned to face her.

Incredulously, she looked to Ben. "It's not your baby."

CHAPTER TWENTY-THREE

Truth is mighty and will always prevail. There's nothing wrong with this idea, except it ain't so.
—Aunt Bess

Mike immediately sobered. And English Ben began to shake.

"What?" Ben said, but there was a crack in his voice. His hands trembled as he continued to cut the ends off the pieces of filler fern that he was adding to the bouquet for Mike.

Sissy hadn't truly meant to say her accusation out loud, but now that she had, it seemed there was no going back. "It's not your baby, is it?"

English Ben cleared his throat, but he didn't meet Sissy's gaze. "If you're talking about Abby's baby—then, yes. Of course, it's my baby," he said.

"Where is Abby?" Sissy asked.

Ben might be able to convince himself that the baby was his, but Abby wouldn't be able to hold up under such accusations. When she found out that her husband had murdered her lover . . .

"Abby's not here," Ben snapped. "And I don't think you should go around saying these sorts of things to people." His voice grew stronger as it neared hysteria.

Suddenly, Sissy realized she had made a mistake. Her impulsiveness was going to get her into trouble one day; her mom was always telling her that. And that day might just be today.

"If this is a joke, it's not very funny." Mike straightened from his place at the counter and looked from Ben to Sissy.

"It's not a joke."

They all turned as Abby came from the back room. There had to have been a restroom or another office back there, off the hallway that Sissy had just come down. She hadn't seen Abby while back there. But she hadn't been looking for her, either.

"I thought you were resting," Ben said.

He put down the scissors he had been using to cut plant stems and turned lovingly toward his wife.

Sissy felt an overwhelming sense of deep regret for him. He didn't know. He didn't know, and that meant he couldn't have killed Kevin. So that only left one person. Sissy turned her gaze to Abby. Ben's wife picked up the scissors and held them out in front of her.

"You," Sissy whispered.

Tears started to fall, and Abby's hand trembled. She grasped the scissors even tighter. "Why couldn't you just leave well enough alone?"

"Abby?" Ben had turned as white as the roses in the bouquet he was working on. His hair was a dark, almost comical contrast with his bleached skin.

"Don't pretend you don't know," Abby said. She closed her eyes briefly, but it only caused more tears to fall. "You walk around here pretending like everything's fine, when you know it's not. It's all your fault."

He shook his head. "But we can have a baby," he said stupidly.

Sissy started back toward the door, hoping that each tiny step she took would go unnoticed by the pair. She wasn't sure who was more dangerous, and since she wasn't necessarily on Team Mike, she wasn't sticking around to see how he would fare with the two of them.

"I'm having a baby," Abby said. "Me."

"Kevin's baby." Mike's face crumpled into something akin to disgust and amazement.

"Kevin's baby?" Ben said the words as if they were incomprehensible.

Abby tossed back her head, still holding the scissors out in front of her. Sissy wasn't sure whether she would use them or not. There hadn't been two other people standing around when she had stabbed Kevin. And it was the truth. She had stabbed Kevin.

"Yes," Abby finally admitted. "It's Kevin's baby." She came out from behind the counter, still holding the scissors out in front of her to keep everyone at a distance. "It's all I ever wanted," she said. "A baby. Is that so much to ask from life? I wanted a baby. Every woman wants a baby. We tried and we tried, but I knew it wasn't me. It was you." She turned back to Ben. Stabbing the scissors at him menacingly. "I can have a baby. It was all you. You didn't want to have the test, so I figured out a way to figure it out."

"You slept with Kevin Saunders?" Ben was having a hard time grasping the entirety of the situation.

"Everything would've been fine. No one would have known, then Kevin somehow figured it out."

"It's Kevin's baby?" Ben was truly struggling to understand.

"Ben," Abby said, pointing the scissors at him again. "Pay attention."

"How could you have done this?" Ben said. The hurt on his face was enough to bring tears to a grown man's eyes.

"I wanted a baby." She said the words as if that one statement alone was enough to explain it all.

"You killed him," Ben said.

"He was going to tell you," Abby said. "He was going to ruin everything.

"I didn't mean to." Yeah, Sissy supposed Abby had envisioned a different scenario when she buried the knife in Kevin's back. "He started in, and I had to do something. I went over to the café just to talk to him. Catch him alone. Or at least not with you around. You've been hovering." The words were accusing and directed solely at Ben. "But when I got there . . ." She shook her head. And Sissy realized just why lately she had been looking so *peaked*, as Aunt Bess would say. Abby had been eaten up with guilt over Kevin's death. "He wanted money."

"That's what he meant when he told me that he had a plan. That he had it all figured out," Mike said.

"Had what figured out?" Ben was really a sweet man, but perhaps not the quickest when it came to matters concerning his wife. Or maybe he just didn't want to face the truth.

"His gambling debts," Sissy supplied. "He was going to get money from Abby to pay for his gambling debts."

Abby raised her hands. "We've been through years of fertility treatments. Did he really think we had anything left? We're mortgaged two and three times." She stopped and shook her head. She closed her eyes, as if trying to put everything back into focus. "There was no money to give him. There *is* no money to give him."

"So you killed him," Sissy said. It was not a question.

Abby shook her head, but it was more a defense than an answer to Sissy's accusation. "I'm not going to jail," Abby claimed. She stabbed the scissors in the air between herself and her husband. Then she backed up, putting herself closer to the display wall and the hallway leading to the back of the shop.

Sissy, Mike, and Ben were all standing on one side of the counter, and Abby on the other.

"I'm not going to jail," she repeated. She started to back down the hallway.

Mike and Ben stood with their arms in the air, as if she had a pistol pointed at them. Abby backed down the hallway and out of sight. They both dropped their hands and looked at each other.

"Are you just going to let her go?" Sissy asked. She supposed she could chase her down, but her legs and thighs were still killing her, and she had two capable men here.

But it seemed as if in some facets of the culture, chivalry was truly dead. Sissy heard an engine rumble to life. "She's in the milk truck." Sissy ran out the front door, not knowing which direction Abby was headed. But she barely made it to the parking lot before she ran into something akin to a brick wall. "Oof."

"Where are you running off to?" Earl Berry wrapped his hands around Sissy's arms, straightening her.

"Abby's the murderer," Sissy hollered. "She killed Kevin."

Earl looked from Sissy to Mike and Ben, who were just coming out of the flower shop. They nodded, and Earl chased after the truck.

Thankfully, Earl hadn't been riding bikes with Gavin, so he wasn't sore. He caught up with the truck easily. Of course, it helped that Abby was not proficient in driving that sort of vehicle and stalled out trying to get on the highway. Earl Berry opened the door of the cab and pulled her from it with ease.

EPILOGUE

The best way to succeed in life is to act on the advice we give to others.
—Aunt Bess

To say folks were shocked to find out that Abby Yoder was the murderer was perhaps the understatement of the year. The *Sunflower Express* printed its exclusive interview with Sissy Yoder and the details of how she solved the case and helped apprehend the culprit.

Sissy knew her celebrity status in town would soon wear off. Small towns were fickle that way. So she was banking on no more than a free piece of chocolate peanut butter pie that was promised to her from the Carriage House Restaurant and continued accolades until the Next Big Thing. Like, say, a fight breaking out at the church softball game.

"What did you order?" Gavin sat across from her, the weekly edition of the paper between them.

"Roast beef and chocolate peanut butter pie."

He grinned. "No chicken fried tonight?"

Now, chicken fried steak was her absolute favorite, but the last time she had ordered it, she hadn't been able to get the chocolate peanut butter pie. She was hoping that tonight, by not ordering the chicken fried steak, the peanut butter pie would be available. See? Logic. Well, Sissy logic, anyway.

"Now what?" Gavin said.

Now what? Sissy repeated to herself. Now she just hoped things would return to normal. No more murder investigations, no more Earl Berry following her around, no more craziness. "Normalcy," she said.

Gavin smiled and lifted his glass of water. "To normalcy," he said.

She raised her glass and clicked it against his. Yes, to normalcy. Whatever the heck that was.

The roast beef was tender, the company always good, but when the waitress slid the hunk of chocolate peanut butter pie in front of her, she thought she might have actually found heaven on earth.

After the first bite, she knew it was true. De-lectable.

She looked to Gavin, eyes wide as she pointed to the pie with the business end of her fork. "This is the best pie I've ever eaten," she said, her mouth still full of peanut butter and chocolate ecstasy.

"Better than your aunt's?"

She nodded, a little sadly.

"I wouldn't let your aunt hear you say that," Gavin joked. "Not if you want to stay employed."

She nodded. But it was true. And she did. At least for the next six months. She had promised herself that much, but over the last couple of days, she had found herself thinking about staying longer. Thinking that Yoder might be a nice place to settle down. And she couldn't do that without a job. Well, a cover job, anyway. Couldn't have people asking questions, and she wouldn't keep her job if she told her aunt that the Carriage House chocolate peanut butter pie was better than the Sunflower Café's.

Well, she would never tell her aunt. First, she would never want to hurt her aunt's feelings, and second, Sissy sort of liked working at the Sunflower—the best place to eat breakfast when in Yoder, and the second-best chocolate peanut butter pie in all of Kansas.

Well, in all of Yoder, anyway.

Sissy lifted her fork. "To pie," she toasted.

Gavin chuckled and clinked his fork against hers. "To pie," he said.

And to whatever comes next.

Visit us online at
KensingtonBooks.com
to read more from your favorite authors,
see books by series, view reading
group guides, and more!

BOOK **CLUB**

BETWEEN THE **CHAPTERS**

Visit us online for sneak peeks, exclusive
giveaways, special discounts, author content,
and engaging discussions with your fellow readers.

Betweenthechapters.net

Sign up for our newsletters and be the first
to get exciting news and announcements about
your favorite authors!
Kensingtonbooks.com/newsletter